LAND OF ICE

A Nature Station Mystery

by
Jannifer Powelson

Eklund Publishing

DEDICATION

To my husband Brad, who did a
fabulous job driving in Iceland
during our family trip to this
beautiful country! He maneuvered us
through a tunnel under the sea,
down one-way streets in Reykjavík's
city center, on a narrow icy road
around a fjord, up snow-packed
mountain roads, and even mistook
our hotel's icy sidewalk for a
driveway. What a grand adventure!

CHAPTER 1

Kristen Matthews' heart was full as she gazed into the hazel eyes of her soon-to-be husband, Brett Stevenson. He smiled encouragingly as he held her gaze. Facing the stained-glass windows of the chock-full church in her hometown of Eklund, Illinois, Kristen could feel the stares of their closest friends and family at their backs. Knowing everyone was merely excited about their wedding, she took a deep breath and tried to calm her last-minute case of nerves on their long-awaited day. She wanted to enjoy the ceremony she and her best friend, coworker, and co-maid of honor, Hope Livingston, plus her mother Joannie and sister and other co-maid of honor, Morgan, had spent much fun preparing for.

However, since Kristen was used to planning events for their work at the Nature Station and having just helped plan Hope's June wedding, this one was a piece of cake to organize. Kristen closed her eyes for a moment, her mouth watering at the thought of the beautiful cake they would slice into later. She let the beautiful sound of the organ and piano duet fill her ears. She inhaled and sighed at the pleasant smell of candle wax and the pine greenery that decorated the church on the cold early January evening. It was just after the new year, and the Christmas tree still stood, fully lit, adding to the festivity of the church's decorations.

Soon the music stopped, and she could hear the creak of the old oak pews as attendees, who were squished tightly together in the small-town church, shifted as the service continued. *At least being snug in the pews will help them stay warm on this winter afternoon.* She shook off her nerves and smiled brightly. This was their big day, after all, and it wouldn't hurt them to be the center of attention during the ceremony. Then they could relax and enjoy the less formal reception afterwards at the Nature Station's Red Barn, part of the business she owned and operated.

As the minister began to speak, Kristen and Brett clasped hands and turned toward him to listen. *This is it!* Kristen had a dreamy look on her face until it was at last time to exchange vows. She was no longer worried about the dozens of people watching their every move; she focused all her attention on the minister's words, so she would be able to repeat them without stumbling once it was her turn. But first, it was up to Brett to do his part in tying the knot. He smoothly said the traditional vows they'd chosen together, ones so many others had repeated before them.

When it was her turn, Kristen was relieved she was able to repeat the vows without incident—no jumbled words, shaky voice, or tears. Vows completed without a hitch, the ring exchange was next.

"With this ring, I thee wed …" Brett said as he slipped the gold band on Kristen's finger.

The ring felt so right on her finger, like it had always been there. Kristen turned to Hope and accepted Brett's ring. Gazing into Brett's hazel eyes, she repeated the age-old words. "With this ring, I thee wed …" then carefully slipped the ring onto Brett's left hand.

2

Once both rings were in place, Brett winked at her. Kristen almost giggled at his levity during this otherwise solemn portion of the ceremony. The deal sealed, she smiled lovingly at her new husband, a few tears of joy now trying to escape. Now, their lifelong adventure was about to begin.

* * *

The Red Barn was packed to capacity when Kristen and Brett arrived after the last of the wedding pictures. It was only five o'clock, but it was already pitch-black and freezing outside. But inside, the barn was blazing with light from loads of candles and warm from all the friends and family waiting for them. Once inside, Kristen stood still for a moment just inside the main door and cast a critical eye over the reception area and was pleased everything seemed to be perfect. The centerpieces had turned out lovely, featuring white pine greenery and pinecones collected from the Nature Station's windbreak, then woven with ice blue and winter white trimmings. In the middle were vintage blue Ball Jars with tall white candles inside and sitting on top of a square of burlap. The decorations' cool tones were perfect for the frigid evening and nailed the look Kristen was after—vintage, folksy, and earthy. Hundreds of tiny white lights were wrapped around the barn's original wood beams and scattered throughout the barn's vast space. She glanced out a window and even saw some exterior lights reflecting off the sparkling snow outside, making the outdoors glow as magically as the indoors.

Checking the cake table, she was amazed at how the simply designed cake her friend Amy, owner of Eklund's

Amy's Bakery, looked not only scrumptious, but also beautiful. Its base was decked out with graceful, long-needled white pine greenery and their ice blue trimmings. The scent of the seasoned roast beef, simmering all day, and from her family's own beef cows, made her stomach grumble. She was glad the guests were already snacking from the cheese and veggie trays and sipping drinks, but she was ready for a bite of her own. Looking at Brett, he guessed her thoughts and nodded. It was time to get the party started!

Kristen scanned the crowd for her parents and saw them across the large main room of the barn, busy chatting with guests. Joannie spotted her looking and waved at the newly married couple, then touched Kristen's dad Ken's arm. Kristen smiled as she watched her parents head their way. Soon they were surrounded with the rest of the wedding party, including Morgan and Hope, plus Brett's two best men. Todd Livingston, Hope's husband and deputy for the county sheriff, slapped Brett on the back and pulled Kristen in for a hug. Brett's brother Jeff did the same. Kristen felt a warm glow, despite the cold evening.

Kristen smiled as she smoothed the gently flared skirt of her ivory silk gown. Simple but elegant in design, its fitted bodice came to a V at the waist. Accented by a sweetheart neckline and off-the-shoulder three-quarter length sleeves, tiny beads glistened on both the bodice and hem of the skirt—pretty, but not gaudy. Kristen was surprised to fall in love with the dress the first time she saw it, even though she'd been dreading dress shopping. She couldn't believe how the flattering dress made her feel like a princess, especially after wearing her normal winter attire of jeans, boots, and a Nature Station sweatshirt. She longed for her boots at the moment, thinking how much warmer and more comfortable they would be than the high-heeled satin pumps she now wore. *Oh well, plenty of time to wear boots after our big day.* She could even get by wearing them when they boarded the plane for their honeymoon destination. Checking one last time to make sure her dress looked presentable after the short ride to the barn in Brett's pickup truck, she caught Brett's eye and smiled.

"Let's get the crowd calmed down and eat!" Brett gave Todd a nod.

Part of Todd's best man duties included acting as emcee. Since it was a very informal reception there wouldn't be much emceeing required, but quieting down the crowd, introducing the wedding party, and giving everyone dinner instructions were essential. Todd's commanding deputy's voice was ideal for the role.

While Todd was running through the announcements, Kristen smiled at all the appropriate times, until she noticed Sheriff Miller watching them. He applauded and appeared happy for the couple, but Kristen didn't remember inviting him. Given Kristen's track record with stumbling across murder victims, maybe Todd thought they might need additional law enforcement on hand. Kristen gave Brett a subtle jab. "What's he doing here?"

"Who?" Brett asked.

"Sheriff Miller." Kristen felt like a bad ventriloquist but didn't want their guests to be able to read her lips, even though Todd was now giving buffet line instructions, and most eyes were no longer glued on them. "I didn't invite him; did you?"

Brett shook his head. "You know I didn't have much to do with the guest list."

Kristen chuckled. "You can say that again. Luckily your mother had an organized list ready to go."

"I'm pretty sure she started putting the list together after the first time I brought you home to meet my family."

"Aw, that's so sweet." Kristen leaned over to kiss Brett, just as Todd pointed to the couple.

"Maybe if Kristen and Brett would pay attention to instructions, they could spare a minute to open up the wedding dinner buffet and let the rest of us follow behind them."

Kristen saw Hope elbow Todd in the side after he let out a loud guffaw. Their guests laughed along with him. Kristen felt her fair cheeks blush furiously under Todd's good-natured teasing, but she tried to ignore the heat. After all, it was their wedding, and if she wanted to kiss her husband, that was her prerogative.

Brett put his arm around Kristen's waist. "Come on. There's plenty of time to pick up where we left off later."

Kristen felt her cheeks grow warm again, but she was content and happy. She smiled and waved at family and friends as they wove their way to the buffet line, with their attendants and parents following.

The rest of the reception passed quickly, but Kristen knew that one day she would look back on this day and still remember every minute. Soon, their guests were starting to leave. As she was saying good-bye to two of her aunts, she caught another glimpse of Sheriff Miller. She vowed to catch up with him later.

She turned to give her full attention to her aunts. "Where are you going for your honeymoon?" her aunt Lois asked.

"We're headed to Iceland on Monday."

"Iceland, of all places!" her Aunt Carol exclaimed. "Isn't it awfully cold there?"

"Or is that Greenland?" Aunt Lois chimed in. "Iceland is green, and Greenland is ice."

"I think at this time of year, they're both full of ice, but that's okay. It's still a beautiful time to visit, and from what I've read, their winter temperatures are usually far milder than what we have in northern Illinois. We also hope to catch the Northern Lights while we're there."

"I'm sure the northern nights will be nice as well," Aunt Carol said with a wink before she hugged Kristen. "Don't worry about sending us a postcard."

Kristen laughed. It was more like her uncles to tease her than her aunts, but she supposed weddings, and maybe a glass or two of champagne imbibed at them, brought out the jokester in everyone. "Okay. I'm sure we'll be taking plenty of pictures."

"We look forward to seeing them when you return." Aunt Lois hugged Kristen. "We're going to leave before it starts snowing again."

Kristen had been so occupied with her guests she hadn't given a thought to the weather. The nice thing about holding the reception in her own Red Barn venue was she didn't have far to go home. *And it will feel even more like home now that Brett will be sharing it with me.* "Please be safe driving home."

"You best be safe when travelling on your honeymoon. You know what happened the last time you ventured out of state," Aunt Carol said, referring to

Kristen and her friends' trip in September to scout out possible tour stops for a Nature Station sponsored trip to Lake Michigan.

"I'm sure traveling out of the country could lead to even more complications," Aunt Lois added.

Kristen felt her heart lurch, and not in the good way it had for the entire wedding weekend. "Let's hope not." Of all the things she was looking forward to seeing in Iceland, a dead body wasn't one of them.

CHAPTER 2

Kristen grabbed her backpack, boarding pass, and boots and made her way over to a bench where she waited for Brett to finish up in the airport's security line. She grimaced as she watched Brett hold his arms up while the airport security employee did a search with his wand, then made Brett empty his pockets, take off his belt, then go back through the scanner. Kristen set to work lacing up her boots, then double checked to make sure she had everything. That done, she looked around the crowded security area, where she could hear several languages. People of all nationalities and destinations were herded into this windowless area of O'Hare International Airport.

Kristen's people-watching was interrupted by Brett's arrival at the bench. She grinned at him, happy he'd made it through security in one piece. Brett still seemed a little frazzled, so she took hold of his backpack while he sat down next to her and began to put himself back together. She'd travelled out of the country during her college days and was familiar with the process, but this was Brett's first time abroad. Security measures seemed to tighten on a regular basis, and it had been a while since they'd last flown.

"I guess I'm ready to go," Brett said, his former good spirits restored.

"Then let's get out of here." Kristen stood and checked again to make sure her passport and boarding pass were handy. That done, they started for the security exit and headed in the direction of their gate.

"It was a little crazy in there," Brett pretended to shudder. "Most of the TSA agents were okay, but some of them are kind of harsh on people."

"I can't imagine how people who don't speak English very well must feel."

"Maybe it's a good thing if they don't understand everything."

"They have signs posted all over the place with rules and regulations, so I'm sure the workers get irritated when people don't follow directions. But sometimes they don't seem to understand how intimidating this process is to people. And most of us don't fly that often." Kristen grabbed Brett's hand as they walked.

"I'm just glad to start a new adventure with you. I can hardly wait to land in Iceland."

"Let's hope the plane gets off the ground okay." Kristen cast a nervous glance toward the windows near the gate where they were walking. Tiny snowflakes were starting to fall.

Brett brushed aside her worries. "It'll be fine. Those are just flurries that shouldn't amount to much." He glanced at his watch. "We still have a couple of hours until our plane leaves. Maybe we should grab something to eat.

Kristen knew their evening flight was only a little over six hours and didn't offer meal service, just snacks. Kristen longed for the days when you could fly comfortably with more leg room and a decent meal. She spotted a bar and grill down the hallway. "Why don't we eat there? But first, let's check out our gate to make sure we can find it easily once we're done eating."

Brett squinted in the direction of their gate. "I think it's just ahead, a couple more gates beyond here."

"Then, let's eat!" They walked into the bustling airport eatery and were soon seated at a table.

Kristen flipped through the menu. "Since I want to eat as much authentic Icelandic food as possible while we're there, I guess I'll have an All-American cheeseburger and fries before we leave." Kristen shrugged off any guilt she may have been feeling. She'd sacrificed several holiday treats to make sure her post-holiday wedding dress fit well, so she could look her best for their wedding.

"That should stick with you for a while." Brett continued to look through the menu.

"I'm sure I'll be starving by the time we land at five o'clock in the morning—Iceland time, that is. Travelling makes me even hungrier than usual."

"Me too. I just hope we can sleep on the plane. I want to make the most of our first day in Iceland."

"I don't normally sleep well on planes, but if I can snuggle up against my new husband instead of trying not to lean on a stranger, maybe I'll have better luck."

Brett smiled warmly at her. "I'll do whatever I can to help with that." He set down his menu just as their server arrived to take their order. "I'll have the Italian beef sandwich and a glass of whatever you have on draft." Kristen ordered her burger.

Their orders placed, Kristen pulled out their itinerary. They'd booked an independent travel package, which included their airfare, hotel and breakfast, airport shuttle, and add-on tours. Kristen hadn't wanted to mess around with renting and navigating a car, so this package was a great compromise, allowing them to still have their independence but not have to worry about getting around. "I think tomorrow we can get settled in, walk along the bay, and explore Reykjavík."

"I know how much you like to make travel arrangements, so I'll just do whatever you tell me."

"I'm sure that won't last." Kristen laughed. "We're both pretty independent, so it will be interesting learning to live together."

"When it comes to traveling, you can handle all the plans without any gripes from me. From what I've read about Iceland, it's a beautiful and peaceful country. As long as we're able to see the main sights, a few off the beaten path ones, and experience the Northern Lights, we can't go wrong."

That pretty much summed up Kristen's thoughts as well. "We'll have a blast, I'm sure. I'm glad we got a good deal on this trip; otherwise, Iceland can be pretty expensive."

"Why do you think I ordered a beer with this meal?" Brett asked. "We may not be able to afford one while we're in Iceland."

"I've heard alcohol can be pricy, but we can check out a local grocery store to grab a few essential munchies and try a bottle of their local brew. Their prices should be more affordable than ordering at a restaurant."

"Hopefully we can find some good Icelandic chocolate."

"You bet! And black licorice."

Brett made a face. "Isn't that the really salty stuff?"

"It's an acquired taste, but once you get used to it, there's nothing like it." Kristen couldn't wait to try everything Iceland had to offer them. After a busy fall of planning their wedding, she was ready to relax and enjoy honeymooning with her husband. *It still feels funny to think of Brett as my husband, but I don't think it will take me long to get used to it!*

"It will be cool to be able to sleep in every day, since it won't start to get light until mid-morning."

"Yeah, even after sleeping in longer than usual and taking our time getting ready, it will still be dark when we're eating breakfast." Kristen had read they'd only have about six hours of daylight at this time of year.

"No complaints from me." Brett wiggled his eyebrows suggestively.

Kristen blushed and swatted him playfully on the arm when she noticed their server coming toward them with drinks. "Stop."

"I just meant we can stay out as late as we want while we watch the Northern Lights," Brett said once he'd taken a sip of his draft, an innocent look on his face.

Kristen grinned, knowing better than to believe him. "That's a good point. I hope we're able to see them while we're visiting."

"I know we'll see a lot of wonderful things, have some great experiences, not to mention having some time to ourselves. But the truth is, it wouldn't matter where we were going or even if we see the lights. I just want to be with you."

Kristen felt tears sting her eyes. She couldn't believe how lucky she was. "Oh, Brett. That's so sweet. You're right. We'll have fun no matter what. But, since we're going to be there, I want to make the most out of our trip and see and experience as much as possible. Besides, the past few trips I've been on have all ended up focusing on a murder investigation, which was definitely not in the plans."

Brett grimaced. "Yeah, this is our honeymoon, and getting involved in a murder investigation is not on our itinerary."

"As loose as our agenda is, there's still no room for that, but I'd love to see the Northern Lights every night, if we have the chance." Kristen had a faraway look on her face that wasn't entirely caused by being on the first day of her honeymoon with the man she loved. Luckily Brett enjoyed the same things she did when it came to visiting natural areas. With Brett's job as a state forester and her work at the Nature Station, she supposed it was an occupational hazard.

"Since we're staying a week, I'm sure the conditions will be right for at least a night or two."

"Luckily we have flexibility with the tour. They only run the tour on nights when the sky is clear, so we'll have more than one option to see them." Kristen spotted their waiter coming toward them. Her stomach rumbled. She hoped after a hearty meal, she'd be able to relax and sleep on the plane. But one thing was for sure, she'd enjoy cuddling with her husband, even if she didn't get a wink of sleep.

CHAPTER 3

Kristen sat next to Brett in the waiting area near their gate. Butterflies fluttered in her stomach as she watched their Icelandair jet taxi into the gate. Light flurries were still falling, and the light was starting to fade. She checked her watch. It wouldn't be long before they began boarding. In the meantime, she occupied herself by watching the other flyers.

She watched an older couple sitting together across from them as they doublechecked their bags to make sure they had everything. Kristen caught the eye of the woman and smiled.

"This is the first time we've flown out of the country before," the woman said. "It's a little nerve wracking." She glanced over at her husband, who was punching numbers into his phone. "He's calling home one last time to make sure our son knows how to handle things while we're gone. I'm sure our son will be glad when we're in the air, and we can't bug him."

Kristen shared a laugh with the older woman. "Are you headed to Iceland?" A dumb question, she supposed, but the couple could have been at the wrong gate.

"Yes, it's been on our bucket list for years." She patted her fluffy white hair. "We thought we'd better jump at the chance when we found a great deal online."

Kristen eyed the paperwork the woman was holding and held up her own. "It looks like we booked through the same company."

The woman nodded. "I've noticed a few others as well, like those two over there." She pointed to a middle-aged couple who were dressed way more formally than the rest at the gate. Most were wearing warm sweaters and casual jeans, but the woman stood out, not only with her perfectly colored and styled black coif and flawless make-up, but also with her dark green designer pantsuit and cream silk blouse, spiked-heeled peep-toe pumps, and lots of gold jewelry that Kristen guessed was the real thing. She carried a purse that even to Kristen's untrained fashion eye, must have cost hundreds of dollars.

"Hmmm. They don't look like the type to travel on a budget." Kristen noted the man's tailored suit, crisp shirt, silk tie, and polished loafers. She couldn't picture being comfortable on an overnight flight wearing expensive and dressy clothes. Then again, Kristen remembered hearing about the days when people used to dress up for flights, but she thought those days were long gone unless traveling first class to an exotic place. Even though Kristen considered Iceland exotic, the star-studded couple across the waiting area didn't look like the type to rough it in the rugged outdoors of the less populated country. *Maybe they'll spend all their time—and money—at the Blue Lagoon or some other geothermal spa.*

"I'll say. It looks like they spent more on clothing than we spent on our entire trip. By the way, my name's Betty."

Kristen was enjoying talking to Betty, but their conversation was cut short by an announcement over the speaker telling them boarding would start in five minutes. Kristen felt Brett nudge her.

"All set?" he asked with a smile, then lowered his voice. "You make friends wherever you go."

"We struck up a conversation because she booked their trip through the same company as ours. We'll probably end up at the same hotel and possibly on some of the same tours, so why not get a head start on being friendly?"

"Just one more thing to love about you." He leaned in for a quick kiss.

As much as Kristen would have loved to extend their kiss, the airline staff made another announcement through the loudspeaker. Kristen broke away from Brett's embrace, then bent over to pick up her backpack. They stood and walked over to the edge of where they were starting to board the plane by row numbers. While they waited for their row number to be called, Kristen scanned the crowded waiting area. She caught Betty's eye and waved. She spotted a group of four backpackers, probably college aged, two boys and two girls. She wondered if they were squeezing in a trip before they started spring semester. Noticing a brochure sticking out of one of the backpacks with the same logo as the company Kristen and Brett had used, *Land of Ice Travel*, Kristen figured they would also be bumping into them later.

Hearing their row numbers announced, Kristen glanced at Brett, and they headed toward the boarding area. She couldn't wait to start their journey to Iceland— and life journey—with the man of her dreams.

* * *

Several hours later, Kristen was awakened by the sound of the flight attendant announcing they would be landing in Reykjavik shortly. Though not exactly refreshed, Kristen felt lucky to have caught a few hours of sleep on the plane. As she straightened up, she glanced over at Brett, who was also starting to wake. She stretched and grinned at him. "Morning, sleepyhead." She peered out the window, seeing nothing but darkness, as the plane started its descent.

Since it was only about four-thirty in the morning in Iceland time, she knew they had a long way to go before sunrise. Still, she was excited. "The first thing I want to do once we pick up our baggage is grab a strong cup of coffee."

"Good idea. A little caffeine for the shuttle will make the ride go more smoothly."

"I'm sure we'll be in tip-top shape by the time we get to the hotel." Kristen knew it was about a forty-five minute ride from the airport to their hotel but doubted she would feel any more well rested. Not that it mattered. She had every intention of doing some sightseeing that day, even if they called it an early night. They could get plenty of sleep before their first tour tomorrow.

"This is one time when we'll appreciate a blast of cold air after being on a warm plane ride."

"The cool temps will certainly help make us feel more awake," Kristen agreed. "We can try checking in when we arrive, but it will still be early when we get to the hotel. Unfortunately, from what the brochure says, they seem to hold firm on the three o'clock check-in time."

"It's all good. Having coffee and breakfast at the hotel while we wait for it to get light enough to do some exploring will help make us feel like humans again."

The plane dipped downward, and Kristen could see the twinkling lights of the airport through the dark night sky. She wished it were light enough to catch her first glimpse of Iceland but knew she'd have plenty of time to explore to her heart's content—with the man who made her heart content—later.

CHAPTER 4

Kristen kept her eyes peeled for her suitcase as others came crashing down onto the luggage carousel. Spotting her bright red case fall onto the carousel, she braced herself to grab it. Brett's came next, and soon they were rolling their suitcases through passport and customs. One stamp in the passport later, they were looking around for signs to direct them to the shuttle they would be taking to the hotel.

Between good signage—easy to follow and in English as well as Icelandic—it didn't take long for them to locate the shuttle stop. The fresh air perked Kristen up, as did the cup of coffee she was sipping from while they waited. Food in her stomach would further improve her disposition. Brett and Kristen didn't speak much, and Kristen resumed the people-watching she'd started at O'Hare the night before.

Her eyes landed on the people she'd picked out earlier at the airport. She waved at Betty and her husband, then saw the fancy-dressed couple headed their way. She speculated on what their backstories were. Several more passengers filed their way, among them the four backpackers she'd noticed previously. They all appeared animated and chatty. A night without much sleep appeared to have done little to faze them. It wasn't long before a minibus with the name of their hotel, Sjór Hótel, rolled up to the shuttle stop.

"This must be it." Kristen picked up her carry-on backpack and slung it over her shoulder. She managed to juggle her half full coffee cup as well.

As they got into a more organized line, Kristen made sure her hotel voucher was handy. She was digging in her backpack for the document when she heard raised voices. Looking up, she noticed Fancy Lady getting in Betty's face.

"But we were here *first*," she snapped.

Since Kristen knew the fancy couple had come along shortly after Betty and her husband, Kristen watched the scene unfold, staying silent but ready to jump in if needed.

Betty, straightened to as tall as her five-foot-two height would allow, looked like she meant business. Kristen had enjoyed chatting with the pleasant woman at the airport, but now Betty's eyes blazed. "No, actually, *we* were here first, but it doesn't matter. Apparently, we're all going to the same place." Betty caught Kristen's eye and rolled her own.

Kristen hid a grin, not wanting to provoke the situation further but glad Betty had stood up for herself.

"Well, if you're sure you don't mind," the woman said in a haughty manner, "we'll just be on our way." She nodded toward her husband. "Come on, Lewis."

"I never said I didn't mind, but I know how to behave in public and won't cause a scene over your childish behavior."

The fancy lady's face flushed bright red in fury. She strode to the front of the line, leaving her husband behind to handle the luggage. Betty stepped back a few steps and muttered into Kristen's ear. "People like that give Americans a bad name."

Kristen couldn't agree more. "I feel sorry for her poor husband, who has to put up with her nasty remarks as well as being responsible for hauling all the luggage."

"I'm guessing she's pretty high maintenance and doesn't travel as lightly as we do," Betty said after looking at Kristen's compact suitcase, then back at her own medium-sized roller. "I guess I'd better get back to my own husband."

"I'm sure we'll bump into each other over the next few days," Kristen turned back to Brett.

"I'm glad you're getting back to *your* husband," Brett murmured in her ear.

"I didn't mean to neglect my husband." Kristen kissed him on the cheek, then rolled her suitcase a few feet ahead to keep up with the line.

"It's not like I'm needy," Brett said, rolling his suitcase next to hers. "But if you pay more attention to me, you'll be less likely to get caught up in other people's business—which, unfortunately, you have a habit of doing—only to discover them dead a few days later."

Kristen gave Brett a playful smack on his arm. "That's nothing to joke about."

"No, it's not. So let's not tempt fate." Brett waited until they'd climbed aboard the shuttle and stashed their luggage before continuing. "This is our honeymoon, and I want us to spend time mooning over each other, not getting involved with other travelers."

Kristen sighed, realizing what Brett said was true, even if he was only kidding about stumbling onto dead bodies on a regular basis. She knew Brett wasn't the domineering or possessive type, but after all, they were on their honeymoon, and they were starting out a new life together. *Now's the perfect opportunity to turn over a new leaf.* Even if she'd run into murder victims several times since she'd met Brett, there wasn't a chance that would happen in the peaceful and idyllic country of Iceland.

* * *

Kristen stared out the window of the shuttle as they rode along the snowy roads from the airport to Reykjavik, though there wasn't much to see in the dark. Still, she could see dark land, probably black lava, covered with white snow. Even though she could only see the landscape from the glow of the headlights ahead, she could sense how beautiful the scenery would be when it was lighter.

Brett squeezed her hand. "It shouldn't be too much longer. I think I see city lights up ahead."

Kristen's anticipation was growing. Driving through the country's capital city would be a pretty site, even in the dark. Though not as large or as famous as other European capitals, Reykjavik still held a charm of its own. Plus, the city was located right on the Atlantic Ocean, something to cause great excitement for a landlocked Midwesterner. She couldn't wait to catch her first glimpse of the city, and they'd have plenty of time to explore at their leisure after some breakfast and rest.

As they came into the city, she kept her eyes glued on the sights out the window. The architecture was simple and charming. She noticed many buildings close to the ocean had metal siding, which she assumed allowed for better protection from the ocean's salty spray. Soon, the bus rolled up to their hotel. Even in the dark, she had noticed the bay waters lapping against the shoreline as they drove. She couldn't believe they only had to walk out the front door of their hotel, and they'd practically be at the ocean—as soon as it was lighter, and they'd fortified themselves with coffee and breakfast, of course.

Even though Kristen was raring to go, they waited until the small bus was almost empty before grabbing their luggage, then joined the rest of the guests as they filed into the hotel.

"Why don't I wait with the luggage while you talk to the front desk." Brett took the handle of Kristen's suitcase.

"Oh, so you're going to let me do the talking?" Kristen knew English was widely spoken in tourist locations, but she still tried to use a few words in the native language when she could.

"I always let you do the talking, so this is nothing new."

"Funny." Kristen smirked at Brett, then got into the line that was already forming from their shuttle. Since they were the last to get off the bus, she was the last in line. She had no hopes for checking in so early in the morning, but at least she could have their luggage stored and get their name on a list as rooms became available.

Hoping the line would move quickly, she looked at the travelers ahead of her, most of them the people she'd first spotted at the airport—excited about their trip then, but now looking a bit bedraggled and travel weary. She wanted to ditch their luggage and have breakfast while they mapped out their day. She could see the breakfast area around the corner from the check-in desk. Smelling fresh coffee and hot breakfast fragrances, her stomach grumbled. She couldn't wait to sink her teeth into hearty whole grain buns slathered with Icelandic butter, like she'd seen pictured in the hotel's website when she'd booked the package.

"What do you mean we can't check in now?"

Kristen's sleepy and hungry thoughts were interrupted by a shrill female voice, coming from someone ahead of her in line. *I'll bet ten thousand Icelandic Króna that's the high maintenance chick from earlier.*

Kristen stood on tiptoe to peer over the lady in front of her, who was wearing a furry hat, to see who was causing the ruckus. Sure enough, the rich looking couple were the ones speaking to the hotel clerk.

From what Kristen could hear, the hotel clerk was holding her own against the pushy woman. "I'm sorry, but we have no rooms available. Besides, check in isn't until this afternoon. You're welcome to stow your bags until your room is ready."

"Well, what on earth are we supposed to do until then?" the woman demanded.

Her husband glared at her, then turned toward the clerk. "You'll have to excuse us. We flew in overnight from Chicago, and she didn't get much sleep."

Kristen stifled a chuckle. She'd seen enough of the woman to know her manner was much the same, regardless of how much sleep she'd had.

The clerk nodded toward the breakfast area. "You're welcome to enjoy a cup of coffee and a warm breakfast. Twelve hundred Króna, since you're not yet registered, but breakfast is included with your room rate for the other days."

"Why, that's highway robbery!" exclaimed the woman, her face bright red.

"Actually, it's quite affordable, around ten U.S. dollars a person." The clerk looked beyond the couple. "Next, please."

Kristen didn't bother holding in her laugh this time. She was probably a little slap happy due to lack of sleep, but she was amused at how well the polite, but firm, clerk had put the obnoxious woman in her place. Kristen felt sorry for the poor husband. He probably had to apologize for his wife all the time. Why would he put up with that type of behavior from his wife? Kristen knew she and Brett were literally in the honeymoon phase, but she couldn't picture herself ever treating Brett that way, let alone acting like such a jerk in public to someone just trying to do her job. Kristen knew from working with the public for so long that people could behave badly, but fortunately she'd grown adept at handling difficult people. She'd found that acting syrupy sweet with a smile pasted on her face helped to calm down most people who were acting rotten. Luckily most people who hiked at the Nature Station or attended their events were normally laid back, but it only took one idiot to spoil things. *Kind of like this woman has done every time I've seen her.*

Before long, it was her turn. Kristen added her name to the pre-check-in list. Brett joined her with the suitcases, and they wheeled them to the designated holding area.

"We may as well enjoy a leisurely breakfast while we wait for it to get light enough to do some exploring," Brett said.

"I thought you'd never ask." Kristen eyed the breakfast area, glad there was only one couple ahead of them waiting to be seated.

The hostess told them to sit wherever they wanted, then to help themselves to the buffet. Kristen was glad breakfast was included in their hotel package, as she'd read how expensive restaurants were in Iceland. The restaurant also offered reasonably priced dinners if they didn't feel like going out for dinner. Kristen sighed with pleasure, excited to be officially starting their honeymoon, but she was also excited at the prospect of exploring a brand-new place together. But first—coffee and breakfast!

CHAPTER 5

Kristen and Brett held hands as they walked along the sidewalk that ran adjacent to the Atlantic Ocean. Kristen was happy their hotel was only a block away from the water and close enough to walk to the quaint original downtown area. Despite the overcast day, they'd been enjoying themselves by wandering around since early afternoon. Kristen knew Iceland would be even prettier in the sunlight, but for now, she was content to catch her first glimpses during daylight hours in the more subdued lighting. She was already in love with the area's charming buildings and beautiful scenery. Not only was the dark blue ocean close by, but snow-covered mountains loomed to the north along the water's edge. She could only imagine the sights they'd see once they ventured out into the more rugged countryside tomorrow. The pictures she'd seen online and in her travel guide gave her an idea of the scenery, but she was sure visiting in person would be an even more amazing experience.

"Do you want to walk further inland to check out some of the shops?" Brett asked.

Kristen nodded. "And maybe also have a look at the main church—the Hallgrímskirkja."

Brett cracked up at Kristen's mangled pronunciation. "Now we know why most Icelanders speak really good English."

"Yeah, to compensate for tourists like us only knowing a few words and probably not even pronouncing even the basic words correctly." Kristen had looked at the map and travel brochures while they breakfasted and couldn't believe how long some of the words were.

"Can you imagine learning to speak Icelandic as a child?" Brett's words echoed her thoughts.

Kristen laughed. "Nope. It seems like such a complicated language, and their words have about twice as many syllables as most English words."

"It would be even harder to learn as an adult." Brett shrugged. "Maybe if you grew up hearing it spoken, it wouldn't be so tough learning it.

"Well, I think we're both too old to learn it easily—which may prevent us from moving here at some point," Kristen said with a chuckle. She knew she'd never want to permanently move somewhere else, much less out of the country, but it was fun to travel somewhere and think about living there if her circumstances were different. She couldn't bear the thought of uprooting her life in Eklund. After all, not only were her home and family there, but also her livelihood—the Nature Station. She knew Brett had no intention of leaving his family or work behind either, so she was content to live in the rural area of northwestern Illinois, where life was good but not always terribly exciting. *Unless you count the numerous murder investigations I've been involved with.* Kristen shrugged the thought aside.

"It would even prevent us from driving around on our own during our stay—if we had rented a car, that is. Can you picture the GPS unit trying to tell us where to turn?"

Kristen giggled. "I can barely understand GPS directions at home, let alone if the voice was pronouncing Icelandic words."

"At least we don't have to worry about driving around on our own." Brett paused to squint toward the water for a minute. "Where are we headed tomorrow?"

"We're booked on a bus trip around the Golden Circle."

"What all are we going to see?" he asked.

"I thought it was a great way to see some of Iceland's most interesting features to kick off our sightseeing. In addition to the beautiful countryside full of snow-covered mountains, we'll see mountain lakes, waterfalls, and even geysers."

"You sound like a tour guide."

"Well, if you follow me, you'll probably end up getting lost" Kristen said with a laugh.

"But we'd still have fun." Brett leaned in to sneak a quick kiss.

Kristen loved being able to just stroll around, exploring the city with her new husband. Despite their jet lag, they were already having a great time. "I'm hoping tomorrow's fun. I'll show you pictures of what we'll be visiting when we get back to the hotel. We'll be stopping at a national park, plus other sights."

"I can hardly wait."

Kristen knew Brett wasn't being sarcastic. She was glad they were well matched in their vacationing preferences. With both of them working outdoors in the environmental field, they enjoyed visiting natural areas together. Kristen considered their honeymoon to Iceland an extreme adventure.

Kristen pulled out the map. "If we want to head to the … the main church."

Brett chuckled. "You mean the famous one we can't pronounce?"

"Yeah, that's the one. Hallgrímskirkja." She stumbled through the name—no improvement over the first time she'd tried to say it a few minutes ago—then pointed to the spot on the map. "I think we need to go north and a little east."

"It looks like that's near the downtown areas we want to visit anyway, so perfect."

Kristen didn't want their trip to be so structured that they wouldn't have any fun, but she was a firm believer in planning ahead enough to make sure they had time to see and do as much as possible. She was glad they had their time mapped out, literally, for the next few hours. She knew they'd be ready for an early dinner as soon as the sun started to set—which was late afternoon at this time of the year.

They started walking away from the water and headed inland. It wasn't long before Kristen spotted the Hallgrímskirkja 's tallest point, the tower, which stood 244 feet high. When Kristen thought of European churches, ancient and traditional architecture came to mind, but according to her guidebook, this church was built in relatively modern times. Its design was much more contemporary than one would expect of a main church in a capitol city. "Listen to this," she read from the book. "It took forty-one years to build the church; construction started in 1945 and ended in 1986, but the landmark tower was completed long before the whole church was finished."

"Wow. Let me see," Brett leaned over to see the picture. "It looks like we can go to the top of the tower for a great view of the city and surrounding ocean and mountains."

"I'm all for that, but do we climb stairs to the top, or is there an elevator?" Kristen grimaced. "After not getting much sleep on the flight, I'm not sure I'm up for a steep climb."

"Let's check." Brett looked closer. "No worries. It sounds like there's an elevator."

"Thank goodness. If that's the case, it sounds like a perfect way to get a feel for the whole city." Kristen smiled as they continued walking toward the church. She noticed several quaint shops she'd like to check out when they were done at the church. Seeing the city from the top would grant them a great view of the entire area.

Since the church's tall tower stood out among the city's shorter buildings, they put away the map and meandered around the charming downtown. The streets in this area were narrow, winding, and hilly, adding even more to the city center's picturesqueness. Crossing a street, Kristen glanced to her left and saw they were lined up directly in front of the church. They walked a few blocks north, up the hilly street.

Finding themselves in front of the church, Brett pointed to a statue. "I wonder who that is?"

"I can tell you that without even looking it up. It's the famous Leif Eriksson."

"I know he was the first known European explorer to travel to North America, but I didn't realize he was Icelandic."

Kristen chuckled. "I remember reading that he was thought to be Norwegian, but he must have spent some time in Iceland, because they claim him as well." Curious, she pulled out her guidebook and thumbed through it. "Actually, this says he was born in Iceland."

"Well, from what I've heard about the Vikings, they travelled all over the Nordic region and beyond, so it makes sense that he could have spent time—or even lived—in more than one country before landing in our country."

"Fun fact, our country gave the statue to Iceland as a gift celebrating the thousand-year anniversary of Iceland's ancient parliament—the oldest parliament in the world." Kristen wasn't much of a history buff, but she did enjoy reading about historical facts when visiting an area. Iceland's history was as interesting as the scenery was beautiful. "We'll see the parliament site when we visit Þingvellir National Park on the Golden Circle Tour we're taking tomorrow."

"Wow, I can't wait." Brett squeezed her arm. "Seeing you in tour guide mode is almost as much fun as being around when you're leading a nature walk."

Kristen rolled her eyes. "Sorry, I can't seem to get away from being a 'guide.' That said, let me reiterate— don't blame me if we get lost."

"Nonsense, that's part of the fun." The afternoon sun, already sliding lower in the sky, peeked through the clouds, and Brett squinted toward the church's main door. "Is that where tourists enter?"

"I'm not sure, but let's find out." Kristen snapped a few pictures of the statue, as well as several angles of the church looming in front of them, then started walking toward the impressive church.

They hadn't gone far before Brett tapped her arm. "Hey, isn't that the high maintenance woman and her poor husband—the couple we saw at the airports and staying at our hotel?"

Kristen eyed the woman, wearing skintight jeans, pointed-toe spike heeled suede boots, and a faux fur jacket. Even without their rooms being ready, the woman must have found somewhere to change clothes from what she'd been wearing on the overnight flight. Instead of wearing a heavy scarf and beanie cap like most of the tourists, and those who Kristen assumed were locals, wore, she only had a lightweight silk scarf elegantly draped across her hair and loosely tied at the neck, like a 1950s movie star.

"Looks like them. I can't believe she's wearing that getup to go sightseeing." Kristen's own feet were already tired from walking to and around the downtown, and the outside of her boots were damp from the snow and ice on the sidewalks and pavement. She couldn't imagine wearing anything but her warm and comfortable hiking boots for winter sightseeing in Iceland. *Besides, why would anyone risk ruining that gorgeous suede?*

"You have to admit she's a class act." Brett laughed when he noticed Kristen's raised eyebrows. "It's one thing to wear something like that in the city center, but hopefully she'll have something more suited to the weather conditions if they venture out of the city."

Class act? From what I witnessed earlier today, that woman doesn't have an ounce of class in her. Kristen thought about the places they planned to visit. "Oh, please. Can you even picture them visiting Iceland's rugged scenic areas?" There was no way the woman could hack even the short hikes they had planned on the tourist sight walkways, let alone anything more adventurous. Kristen had noticed that the snowy and icy sidewalks didn't detour the locals from walking, biking, and running on the sidewalks or pedestrian path along the bay. They were used to it—and wore appropriate clothing—allowing them to be active, even in questionable weather. By now, the sun had scurried behind the clouds again, and she felt a snowflake graze her face.

"We'll steer clear of them." Kristen grimaced, remembering the scene while boarding the airport shuttle and then later at the hotel. "I'm not in the mood for any more of their drama."

"Works for me." Brett took hold of Kristen's arm and steered her toward the church.

Once inside, they stood for a minute at the back of the church, taking in the view. Kristen had visited dozens of other European churches, always amazed at their size, architecture, and craftsmanship. Because this was a more contemporary church—at least by European standards—its interior was simpler than many, but it was still impressive.

"Wow, this is incredible." Brett's hazel eyes widened as he looked upward at the gothic style domed arches.

"I'm sure the view from the top will be equally incredible. Are you ready?"

Brett pointed toward a sign. "My Icelandic isn't quite as good as yours, but I think we need to head in that direction."

"Very funny, since it's written in English as well as Icelandic."

"A guy's gotta learn a new language somehow."

Kristen laughed and grabbed onto Brett's arm. "Come on."

There was only a short wait for the elevator. Kristen was glad they were visiting in the winter. Not only was the city and scenery beautiful at this time of the year, but it wasn't as crowded. After the hustle and bustle of the holidays, not to mention the last-minute preparations for their wedding, it was nice not to have to fight crowds on their honeymoon. Soon they were at the top, gazing at the panoramic view.

"Okay, you're right," said Brett. "This is incredible."

"I've climbed to the top of a lot of towers in my travels, and I've never been disappointed with the views." Kristen sighed. "But this one takes the cake. You can see most of the city from here, plus the mountains and ocean."

"An added bonus, no actual climbing was required in this case." Brett scanned the panoramic view. "I could stay up here all day."

Kristen eyed the observation area. "We can stay as long as we like. All we have planned for the rest of the afternoon is seeing the city sights, eating an early dinner, and getting to bed early to catch up sleep."

Brett leered at her. "Or something else."

Kristen grinned. "Knock it off. Someone will hear you." Even as Kristen's face reddened, she felt a feeling of contentment wash over. "Just a peaceful day, all to ourselves …"

Whatever else she was going to say was cut off by an ear-piercing scream. In an instant, Kristen not only had an ominous feeling about what they might see when they looked in the direction from which they'd heard the scream, but she also had a feeling she knew who had screamed. "Come on. Let's see what that was all about."

Like everyone else on the tower level, they rushed to the side to see what had happened. Kristen gulped, knowing the church's parking lot and other paved areas lay below. Since the scream sounded close, she assumed it had come from right next to the church. Stepping as close to the tower edge as she could for the best view, she held on tightly to the railing with one hand and Brett's hand with her other and looked below. Her heart almost stopped, then started racing, when she noticed the obnoxious woman's silky scarf fluttering in the breeze, loosened as she squatted down near her husband sprawled on the ground beside her.

Kristen had a feeling the peace of their day had been shattered, but not as badly as the man who lay motionless below them.

CHAPTER 6

Kristen glanced at Brett, whose normally tan face had paled. She could only imagine how pale her own face was—probably ghostlike since she was so fair skinned anyway. Brett nodded at her, and they quickly made their way toward the elevator and were ushered on board. As the doors closed and the elevator started downward, she thought about the scene below. Even though her common sense told her she didn't really want to know what all had transpired below—much less get involved--her natural curiosity won out over reason. And, since these people probably didn't know anyone else in Reykjavik, the least she could do was offer assistance, she rationalized.

Kristen's mind sifted through the possibilities. Had he fallen from the church tower? *Impossible*. First of all, she hadn't seen the couple in the elevator or on the tower level. Secondly, there was no way a person could fall from the top. Everything was safely fenced to prevent accidents. Even though Kristen had qualms about getting close to the edge and looking directly downward, like she had a couple of minutes ago, things were perfectly safe.

Well, then, what happened? Did he have a heart attack? Kristen remembered him as being lean and fit, but a heart attack could still strike. As the elevator reached the bottom, Kristen and Brett raced out the doors as soon as they opened and ran outside to where the man still lay inert on the snow- and ice-covered plaza near the Leif Eriksson statue. Only a few minutes had passed since they'd first heard the scream. By now his wife was standing, punching numbers into a phone. Kristen couldn't tell if the man was breathing or not.

Kristen crouched down, removed her gloves, and placed her fingers on his neck, trying to feel a pulse, while she watched to see if his chest was moving. His body was lying face up, so if he was breathing, she should be able to see it. Since she'd had experience with this sort of thing before, it barely fazed her at this point. The important thing for now was making sure they knew whether he was dead or alive. However, she also knew from experience things would hit her hard later.

Brett stood near the man's wife. "Is there anything we can do to help?" he asked.

The woman apparently hadn't noticed Brett or Kristen until he spoke. She flinched, as if he'd startled her, then shook her head, tears in her eyes. "It's no use. I think he's already gone!"

Kristen whipped her head up at that news. "Are you sure? I'm still trying to check his vitals." *Or whatever it's called when you're trying to determine if someone is still alive.* Kristen, though calm earlier, was starting to feel like the situation was surreal.

"What can we do to help?" Brett asked again, speaking to the woman using his calmest tone.

By now, the woman was sobbing, with tears streaming down her face. "I don't know. I can't get a signal on my phone, and where on earth are the police in this godforsaken city?"

Kristen could tell the woman was truly upset, and she now felt horrible about thinking so harshly of the woman such a short time ago. No matter how obnoxiously she'd behaved, things weren't looking good for her husband. Kristen picked up the man's wrist, hoping to have better luck there finding a pulse, but knowing she probably wouldn't. She'd been down this road too many times not to recognize the signs—even in Icelandic. Though the man hadn't been dead for long, Kristen was surprised to catch a whiff of an offensive odor. It was hard to believe such a well-groomed man could smell bad, even if he was dead. After all, he had barely been dead long enough for his body to grow cold, even in these cool temperatures.

Brett placed his hand on the woman's arm. "Let me see if I can reach the authorities on my phone." Brett pulled his phone from his jacket pocket, glancing at Kristen and raising his eyebrows.

Kristen, realizing it was a waste of time to continue her efforts, felt a wave of nausea and dizziness wash over her and remained on the ground for a moment, trying to get her bearings. She'd taken off her gloves to check pulse points, and she sighed heavily, pulled her gloves back on, glad for the warmth, though the chill she now felt had nothing to do with the brisk Atlantic breeze. She slowly rose to her feet and went to stand next to Brett, wanting to be useful, to help a case of the nerves that started when she realized there was nothing to be done for the man.

"Let me check to see if there's an Icelandic equivalent to nine-one-one." She mentally shook her head. After several weeks of learning vocabulary and reading up about the sights they would be visiting, she had a hard time remembering how to contact the police in an emergency, which should be one of the first things that came to mind. She pulled her guidebook from her backpack, knowing there was a section on the basics of Iceland. Scanning the pages quickly, her eyes landed on the number she needed. "Try calling 1-2-2."

Relieved she'd at least been able to track down the correct number, she watched as Brett connected with the emergency services. Kristen was glad his cell phone seemed to be working okay in Iceland. The only thing that would make this situation any worse was not being able to contact the police. *Hopefully once they arrive, we can leave.* But Kristen knew she'd want to find out more about why this man was lying dead next to one of Iceland's most visited tourist destinations.

Kristen could hear Brett talking into the phone, trying to explain the situation and their location. Her eyes scanned the area, and she noticed a small crowd gathering. She figured there would be a larger crowd by now if this had happened in the summer, when more tourists and locals would be milling about. Once Brett had taken charge, the woman had crouched down next to her husband and was holding his hand. Kristen felt tears stinging her eyes. Newly wedded and up until now, thoroughly enjoying their honeymoon, Kristen couldn't begin to imagine how she'd feel if something happened to Brett.

Kristen knelt near the woman. "What happened? We saw you both just a short while ago, and everything looked fine." Though to be honest, Kristen recalled being catty about what the woman was wearing and feeling sorry for her husband for having to deal with the woman on a regular basis.

The woman's earlier perfect hair, make-up, and fashion choices now looked sad and disheveled. "Things were going so well," she said, dabbing her eyes with the handkerchief Brett handed her. "We've been wanting to take this trip forever."

Kristen wondered if the man had been ill. Maybe this trip was on their bucket list—before he kicked the bucket. "Was he feeling all right when you left the hotel?"

"Yeah, I think so. It's hard to say because we didn't sleep on the plane. If he wasn't acting one hundred percent, I thought it was just because he was tired." She sniffed. "One minute we were walking and talking, and the next minute he just sort of collapsed on the ground."

"Do you think he had a heart attack or a stroke?" Kristen wasn't sure how someone "sort of collapsed." She knew the police would arrive before long, and her chance to question the woman would be limited after that.

"At first I thought he might have slipped on the slick pavement," she said, scowling at the patches of ice and snow.

Now they were getting somewhere. Kristen glanced over to see if there was any blood on the pavement. She hadn't noticed any earlier. "Did he call out when he fell?"

"Honestly, I don't know, which is awful." She started crying again. "I do remember him reaching out to grab my arm when he fell."

"The police and an ambulance should be here soon." Brett gave Kristen a look, urging her to go easy on the woman. "You'll want to save your strength."

Kristen took his hint. "By the way, we must be on the same trip. We're the Stevensons—I'm Kristen, and this is my husband, Brett." Kristen couldn't help but feel giddy at the fact that she was referring to herself and Brett as a married couple.

"Thanks for coming to my rescue," the woman said. "My name is Margaret, and my husband's name is …" She choked back a sob. "Or, *was*, Lewis. Lewis and Margaret Sawyer." Margaret had a faraway look in her eye as her eyes teared up again.

Kristen almost wished Margaret was acting like her earlier haughty self. At least that would mean her husband hadn't dropped dead outside the Hallgirmskirkja in the middle of Kristen's honeymoon. Kristen hated to be selfish, but she had a sinking feeling their peaceful honeymoon was destined to head south—and not just for the south shoreline of Iceland on a trip to the black beaches near Vík they planned to visit in a few days.

Brett, as if sensing Kristen's thoughts, jumped in. "If there's anything we can do to help, let us know, but it sounds like the police are headed this way, so we'll let you talk with them."

"Oh, no," Margaret wailed. "I can't deal them myself. When hard times hit, Lewis always handled things. I may like to spout off my mouth, but he was the one who got things done. What am I going to do without him?"

Most of Margaret's once perfect makeup had washed away from her flood of tears. Her hair was a disarray from the slight breeze and all the recent activity. Her suede boots were scuffed from kneeling beside her husband, and her jeans were splotched with patches of snow and ice. She seemed to have aged a dozen years in as many minutes.

"There, there," Kristen cooed, patting her arm, not knowing what else to do. "The police will have some questions for you, and you need to pull yourself together to answer them—for Lewis' sake." Kristen rummaged in her bag and pulled out a water bottle. "Would you like some water?" Kristen felt hopelessly inadequate. When she'd discovered dead bodies in the past, an emotional spouse wasn't ever hovering nearby.

"I think I'd prefer a stiff drink rather than some supposed Icelandic thermal spring water." Margaret's tone was harsh; her earlier behavior was starting to return.

Kristen breathed a sigh of relief. At least Margaret was starting to act more like what was probably her normal self. Maybe she wouldn't expect them to hang around much longer. "Unfortunately, I don't have a flask of anything stronger with me, so this will have to do for now." *Which is a shame, since I could use a shot of something as well.*

While Margaret took a tiny sip of water, Kristen looked around the small crowd that had gathered. She zeroed in on the others she'd seen on their trip so far—the four backpackers and the older couple, Betty and her husband, were all standing around, watching them with interest. Kristen hoped to catch up with Betty later. From the looks of it, Betty looked like she was dying of curiosity. *Not well phrased, Kristen.*

Kristen could see Brett a few feet away, on the lookout for the police. Then Kristen could hear the sirens in the distance—a different sound from the sirens she'd heard in the U.S. at other times she'd found a body—but emergency sirens just the same. Soon they were coming toward them, swiftly but carefully driving down the narrow streets toward them. Brett waved them closer to where Lewis lay.

Kristen continued to stand near Margaret, hoping her presence would help keep Margaret calm. Once the police started questioning her, Kristen would step away and stand with Brett. *I'm sure the police will want to question us as well, since we were the first on the scene.*

The thought of the police questioning them did nothing to help calm the upset stomach she'd noticed earlier. *How on earth do I get myself involved in these situations?* She knew she and Brett could have easily stayed at the top of the tower and ignored Margaret's scream, but they weren't the type of people to do that. Now they were paying the price—but fortunately not the ultimate price—like poor Lewis had.

CHAPTER 7

Once the police started talking to Margaret, Brett walked over to Kristen and swept her into a bear hug. Safe in Brett's arms, she felt herself relax. While it felt heavenly, she knew the relative calm she now felt would soon be replaced with another case of the nerves.

When Kristen finally broke away from the embrace, Brett kept his arm around her and steered her toward a bench. "Let's wait here until they're ready to talk to us. You look like you could use a few minutes to recover, and I know I could." He kissed her cheek. "Now I know how you must have felt all the other times you've found a body."

"I seem to remember you being there the first time I found a body."

"That's true." Brett grinned sheepishly. "Maybe I'm the one who started your string of bad luck in that regard."

"At least you've brought me some good luck as well." Kristen snuggled against him, glad to have his warmth on the cold stone bench.

"Glad to hear it." Brett glanced up. "Looks like we have company."

Kristen saw Betty and her husband walking toward them. As much as she liked Betty in the few short conversations she'd had with her, she wasn't in the mood for a lot of questions at the moment.

"Wow, that was impressive," Betty said. "Are you two paramedics or something?"

"No, but we've had some emergency experience in the past and thought we'd try to help." Kristen hoped Betty wouldn't probe into what exactly those experiences were.

Betty's husband held out his hand first to Brett to shake, then offered it to Kristen. "I don't think we've been introduced. My name's Douglas. Doug and Betty Schmidt. I have a feeling we're going to be seeing a lot of each other in the next few days." He grinned at Betty, then looked over at Kristen. "It seems like the two of you have already become fast friends."

Kristen smiled, thinking Doug might be exaggerating just a tad, but it was true she had enjoyed chatting with Betty so far. Kristen even thought she would fit right in with her older friends who volunteered at the Nature Station. "That's right. Nice to meet you, Doug."

"That's true," Brett agreed, referring to Doug's remark. "Since we were on the same flight, staying at the hotel, and probably have many of the same tours planned, we'll keep bumping into each other."

"I wonder who bumped him off?" Betty glanced toward Lewis' body.

Kristen's eyebrows arched. "What makes you think anyone killed him?" The thought hadn't even occurred to Kristen, and she'd been around enough murder investigations that she should know a natural death from murder by now.

"I shouldn't speak ill of the dead man's spouse, but we all know she's been a real treat in the short time we've

47

been traveling together. Just look at her! Her outfit alone cost more than our monthly social security deposits," Betty said. "Maybe she murdered him to get her hands on his life insurance money or something."

As much as Kristen liked Betty, she thought she was being a little judgmental as well as jumping to conclusions. Even though Kristen agreed with Betty about Margaret's earlier behavior and manner of dress, there was nothing to indicate Lewis' death was from anything other than natural causes. Besides, she'd seen a humbler side of Margaret a few minutes ago.

"I assumed he died from natural causes, and as far as his wife goes, she was behaving okay to us, given the awful circumstances. I think she was grateful for our help."

"Of course she was." Betty looked sheepish. "What I just said was uncalled for. If something happened to Doug, I'd be beside myself with grief. I should give her the benefit of the doubt."

"I agree that she did cause a scene or two," Kristen said, "but that doesn't mean she deserves to lose her husband. It's even worse since they're so far from home." Kristen hoped that since they were the first to arrive on the scene the police would let them know Lewis' cause of death. Maybe Icelandic police were more forthcoming with information when they were questioning witnesses, but she highly doubted it. They were probably even more closemouthed than Sheriff Miller, which meant her curiosity probably wouldn't be satisfied.

Thinking of Sheriff Miller made her smile. *Boy, would he be surprised to know we're involved with a mysterious death in Iceland. Then again, maybe not.* However, Kristen reasoned, the cause of death may be mysterious to them, but she assumed the medical team hovering near the body now would be able to figure it out quickly—mystery solved. At least she hoped that was the case, because she had no desire to be further involved while trying to enjoy her honeymoon.

"Being far from home does complicate matters," Betty agreed. "How will they get the body home?"

"It's a good thing we're in Iceland in the winter," Doug said with a wink.

Kristen threw him a questioning glance, wondering where he was going with his comment but not really wanting to know the answer. "Why?" she asked.

"Well, the smell, of course. The body shouldn't deteriorate as fast in this climate." Doug shuddered. "Let's hope the body is shipped home on a different flight than ours."

Kristen assumed Betty and Doug were nice, decent people, but right now, she didn't feel like any more chitchat with them.

"I'm pretty sure bodies are stored in cold conditions no matter what the outdoor temperatures are." Brett stole a glance at Kristen. "Look, we've had a long day. Maybe we should change the subject."

"Oh, so sorry for what I said earlier, and also for Doug's thoughtless remark." Betty glared at her husband, then smiled at Kristen and Brett.

"Thanks, we appreciate that." Kristen smiled to show there were no hard feelings.

"Since you two were the first on the scene, I'm sure you're upset."

"It's not like you ever get used to it." At Betty's baffled look, Kristen hastened to add. "Jet lag, I mean.

We're exhausted, and I think my adrenaline has crashed after the scene we just witnessed."

"Witnessed?" Betty's snow-white eyebrows rose. "I don't know that anyone actually witnessed the poor man's death—other than his wife—but you and your husband sure did help afterwards."

Kristen nodded. "We just did what we thought was right." Maybe Betty had a point. Had anyone seen anything? Kristen figured the police would be verifying Margaret's story, starting with questioning Kristen and Brett. *Why am I feeling strange vibes about this death?* She shivered, not necessarily from the chill of the late afternoon Icelandic winter day, but she was starting to have a bad feeling—one she recognized from previous experiences—and those past experiences had all turned into murder investigations.

CHAPTER 8

Kristen stirred rich cream into her coffee, watching the strong dark brew lighten to a caramel color. They were seated at a café near the Hallgrímskirkja, having moved indoors to wait their turn to talk to the police. Not only was Kristen starting to feel chilled while waiting outdoors by the church, but the jetlag was taking its toll. Now, she felt content, with warm rich coffee to help warm her up and give her some much-needed energy. Kristen had a perfect view of the church and was keeping her eyes on the spot where emergency personnel were still working.

Kristen took a sip of her coffee. "Doesn't it seem like they're taking a long time? I would have thought they'd have already taken the body away by now."

Brett shrugged. "I'm not sure how things work here. Everything seems to run smoothly and efficiently, but people also seem more laid back. I'm sure they're just following procedure, and that takes time."

Kristen decided to share what was really bothering her. "But I'm beginning to get that feeling."

"What feeling is that?"

Kristen figured Brett knew exactly what feeling she was referring to but wanted to hear her say it. "Like there's something very wrong with the situation."

"Well, a man died unexpectedly outside one of Reykjavik's most famous landmarks far from home." Brett shook his head. "That's not good."

"I don't mean that. I mean …" Kristen took another bracing swig of the strong Icelandic brew. "Maybe he was murdered."

"Murdered?" Brett's voice was loud, his tone incredulous. "That's a bit of a stretch, even for your wild imagination. Don't you think you're getting ahead of yourself?"

"Shhhh," Kristen hissed. "Someone will figure out what we're discussing."

Brett had the nerve to chuckle but lowered his voice. "I think it's a little late for that. We're sitting in a café, nursing coffees, trying to stay warm and keep from falling asleep at the table. People are probably already wondering about us. Plus, I think everyone in this place knows there's something up right outside the window."

"Do you think the police cars and ambulance gave that away?" Kristen joined Brett in laughing at their situation. She was starting to feel a little goofy from lack of sleep, not to mention feeling zapped of energy after her earlier adrenaline rush faded. She wished they could get the questioning over with, so they could enjoy an early dinner then head to their room to sleep for the next several hours.

"Pretty much." Brett reached across the table to put his hand over Kristen's. "Look. I know we've had a shock, and you've been down this road plenty of times. Unfortunately, that was because the bodies you found ended up being murder victims. I'm sure that's not the case this time, so try to relax."

Kristen was glad for Brett's words of encouragement, but that didn't stop the niggling feeling this body discovery wasn't much different from the others she'd found. Sure, they were in another country, and they'd assumed Lewis' death was due to natural causes, but Kristen still couldn't shake the feeling that something was amiss.

Hearing the café door open, Kristen looked up to see two uniformed police officers walking toward them. She'd been so caught up in her thoughts she hadn't noticed them approaching. "Good, now we can get this over with," she murmured to Brett.

One of the officers held out his hand to each of them. "Hallo. I'm Officer Grímsson." He nodded toward the other policeman. "And he's Officer Helgason."

Officer Grímsson looked toward the counter, where their waiter was hovering with a washcloth, wiping down the already spotless surface. "Is there somewhere we can talk to this couple in private?"

Kristen was glad he'd spoken in English for their benefit. Otherwise, she would have felt like they had done something wrong. After a quick exchange in Icelandic, Officer Grímsson nodded to them. "Please join us in the back room, where we can take your statement in a more private setting."

Taking a deep breath and catching Brett's eyes as she rose from the table, Kristen felt uneasy yet again. Not only was she nervous about what the police would ask— not because she and Brett had done anything wrong— but she couldn't ignore the feeling someone else had done something wrong to Lewis. She also wasn't familiar with how police interviews were conducted in Iceland.

Officer Grímsson ushered them into the small, private dining area. Kristen thought it would be perfect for a family gathering, then felt a wave of homesickness. Up until an hour ago, she'd been having the time of her life with the man she loved and hadn't even thought about home or the family and friends who lived there. Now, she would give anything to be back in the familiar town of Eklund, far away from death. *Well, not exactly.* Kristen gave herself a mental shake. As soon as they were finished with their question-and-answer session, she and Brett would be on their way, without giving any more time or thought to Lewis' death. *Yeah, right.* If Kristen was honest with herself, she knew she wouldn't rest until she found out how Lewis had died. Unfortunately, she had a feeling the Reykjavik police wouldn't be as forgiving as the sheriff's department housed in Eklund were about her contributions to murder cases and finding dead bodies in the first place.

However, from the brief interactions she'd had with the officers so far, they seemed to be polite, professional, and respectful, something she couldn't always say about her interactions with Sheriff Miller. *Now's not the time to reminisce about Eklund*, she chided herself. *The sooner we answer their questions, the sooner we'll be out of here.* Kristen felt a warm dinner and early night calling her name. Jet lag and the afternoon's dramatic events were catching up with her.

Officer Grímsson gestured for them to sit down, then he and Officer Helgason sat across the table from them. Kristen was relieved when Brett picked up her hand and squeezed it. She snapped out of her moodiness. They would get through this together.

"Thank you for taking time to talk with us today." Officer Grímsson's English was perfect. "We would like to ask you a few questions about the death of your fellow American …" he paused to look at his notes. "Lewis Sawyer." He pronounced it Saw-yer, like a saw.

Kristen nodded. "Whatever we can do to help."

"You've already helped quite a bit," Officer Helgason said. "From what Mrs. Sawyer told us, the two of you were on the scene right after her husband collapsed. Where were you when you realized he was in trouble?"

"We were at the top of the church tower." Kristen didn't want to try to pronounce the church's official name to the Icelanders.

Officer Grímsson raised his blond eyebrows. "How did you know there was trouble from up there?"

"From Mrs. Sawyer's scream. We could hear it all the way up there and ran over to the side where we'd heard it. We had seen Mr. and Mrs. Sawyer earlier—we recognized them from seeing them at the airport and hotel—and thought we'd better try to help."

"That must have been very loud to hear all the way up there?" Officer Helgason looked skeptical. "Isn't the bell tower closed in with glass?"

Kristen thought about it and nodded. "It was an ear-piercing scream—the kind that signals something bad just happened, not just a frightened type of scream."

"The church and surrounding area were so peaceful," Brett offered. "Even though plenty of people were milling around, no one was talking loudly. Voices tend to be more subdued in and around a place of worship, you know? The scream was not only loud; it shattered the peace."

Officer Grímsson nodded in understanding. "That makes sense. But it doesn't explain why you were the first on the scene. You arrived before anyone else, even though you were at the top of the bell tower."

"Once we realized the Sawyers were in trouble, we boarded the elevator. There wasn't a wait, so we arrived relatively quickly," Brett said.

"There's quite a distance to cover, from the elevator entrance to the statue." Officer Helgason scrunched up his eyebrows. "Did you run the entire way?"

"I don't remember exactly how fast we were moving."

Kristen remained silent. She knew Brett was trying to downplay their fast-thinking action, so as not to draw suspicion upon them—not necessarily as having anything to do with Lewis' death but having been involved in other sudden deaths.

"We just did what we thought we had to do." Brett continued and nodded toward Kristen. "We both work and exercise outdoors, so we're in pretty decent shape."

"Regardless of how much you regularly exercise, that seems like a lot of effort for people you don't know." Officer Grímsson looked at them questioningly.

As professional and efficient as the officers seemed to be, Kristen was starting to squirm. Were they wondering if she and Brett had anything to do with Lewis' death? Why were they fussing over details if Lewis had died of natural causes?

"I'm not sure if Mrs. Sawyer already told you," Kristen said. "Apparently we booked under the same travel agency." Although, to be honest, Kristen wasn't sure if Margaret Sawyer had recognized them before they arrived on the scene to help. She seemed to be one of those self-absorbed types who didn't pay attention to those around her, because she was used to making a statement—or a spectacle—wherever she went.

"So you knew each other before today?" Officer Helgason asked.

Kristen shook her head. "No. We hadn't even spoken to each other before we tried to help her husband."

"Then why did you get involved?" Officer Grímsson had his head down, looking at his notes, but Kristen wasn't fooled by the seemingly casual question. She could feel his partner watching her closely, but she tried to act naturally.

However, Kristen was starting to question their actions herself, and she felt she needed to answer his question cautiously. Brett gave her hand another squeeze. She wasn't sure if he was urging her to keep it simple or if he was merely trying to reassure her. "We're all so far from home, and while Iceland seems like a wonderful place, we don't know anyone in this country. We come from a small town back home, where we work together and try to help each other—even strangers who may cross our paths. Though you need to be careful of that these days." Kristen felt she was starting to ramble, telling the officers more than they needed to know. If the officers grew curious about Brett and Kristen's backgrounds, all they had to do was make a phone call to see just how helpful Kristen had been in the past—to not only her friends and neighbors, but also the sheriff's department when it came to solving murder mysteries. *No need to go into that.*

"What my lovely wife is trying to say is even though we don't know these people, we felt a sense of obligation to help since there didn't seem to be anyone else coming to their aid."

Kristen wasn't enjoying having to defend their helpfulness. S*ince when is it a crime to help someone in need?*

"Moving on," Officer Helgason said, as if sensing he wouldn't get any more information out of them. "Describe what happened once you arrived on the scene."

Kristen tried to gather her thoughts. "At first we weren't sure if Mr. Sawyer was still alive, so I checked for a pulse."

"While Kristen was doing that, I tried to help calm down Mrs. Sawyer. She was having problems with her phone, so I used mine to call nine-one-one—or one-two-two, as it's called here." Brett paused. "Mrs. Sawyer was almost frantic, trying to reach the authorities but not having any luck with her own phone."

"Did you notice anything unusual or see anyone nearby?" Officer Helgason asked. "Even if the two of you made it to the Sawyers in record time, it seems odd that you were the first to arrive. What was everyone else doing? There are always people loitering around the Leif Ericksson statue before they enter the church."

That was a big question, and Kristen wasn't sure where to start. "Honestly, I didn't notice much. My priority was checking to see if Mr. Sawyer was still alive, and Brett was doing his best to help Mrs. Sawyer. We were occupied with that until we realized he was dead. Then we tried to console Mrs. Sawyer while we waited for you to arrive—the police and ambulance."

"No one else was close by?" Officer Grímsson gave her a shrewd look.

"I'm sure there were others in the vicinity, but no one offered to help." Kristen wondered why he kept pressing the matter. Did Iceland have a Good Samaritan law? They couldn't help it if they hadn't noticed others in the area. They had their hands full.

"Our main focus was trying to help the Sawyers, so we weren't paying attention to much else," Brett interjected. "As Kristen already mentioned, we checked to see if Mr. Sawyer was still alive, contacted the authorities, and tried to keep Mrs. Sawyer calm. All I can remember is, no one came running up to help when we first got there, but a small crowd started to form later."

Kristen could tell her normally good-natured husband was starting to get irritated. What were the police insinuating? "That pretty much sums up everything we saw and did. We've told you everything we know." Kristen paused for effect. "Is there something you haven't told us?" Kristen was beginning to think there was *plenty* the police weren't telling them.

CHAPTER 9

Officer Grímsson and Officer Helgason exchanged a glance, making Kristen wonder what was up. Officer Grímsson nodded at Officer Helgason, and then spoke. "We don't want you to get the wrong idea about Icelanders," he said, cracking a small smile. "We don't normally question tourists about an accident they may have witnessed to this degree. However, …" he sighed. "We're working under the assumption Mr. Sawyer's death was not due to natural causes."

Even though Kristen had an inkling something was amiss, it was still a shock to hear it spoken aloud. "You mean he didn't die of a heart attack or stroke, as we first assumed?"

"*First* assumed?" Officer Helgason asked. "What do you mean by that?"

Kristen gave herself a mental kick. "Well, you've been giving us the third degree." At the officers' raised eyebrows Kristen elaborated. "Sorry to use American slang. What I mean is, you've been asking a lot of questions about what we saw and when we arrived. If it were a natural death, there wouldn't be much to see or question us about."

"That's true," Officer Grímsson grinned wryly, then frowned. "We think Mr. Sawyer was murdered."

Kristen's mind raced, even though she'd been expecting that news. "What was the cause of death?" She hadn't noticed anything in the vicinity that could have been used as a weapon, and she hadn't seen any blood.

"We won't know for sure until autopsy results are final," Officer Helgason said, his tone stern, as if that were the end of the information they'd be receiving.

Kristen knew this was a standard statement. It didn't matter they were dealing with Icelandic police; Officer's Helgason's remark was verbatim what Sheriff Miller would say in a similar situation. From the way the police were questioning them as witnesses to his murder, Kristen felt sure the police knew how Lewis had died. Otherwise, they would have probably only taken token statements from them, as a matter of formality.

"But you must have some idea if you're investigating his death as a murder." Kristen smiled her most angelic smile, hoping she radiated pure innocence.

Apparently, the officers weren't buying her act, or they were made of sterner stuff. Either way, they weren't going to spill any information. Kristen wasn't happy, but she understood. After all, she'd come up against similar roadblocks with Sherriff Miller.

"I'm afraid we can't say anything until we know the official cause of death," Officer Grímsson said. "Rest assured, if we need to question you further, we will contact you once we receive the results, which we hope to have by tomorrow."

"That seems fast," Kristen blurted out, then realized they may wonder how she was so familiar with police procedure. "I mean, doesn't an autopsy take some time?" Even in a country like Iceland, where crime rates were low, there were probably still people—or bodies, rather—ahead of Lewis Sawyer.

"Things do take time, but as far as we know, there haven't been any recent questionable deaths, so Mr. Sawyer will be first in line tomorrow," Officer Helgason said.

Kristen thought they were probably trying to expedite matters, since both the victim and his wife, as well as their star witnesses, were visiting from another country and wouldn't be in Iceland for very long.

Officer Grímsson must have read her mind. "If you could please give us your contact information, such as your hotel name and cell phone numbers, we will get in touch with you soon. Once done with further questioning, we will let you know when you can leave the country."

Yikes. Kristen gulped. "We have several sightseeing expeditions planned. Is it okay to travel within the country?"

"Of course." Officer Helgason smiled. "We want you to see all the sights Iceland has to offer. We may be a small country, but there are many extraordinary places to see. It's unfortunate you've had a bad experience so early in your vacation, but we hope you can put it behind you and enjoy your trip."

"Our honeymoon, actually." Though polite and respectful, Kristen could tell Brett was starting to feel the effects of jet lag, the murder, or possibly irritation from the questioning, if not all three. She hoped they would soon be finished.

"We're so sorry, but we appreciate you allowing us to intrude on your honeymoon with questions, as well as all you tried to do for the victim and his wife." Officer Grímsson stood. "You're free to go now."

Kristen and Brett rose from their seats. Kristen felt bone tired but was also hungry. As soon as they left the private room and walked into the café proper, Kristen noticed how dark it was outside. She checked her watch. "It's five o'clock. How about that early dinner we wanted? Should we get something to eat here?"

"Fine by me, as long as they don't mind a couple of fugitives eating here."

"Is that what the police think of us?" Kristen grinned at Brett's attempt at humor, but she couldn't help feeling out of sorts about the whole situation.

"I'm sure they were just covering their bases. We know how the police operate at home, and they seem to be pretty much the same here." Brett put his hand on the small of Kristen's back and guided her toward the front of the café to inquire about a table. "This place seems quiet and laid back, so let's try to put things behind us for a while and enjoy ourselves."

Soon they were seated at the same table where they'd had coffee earlier. There weren't many other diners at this early hour, which was fine with Kristen. She wasn't in a social mood. She hadn't paid much attention to the café's interior earlier—her thoughts otherwise occupied by Lewis' death--but now she looked around the café appreciatively. Already getting used to simplicity and clean lines in contemporary Nordic design, she noticed the furnishings were simple but comfortable. Glowing candles at each table, subdued lighting, and a gas fireplace added to the warmth and coziness.

Kristen turned her attention to the menu, which was thankfully written in both Icelandic and English. Wanting to try something Icelandic, she decided on the grilled haddock and boiled potatoes. "I love how simple and unpretentious traditional Icelandic food is."

Brett nodded. "I'm famished after that interrogation, but I'm having a hard time deciding."

Their waiter, a tall, lean man of middle age, walked toward them, holding a tray with two tall glasses. "I thought you two could use these." He set two tall slender glasses in front of them. "They are … how do you say? On the house. Gull beer is Iceland's most popular brand. You have to try some." He also set down a basket full of hearty whole grain bread. "By the way, my name is Gunnar."

Kristen eyed both the beer and the bread. Was her mouth literally watering? "That is so kind of you. We appreciate your hospitality. It's our first day in Iceland, and we're tired from the flight."

"And also from the police questioning you, I would guess." Gunnar chuckled, his ice blue eyes twinkling. "Don't worry. Icelandic police are very thorough, but our justice system is fair."

Kristen took a sip of the beer, served at room temperature, not knowing what to expect. "Oh, boy. This tastes great."

"I'm so glad you like it." Gunnar said. "*Skål*, by the way."

Kristen held up her glass in a mock toast, then pulled a piece of bread out of the basket and spread some butter on it. "It's been such a long day. I'd better have some bread to go with my beer, or it will go to my head."

Gunnar grinned. "That wouldn't be good. Do you know what you would like to order? After such a long day, a hearty meal is just what you need."

Kristen glanced at Brett, who nodded. Once they gave him their orders, Gunnar nodded approvingly. "Great choices for your first night in Iceland. I like it when tourists eat some of our traditional food, rather than opting for a cheeseburger or asking if we serve pizza."

"We can eat all that at home, but we don't get much fresh seafood where we live," Brett said. "Your menu listed several dishes I'd like to try."

"Then I hope you'll come back again while you're in Iceland." Gunnar bowed slightly, then headed toward the kitchen.

Kristen was charmed by the old world gesture. She brushed aside their worries about murder and focused on relaxing by drinking good beer and eating delicious bread with her husband.

Kristen looked up to see Brett grinning at her. "It looks like I have some competition."

Kristen's face reddened as she smiled. "No way. It was just so thoughtful of him to bring us beer and bread before we even ordered." Kristen couldn't help but remember Joseph, the waiter who ended up dead during their fall trip to Michigan. Her smile faded.

"Are you okay?" Brett sipped his beer.

"I'm fine. I just had a flashback to Joseph's murder. Our waiter tonight reminded me of him—not that they have, or had, anything in common other than being good waiters."

"Look, it's been a very eventful day, but let's make the most of our first night in Iceland and try not to talk about murder."

"I'll be fine once I get something to eat." Kristen bit into a hunk of bread.

"I'll have to remember that after a rough day all it takes is beer and bread to make you happy."

"Actually, you may be on to something," Kristen teased him and felt some of the earlier tension drain away. "But I'm not sure this kind of bread or beer can be duplicated at home." Though maybe she'd try to talk her baker friend, Amy, into offering some hearty multigrain breads and rolls at her bakery.

"We're on our honeymoon in a beautiful foreign country. That would be hard to duplicate in Eklund."

"I guess that's why travelling—especially on a honeymoon—is so special. Seeing new places and experiencing new cultures is what it's all about."

"I'm finding that one of the best ways to experience culture is to eat and drink traditional favorites." Brett smeared butter on his second piece of bread.

"I agree one hundred percent. In fact, we need to find a grocery store."

Brett raised his eyebrows. "Don't tell me you want to attempt making an Icelandic dish in our room. We don't even have a microwave, coffee pot, or mini fridge, like we do in many American rooms.

"Of course not, silly. As we've already discussed, I just want to pick up snacks for us and a few things to take home—like Icelandic chocolate, for one thing, and Icelandic licorice for another."

Brett made a face at the mention of licorice. "You're not on that salty candy kick again, are you?

Kristen nodded. "It's popular in all the Nordic countries. It's an acquired taste, but it doesn't take long, so you'll be munching on it in no time."

"I can't argue with you about chocolate, but remember, we have weight limits for our luggage."

"No worries." Kristen took another sip of her Gull, enjoying its rich and hearty flavor as much as the banter with her husband. She wouldn't normally enjoy a beer at room temperature but knew that's how most Europeans drank their beer. *When in Reykjavik.* "I'll make sure we have plenty of room—and weight---to spare."

"Even if it means chucking some of my stuff to the curb?" Brett's eyes were twinkling.

"I don't think we'll need to take any drastic measures." Kristen's eyes lit up as she noticed the waiter coming toward them with a tray laden with their Icelandic meals. This was what their honeymoon was supposed to be like, enjoying their time together, not becoming involved in a murder investigation.

But wait. Aren't we already involved? Kristen sighed as she bit into her fish, not necessarily from pleasure, though the fish was cooked and seasoned to perfection. She sighed because she knew in her heart, she'd do what she could to help solve Lewis' murder, whether the Icelandic police welcomed her help—or interference, as Sheriff Miller called it—or not.

CHAPTER 10

When Kristen rose the next day, it was still pitch-black outside. She fumbled around for her watch or phone—whatever she could put her hands on first—to check the time. She was shocked to see it was already eight o'clock. She'd slept for over twelve hours. Stretching, she glanced over at Brett, who was just starting to stir.

"Why don't you hop in the shower while I'm waking up?" Brett buried his head back in his pillow and pulled the covers up around him.

"I won't be long. I'm dying for a cup of coffee, and from the looks of you, you could use one as well." Momentarily sad their room didn't have a coffee pot, Kristen's mood brightened. She swore she could smell coffee wafting up from the dining area two floors below them.

"Forget the cup. I think I could drink an entire pot of coffee." Brett mumbled the words from under the covers, but Kristen still understood him. She felt the same way. "No one should have to wake up when it's this dark out while they're on their honeymoon."

"If we were here in June, we'd probably be cursing the fact that the sun would be shining for most of the day—and night!" Though Kristen would thoroughly love to witness the Midnight Sun almost as much as the Northern Lights, which were on their agenda for that evening. The thought of all they planned to see today motivated her to pull away from the warm bed—not to mention her husband—and take her turn in the shower.

* * *

Kristen sipped hot coffee while she waited for Brett to arrive in the breakfast area. Between a decent night's sleep, her shower, and the coffee she now drank, she was feeling much more like her normal self. She was content to drink coffee for a moment but would be ready to fill her plate once Brett arrived. Thankfully he came through the dining room door just as she glanced in that direction. She waved him over to the table she was holding.

"Hiya, handsome."

Brett kissed her on the cheek. "Let me grab some coffee, then you can get your food. I know you're probably starved."

"Sounds great." Kristen swirled the coffee in her cup, then took a sip.

When she saw Brett headed back her way with his own cup of coffee, she stood. "I can't ignore my grumbling stomach any longer."

Kristen was filling her plate with bread and fruit when someone bumped her elbow. Looking up, Kristen recognized one of the backpackers who had flown on the same flight. "Sorry about that."

"No, my bad," the red-haired boy said. "I'm starved and got a little overzealous, I guess." He grinned good naturedly. "Say, I think we must have booked the same tour package."

"Yeah, that's right. My name's Kristen."

"I'm Sam." He heaped some eggs on his plate. "Are you guys going on the Ring of Fire trip today?"

Kristen smiled, then nodded. "If you mean the Golden Circle tour, then yeah, we are."

"Hey, that's right. I knew it was something like that, but I'm not in charge of the itinerary." He grabbed a couple of hard rolls. "Well, I'm sure we'll run into each other later. See ya."

"I'm sure we will. Nice to meet you." Kristen balanced her plate with one hand and poured milk into a cup with her other hand, then walked back to their table where Brett had just polished off his cup of coffee.

"I'll get a refill for both of us, then get something to eat." He eyed Kristen's plate. "Looks like they have some good stuff."

Kristen nodded as she started spreading butter on a hard roll. "They sure do." She handed Brett her empty coffee cup.

Kristen began to eat while she waited for Brett to return. She'd just taken a bite of her roll when someone pulled out a chair at their table. Glancing up, she was surprised to see Margaret sitting down across from her.

"Am I disturbing you?" Margaret asked, noting Kristen's confused look.

"No, not at all. I just thought you were my husband returning with his breakfast and was surprised he was back so soon." Kristen smiled warmly. "To be honest, I didn't think I'd see you in the dining room."

"A girl has to eat, doesn't she?" Margaret's manner was offhand, but her red eyes spoke differently. "Okay, I'm not all that hungry, but I think a cup of coffee is a good start."

"I couldn't agree more." Kristen caught Brett's eye across the room and gestured toward Margaret, then used her hand to form a drinking from a cup gesture. Brett looked puzzled at first, then headed back to the coffee pot for another cup. "Brett is bringing me a cup, and he's pouring one for you as well."

"That's why I came downstairs. Seeing a couple of friendly faces and having a cup of coffee gives me a sense of normality in an otherwise abnormal situation."

Kristen understood Margaret's reasoning but thought it was ironic they were going to drink coffee together. After witnessing Margaret's behavior at the airport and hotel yesterday morning, never in a million years had Kristen thought they would end up eating breakfast together. *I guess a murder will do that to you.*

"I think it's wise. Once you've had some coffee, maybe you'll feel like eating something." Kristen pointed to the bread she'd been eating. "This bread is out of this world and would probably be good for your empty stomach."

"I could use an otherworldly experience after yesterday's experience."

Kristen was glad to see Brett coming toward them, precariously holding three cups of coffee between his hands. He sat Margaret's down first. "I hope you're feeling okay today."

"This should help me feel a little better." Margaret gave Brett a weak smile. "Besides, I need to be ready for the tour anyway."

Kristen about fell out of her chair. Was Margaret honestly going on a tour the day after her husband was murdered? "We're going on the Golden Circle tour today. Are you going on the same one?"

"Oh, yes. I wouldn't miss it." Margaret dabbed her eyes with a napkin she pulled from the table dispenser. "But it won't be the same without my dear Lewis."

Kristen exchanged a look with Brett over Margaret's bowed head. "I'm sure it won't. I wouldn't even feel up to it if something had happened to Brett." She didn't mean to sound accusing, but it seemed like Margaret was being unfeeling by continuing with her vacation plans at the same time her husband was probably scheduled for an autopsy. Besides, what if the police had questions or wanted to communicate new information with Margaret?

"I know it probably sounds cold of me, but it's not like that. I'll go crazy if I stay in my room. Lewis wanted so much to visit Iceland, and I feel like I owe it to him to continue as planned."

"Are you taking a Northern Lights tour as well?" Brett asked.

Margaret nodded. "Assuming I still feel up to it this evening. My luck, it will be too cloudy to see anything."

"We're hoping to see them tonight as well." Brett spoke conversationally as he edged away from the table. "If you'll excuse me, I'm going to get something to eat. Is there anything I can get you?"

Margaret shook her head, then changed her mind. "Perhaps a little bread will do me some good. Kristen's been raving about it, so I'll give it a try."

Kristen hardly considered her casual comment about the bread to be raving, but it would be good for Margaret to eat something. Kristen held a fork to her mouth, then paused. "I hope you don't think it's rude if I continue eating?"

Margaret waved her away. "Of course not. Besides, I'm the one who sat with you, uninvited."

"That's not a problem. I'm glad you did. I feel badly for you not knowing anyone else to help you through this. Do you have family coming over to be with you?" Kristen wasn't sure how long Margaret's presence would be required. For all she knew, Margaret was a prime suspect in her husband's murder and would not be allowed to leave until the killer—whoever that may be—was tracked down. Kristen shivered. Was she eating breakfast with Lewis' killer? Even though Margaret was visibly upset earlier, she seemed to be okay now and was planning a day full of sightseeing. If she were really grieving, would that be natural? Then again, if she'd killed her husband, would she want to be out sightseeing with others who had been in the area when her husband had died? Wouldn't she want to avoid being around them? Maybe Margaret was trying to avoid answering more questions from the police.

"I broke the news to our children yesterday after the police were done questioning me. I'm waiting to hear when or if one of them can fly over to be with me." Margaret took a sip of coffee before continuing. "I have three children, and it will be difficult for them to break away from their families and jobs to come over to help me. Then, there's the cost of a last-minute flight."

"I hope one of them is able to fly over to stay with you." Kristen wondered if Margaret got along well with her children. Kristen would drop what she was doing if one of her parents were in a similar situation, and if money were an issue, wouldn't Margaret offer to pay travel expenses? From the way they dressed, they looked well-to-do. "I'm sure there are arrangements to be made once the police release the body."

Margaret gave Kristen a sharp look. "What do you know of such matters?"

Kristen wasn't sure she was supposed to know Lewis' death was being investigated as suspicious. "I assumed they would need to determine the cause of death, and then there's all the red tape that is probably involved with shipping a body back home from a foreign country."

Margaret flinched at Kristen's words. "Lewis is not just a body to me."

I keep sticking my foot in my mouth. "I'm sorry." Kristen wasn't sure what to say, so she patted Margaret's arm, hoping Brett would soon return to help lessen the awkwardness of the situation. "I didn't mean to be so blunt. I was a biology major in college and work as a naturalist now, so I'm used to using basic, scientific terms to describe situations. You wouldn't believe some of my lunchtime conservations." Kristen tried to joke, not very successfully, she feared. *Not to mention my experience with finding bodies in the past.*

"It's okay. I don't know how you would have phrased it any differently. I just need to stop being so sensitive and get used to the fact that Lewis is gone."

"It's going to take some time," Kristen told her. She looked up, happy to see Brett walking their way, a plate full of food in one hand and a tall glass of orange juice in the other.

As Brett settled down to eat, Kristen looked around the room and noticed the backpackers sitting together at one table, then saw Betty and Doug at another. She wondered if they were all going on the Golden Circle Tour. Since it was one of the most popular tours for first time travelers to Iceland, Kristen thought they probably were. *Maybe some of the others could help keep Margaret company while I enjoy the tour with my husband. After all, this is our honeymoon!*

Kristen didn't mean to harbor such selfish thoughts, but she couldn't help it. It was bad enough they spent their entire first afternoon in Iceland helping Margaret then ended up being questioned by the police. She was hoping they could put all that behind them today, but she wasn't feeling optimistic at the moment. Margaret seemed to have latched on to them. *But who else is there to keep her company?*

There was also the fact that if Lewis Sawyer had been murdered, Kristen knew it would be hard for her to stay away from the investigation. Kristen had already felt the pull, while they rushed to help Lewis. Kristen looked at the bright side. If they were going to be stuck with Margaret today, what better way to do some digging than to start with the wife—or main suspect—who should know the deceased better than anyone else.

CHAPTER 11

Tucked away on the bus heading northeast out of Reykjavík, Kristen was thankful there were only two seats on either side of the aisle, and Margaret had picked a seat several rows behind them. Although she had no doubt Margaret would seek them out later, Kristen planned to make good use of the time before they arrived at their first stop, Þingvellir National Park, in about forty-five minutes.

Snuggled in next to Brett, Kristen gazed out the window. The sky was finally starting to lighten. They passed mile after mile of gorgeous scenery. Everything from gentle countryside landscapes to volcanic mounds, and more pronounced low mountains glistened with snow. If travelling inland was so beautiful, she could hardly wait until they explored the coastline and fjords later in their trip. She vowed to keep any thoughts of murder, or of Margaret tagging along with them, at bay as they tried to enjoy their honeymoon.

Kristen turned away from the window back toward Brett. "Reykjavik is a charming city, but the scenery is amazing."

"All the snow adds to it, but I'm sure it's equally beautiful no matter what the season."

"One of these days we'll have to visit in the summer—or fall or spring." Kristen lowered her voice. "Definitely not when a murder has taken place."

"I'm sorry, honey, but trouble seems to find you. I can't imagine very many murders occurring on this island oasis, but as luck would have it, one happened on the first day of our honeymoon."

"You can't blame me because someone offed another traveler." Kristen tried to sound offended, but she knew Brett was only kidding. She did seem to stumble upon more than her fair share of murders. *Zero is a fair share, and this is the …* Kristen did the mental math *… seventh murder I've been unfortunate enough to be involved with.*

"I don't blame you," Brett said good naturedly, "but wouldn't it be nice to just have fun?"

Kristen's earlier vow was already long forgotten. "Aren't you curious as to how Lewis died?" Kristen was puzzled how a man could drop dead in the middle of a fairly busy area, even in the middle of winter, and no one notice. She also wondered why it hadn't been more obvious to them that Lewis had been murdered, rather than dying from natural causes as they'd assumed.

"Even if I am curious, do you think the police are going to tell us?"

"As long as Margaret continues to cozy up to us, I hope to work some information out of her."

Brett rolled his eyes. "Once you start, you won't be able to stop until you've uncovered the killer. You do know that, right?"

"You're probably right, but how am I supposed to ignore my natural curiosity?"

"I can think of a few ways." Brett leaned in closer for a kiss.

Kristen had to admit kissing Brett swept away most unpleasant thoughts. The sound of the tour guide's voice interrupted their kiss. One thing she liked about the tour they were taking was the guide would do most of his talking before they arrived at each of the day's destinations, leaving them plenty of time to wander around the sights on their own.

"It sounds like we'll be there pretty soon," Kristen said, checking the area to make sure her personal items were handy.

"We've already seen some beautiful places, just on the ride here. It's hard to imagine the parks we're visiting will top them."

"I think you're in for a nice surprise then." Kristen peeked out the window. "Good news; the sun just came through the clouds. That has to be a good sign, right?"

* * *

From the main lookout point at their first stop, Þingvellir National Park, Kristen gaped in wonder at the scene before her. Not sure which direction to look in first, she slowly panned the area. A vast mountain lake called Þingvallavatn—the second largest natural lake in Iceland—with low mountains on one side, a lazy river on another, and the famous rock formations that surrounded the location of the very first parliament on yet another side, all competed for her attention. The snow covered everything and sparkled in the weak sunlight. Thankful they had plenty of time to explore all the sights, she took the lens cover off her camera and started snapping photos of the lake first, then turned to the river, and finally the rocks.

"There, now let's take some of each other," Kristen suggested.

"Let's ask someone to take one of both of us." Brett waved at Betty, who was standing close by. "Can you take our picture?"

"Anything for the two lovebirds," Betty joked, as she took the camera from Kristen. "This looks a little fancy for my skill level."

"I already have it zoomed in, and it's set on autofocus, so all you have to do is look through the viewfinder and press the button," Kristen assured her. She hoped Betty could center them, or at least position them so Kristen could fix the picture later if needed with cropping. She stepped back toward Brett, and they smiled for a few shots.

"Thanks," Brett said, taking the camera from Betty. "Do you want yours taken?"

"Sure." Betty handed Brett her phone. "It's amazing how well these smartphones take pictures these days."

"Sometimes I think the phones are smarter than me." Brett snapped a couple of shots, then handed the phone back to her. "What do you think of the tour so far?"

"If the rest of it is as good as this park, we're happy campers," Doug said.

"Speaking of happy campers," Betty said, leaning closer to them and lowering her voice. "What's up with Margaret? I can't believe she's taking a sightseeing tour the day after her husband died."

"Seems a bit early to be living it up," chimed in Doug.

"Margaret told me she didn't want to be alone at the hotel. She already had the tour booked, so she decided she may as well stick with her plans." Kristen looked around, not having seen Margaret since they got off the bus.

"I noticed you were awfully chummy with her at breakfast," Betty said. "I would hate to be alone in a foreign country if something happened to Doug, but I also can't picture me hopping on a sightseeing tour right after it happened."

Kristen shrugged. She didn't really get it either. "Hopefully she won't regret coming on the tour later. We still have a full day ahead of us."

"I'd bet she didn't get much sleep last night," Brett said. "She may sleep through the next stops."

"Any news on how her husband died?" Betty asked.

There was no way Kristen was going to even hint at the fact Lewis was thought to have been murdered. She shook her head. "The police didn't give us a definite cause of death when they spoke to us." *Which was true.*

"What all did they ask you?" Betty asked. "We've never been involved in anything like this. I bet you didn't know what to think."

Kristen hid a grin. *If Betty had an inkling of our involvement in other murder investigations, she would be even more curious.* "They just wanted to hear our version of the story. I'm sure Margaret wasn't thinking straight when they talked to her. The police asked us general questions about the sequence of events." Kristen hoped she answered Betty's question without telling her all that much.

"What a way to kick off your honeymoon."

"Better than kicking off, like that poor guy," Doug added.

Kristen wasn't sure what to say to Doug. He seemed to enjoy making crude remarks. "We're just glad to have it behind us." Betty and Doug didn't need to know Kristen might ask a few questions of her own, starting with Margaret, as soon as she was over her initial shock. Kristen figured the poor woman hadn't quite grasped the fact her husband was dead.

Brett put his hand in the small of Kristen's back. "We still want to see the parliament site. You're welcome to join us."

They started walking down the paved path. Kristen was glad for her heavy boots, as the path was snow covered. She wondered what type of footwear Margaret was wearing on the tour—hopefully warm boots with good tread, but Kristen doubted it after seeing the woman's earlier fashion choices. Kristen told herself to stop criticizing Margaret's clothing. Why did she care about Margaret's outfits when they were in the midst of so much history and natural beauty?

Trying to watch her step as she walked down the slightly sloped path, Kristen looked up at the dark brown rock formations on either side of them. Soon they reached the spot where the first parliament took place, with the blue and red Icelandic flag waving prominently, a striking contrast to the rock and snow.

Brett put his arm around Kristen. "Pretty neat, huh?"

"Yeah." Kristen pulled her guide out of her pocket. "Isn't this also the division between continents?"

"You mean like a continental divide?"

Kristen looked back at the pathway they'd walked on a few minutes ago. "I think that path is the continental rift between North America and Europe." Kristen had crossed over the Continental Divide in the United States more than once, but this concept was even more amazing."

"Let me see your book."

Kristen handed Brett the travel guide. Looking around as he read, she spotted Margaret walking down the path. She looked lost—not literally lost—but as if she'd just lost her best friend, which she probably had. Feeling sorry for her, Kristen waved at her.

Margaret, who at least was wearing tennis shoes with her jeans today—though they appeared to be designed more for fashion than for fitness—was headed their way. Her thin body seemed even tinier in the parka she wore.

"How are you doing?" Kristen asked. "Isn't this something?"

"It's something all right, if you like a pile of rocks."

Brett quirked an eyebrow. "I was just reading about this pile of rocks. That pathway we just walked down basically separates the North American and Eurasian tectonic plates. Don't you think that's cool?"

Margaret sighed. "My husband would have thought so. He's the reason we decided to visit Iceland. He was a geology professor at the University of Illinois."

"I don't know much about geology, but I do know that Iceland is the place to go if you're interested in it." Kristen gazed at the scenery, which also happened be rich in history. "This park has it all!"

Margaret nodded. "Lewis couldn't wait to take the Golden Circle Tour. He would have been in seventh Heaven with all the geysers, mountains, tectonic plates, volcanoes, waterfalls, and other geological features of this area." She sighed. "Which is why I was so insistent on coming on this tour today."

Kristen patted Margaret on the back. "I can't imagine how hard it is for you."

"You have no idea." Margaret pulled a tissue from her pocket. "Now I'm wishing I hadn't come. This place is bringing back too many memories of Lewis."

"Try and focus on the beauty of the area," Brett suggested.

Kristen smiled lovingly at her husband. Even though she knew he was chomping at the bit to continue exploring—and so was she—he was doing his best to curtail his impatience at the situation they found themselves in by trying to help Margaret and Lewis yesterday and befriending Margaret today.

"It is lovely." Margaret sniffed. "I was overcome by the beauty of the lake. So serene and peaceful. I hope Lewis is feeling peace and looking down on me today."

"I'm sure he is." What else could she say? Even though Kristen believed in Heaven, there were no guarantees Lewis had made it there. If he had been murdered, someone must have hated him. What had he done to provoke that hate?

"Do you want to take any more pictures here?" Brett looked at his watch. "It's almost time to head back to the gift shop where we're supposed to be meeting."

Kristen snapped a picture of the Icelandic flag among the dark brown rocks. "I want to have time to go back to the overlook and see the lake again."

"Then let's go." Brett waved his arm toward Margaret, to allow her to go before them.

They were silent as they walked back toward the park headquarters. Margaret appeared to be lost in her thoughts, but Kristen let her mind empty and concentrated on soaking up the beautiful scenery. She had every intention of fully experiencing every bit of this trip, despite the fact a murder was hanging over them.

CHAPTER 12

Back on the bus, they trundled toward the next stop on the Golden Circle Tour, Geysir Geothermal Area. Their guide told them it would take at least forty-five minutes to get there, depending on traffic and road conditions. Kristen looked out the window at the snow-covered landscape. The sun had disappeared, and it was snowing lightly. Their guide would brief them as they got closer to the park, then would let them wander around to explore on their own.

Kristen hoped Margaret wouldn't latch onto them again then felt guilty. Kristen knew Margaret had nowhere else to turn, but she couldn't help but hope Margaret wouldn't tag along on the rest of the sightseeing excursions they had planned for the rest of the week.

Maybe if we help solve the murder we can truly focus on our honeymoon, Kristen thought. She turned to Brett, keeping her voice low. "I just don't get it. Why was Lewis killed in Iceland? They supposedly don't know anyone here. Even though Margaret was acting all hoity-toity when the trip first started, Lewis didn't seem that way. I didn't even pay much attention to him, because the spotlight was on Margaret."

Brett shrugged. "None of it makes any sense, but remember, the police are working on it."

"But where do they start? They don't know anything about the Sawyers, much less why anyone would want to kill Lewis."

"I'm sure they know more than they're letting on."

"What's that supposed to mean? Do you think we're in any danger hanging out with Margaret? Maybe she's the killer, or even if she's not, maybe she's the next target."

"If I thought there was any danger spending time with her, I'd be the first to put a stop to it." Brett kissed her, a brief but searing kiss, then pulled away. "Don't you think I want to spend more time with my wife alone? Or, at the very least, not talk about the latest murder case when we *are* alone?"

"You have a point. I think we should start asking more questions to help move the investigation along. With any luck we can have this thing solved in the next couple of days and then have the rest of the week to have some fun."

"Luckily we are having some fun, and I want to keep it that way." Brett grinned at her. "Besides, I didn't give you the green light to move forward with investigating."

Kristen quirked an eyebrow. "Do I *need* a green light from you?" Kristen was used to her independence. In the past Brett had always been supportive of her, even if he disliked her meddling in murder investigations.

"When we're on our honeymoon in a foreign country, when we know nothing of the situation or even how law enforcement works here, then, yes, you need to run this by me first."

"But you'll only say 'no,'" Kristen whispered, not wanting the entire bus to hear their conversation

"Can you blame me?"

Kristen sighed. "I guess not. Sorry, I got a little carried away. I still don't think it would hurt anything to ask around. Maybe some of the others on this trip noticed something."

"If anyone in our group saw anything, don't you think they would have reported it to the police?" Now it was Brett's turn to sigh. "If you want to talk to the people you've already met on this trip, that probably wouldn't be a big deal. I'm sure your friend Betty would give you an earful, and then there's the buddy you made at breakfast this morning."

Kristen wasn't sure who Brett was referring to. "You mean Margaret?"

"Well, it would be good to chat with her if she's calmed down a little, but I mean the red-haired guy and his fellow backpackers."

Kristen didn't even realize Brett had seen her talking to Sam, but he was right. Kristen remembered seeing Sam and his friends near the church when Lewis died. *Who else was in the area?* That was the question of the day.

* * *

Kristen and Brett walked hand in hand along the path leading to steamy and smelly geysers and mud volcanos at the Geysir Geothermal Area. The deep geothermal pools came in all shapes and sizes and contrasted with the snow surrounding them. Kristen marveled not only at the interesting geothermal pools but also at the diversity of scenery in the small but beautiful country. *To think we've only seen a tiny portion of Iceland.* The falling snow seemed to instantly disappear when it fell close to the boiling pools.

Brett must have noticed the dreamy look on Kristen's face. He squeezed her hand. "Isn't this something?"

Kristen nodded and pointed toward a tall geyser spouting water and steam several feet in the air. "That must be the main geyser, kind of like Old Faithful in Yellowstone."

"You could be right, from the looks of all the people gathered around it."

They walked closer and joined the others watching the geyser's eruption. Once it was done, Kristen said, "Let's wait for the next eruption." Kristen opened her guidebook and turned pages until she came to the section on Geysir Geothermal Area. "It looks like we only have eight minutes or so until the next show." She looked at the sign marking the geyser. "It's called Strokkur."

Brett repeated the name aloud. "Hey, I just said my first word in Icelandic."

"There's no guarantee you said it correctly," Kristen teased.

"Does it say how far the water shoots into the air?"

"It says around fifty to sixty-six feet, but sometimes it shoots higher."

"That's amazing." Brett looked around while they waited. "We'll have to check out some of those mud volcanoes as well."

"You can be sure of it." Kristen looked around, taking in the other geysers while they waited, then opened her book again. "There should be one called 'Geysir' near here."

"That's original."

Kristen smiled. "That's because it *is* the original geyser—or the first one recognized and named as a geyser. The term 'geyser' came from this particular one."

"We'll have to find it once we're done with this one." Brett scanned the crowd. "Say, isn't that your red-haired friend over there?"

Kristen followed his gaze across the ring around the geyser and spotted Sam and his friends. His bright hair stood out in the snow and the subdued colors of the thermal areas. "Maybe we'll have a chat with them after we're done here."

"As long as we have plenty of time to see the rest of what there's to see here, I'm fine with that."

"Are you sure you don't mind? I can try to catch up with him back at the hotel or something."

"May as well do it here, while we have the chance."

"Then let's walk a little closer, so we can get to them more quickly once Strokkur is done erupting." They began to edge closer to the backpackers, but Kristen stopped when she could hear and see more activity near the base of the geyser. "It must be about to erupt." Sure enough, water began to gurgle, then shot into the air.

"Wow, I think that went even higher than when we saw it go off a few minutes ago," Brett said.

"You may be right. I wonder what determines how tall each eruption is?" Kristen grabbed Brett's hand. "Let's go talk to Sam. We can talk while we walk." Kristen was excited about asking questions of her fellow travelers. Who knew what they may have noticed? Since she was sure the students weren't as experienced as they were at murder investigations, they may have seen something but not realized the importance of it, let alone reported it to the police.

"All right."

Kristen walked toward them with Brett at her side, hoping it appeared they were on their way to the next site and happened to bump into them. "Well, hello," she said to Sam, then nodded to the others.

"What did you think of that?" Sam asked, referring to the Strokkur.

"To say that it was awesome is an understatement," Kristen said. "Hey, this is my husband, Brett. We're going to walk around and see some other geysers and mud volcanoes."

"Same here." Sam glanced at his friends. "By the way, let me introduce you to my girlfriend, Alicia, and my friends, Nora and Trevor."

Kristen nodded at them all. "Nice to meet you. My name is Kristen, and you already heard me introduce Brett." They all smiled in return. As they began to walk along the path toward the next geyser, Kristen checked out their fellow travelers. Alicia was pretty, with her black hair and light blue eyes a contrast to Sam's flaming red hair, as was her petite, curvy build compared to Sam's tall and lanky build. They made a cute couple. The other girl, Nora, was also pretty, with light brown hair and green eyes and of medium height with a slim build. Kristen wondered if she was Trevor's girlfriend, or if they were just friends. Trevor, with his dark hair and chocolate brown eyes was almost as tall as Sam but with a thicker build. Trevor was handsome, and Kristen thought he and Nora would make an attractive couple if they weren't already dating. Kristen concentrated on committing their names to memory.

As they walked, Kristen tried to figure out a way to casually bring up the topic of Lewis' murder—not that she'd mention anything about him being murdered—to the backpackers.

Trevor beat her to it. "Weren't you two the ones who were trying to help the dead guy?"

Kristen wasn't prepared for his blunt question, especially since she was the one who planned to ask questions. "I guess you could say that was us. Unfortunately, whatever help we gave didn't help much."

"I'm sure you did what you could," he assured her. "What was wrong with the old geezer—or should I say geyser?"

At Kristen's startled look Trevor rushed to apologize. "Hey, I didn't mean it like that. I guess I'm just freaked out."

Kristen knew he was young and probably didn't have much experience saying the right thing when someone died. "It's okay. Sorry if you're freaked out. Sudden death does that to people."

"It's not so much that, though I am shocked he died so suddenly. He was a professor at our college."

Interesting. Kristen decided to play dumb, even though she already knew Lewis was a geology professor at the U of I. "Where do you go to school?"

"The University of Illinois," Sam said. "We're all students there. That's how we met."

"Okay, that explains all the orange and blue hoodies." Kristen chuckled. "Are you all majoring in the same thing?" Kristen wondered if any of them had Lewis as a professor.

Trevor shook his head. "Nope, we're all studying different majors."

In a school that size, Kristen wondered how they'd all met and become friendly enough to travel to Iceland together. "Did you know him?"

"You mean Lewis Sawyer?" Alicia asked. "That was his name, right?"

"Yeah, that's him." Kristen was wondering if any of them would spit out anything useful.

They all looked at each other, and Nora spoke. "I don't think any of us actually knew him. He was a science teacher, but I'm not sure which classes he taught."

In the age of mini computers, a.k.a., smartphones, Kristen thought it odd none of them were curious enough to at least Google the man. She decided to change the subject and hope she could chat with them later. She didn't want to waste any more of their precious time at this stop if she wasn't going to learn anything helpful anyway. Maybe she'd try to catch them individually to see if they would be more forthcoming with information. Looking down the path at the carved rock with the name "Geysir" carved into it, Kristen realized they would miss what they came there to visit if she continued to question the closed-mouthed students.

"Have you seen the Geysir geyser yet?" she asked, pointing to the rock and the geyser behind it.

They all looked at her like she was crazy. Apparently, they hadn't Googled the Geysir Geothermal Area either. "You know, the first geyser to be named is located here—the term stuck and now all geysers are called geysers. It's spelled a little differently, G-E-Y-S-I-R." When they continued to gape at her as if she was crazy, Kristen decided to quit while she was ahead. "Well, I think it's right up ahead. I want to get a picture of it, so we'll catch you later."

Sam gave them a lame smile and wave, while the others just stared at them as they left.

A few yards down the path, Brett burst out laughing. "Wow, that was excruciatingly painful."

"You think? That was almost enough to cure me of my curiosity."

"Well worth the effort then."

"That would be funny if it weren't so painful. Can you imagine if the police tried to question those guys?" Kristen grinned as she considered how the stern officers would handle the laid-back students.

"I doubt they'd get much information out of them."

"Do you think they may know something important? After all, they're students at the same school where he taught."

"Come on, Kristen. You know how big the U of I is."

"Somewhere around forty thousand, if I remember correctly."

"I think it's even bigger than that," Brett said. "Either way, it's a lot of students—larger than most of the towns in our area."

"You mean larger than most of the towns in our area put together."

"That's right. So, the odds of any of them knowing anything about the professor are slim."

"But somehow the four of them met and became friends, even though they're not studying the same major." Kristen remembered most of her college friends being fellow biology majors. Who else could relate to freezing field trips, horrible lab practicals, and shark dissections?

"They probably met at some freshman party or in an intro class everyone has to take. Heck, they could even be from the same hometown and stuck together when they went away to college."

What Brett said made sense, but still, out of a college that size, where some students and professors may rarely run into each other on campus, they managed to all be on the same trip. What a coincidence! On the flip side, it made the odds slimmer they would have had Lewis as a professor.

The cynical side of her could picture Sheriff Miller saying, "There are no coincidences when it comes to a murder investigation."

For once Kristen had to agree with the sheriff.

CHAPTER 13

Back on the bus, they only had a short drive to their next destination, *Gullfoss*, a waterfall system about ten minutes away. Kristen had seen photos of the unusual waterfall and couldn't wait to see it in person. She nudged Brett. "We have to get some pictures of us in front of the waterfalls—they're gorgeous."

"What, didn't you think the mud volcanoes were pretty enough to use on our wedding thank you notes?"

"Let's just say, they are more interesting than pretty. And we won't even discuss the sulfur smell coming from some of the mud volcanos. Now for our next stop, prepare to be amazed by the waterfalls."

"Waterfalls, as in plural?"

"Yeah, they drop over one hundred feet in two stages."

"It sounds like that will be quite a hike in the snow."

"Not really. One of Iceland's most spectacular views is just a short walk from the parking lot. You can get great views from the path along the falls." Kristen was glad of that. She was starting to grow weary from their earlier hikes, then being almost lulled into a nap from riding on the warm but slow-moving bus, as it lumbered up and down snow-covered hilly and curvy roads. She would probably rest on the two-hour drive back to Reykjavik. Looking at the cloudy sky, she thought it unlikely they would be viewing the Northern Lights that night, but weather conditions could be different in the capital city, and she wanted to be rested up in case they went on the tour.

Soon the bus came to a stop near the entrance to the walkway and staircase leading to the falls. "One nice thing about a bus tour is that it drops us off close to the entrances, rather than making us hike across the parking lot."

"We've become pampered tourists," Brett said with a chuckle. "I don't mind, if you don't."

"Not at all. I think after a busy day the jet lag will take its toll, and another early night is in order."

"What about the Northern Lights tour?" he asked.

Kristen shrugged. "I guess we'll have to see if it's cloudy when we return to town. A lot can happen between now and later this evening." Indeed, it could. Kristen spotted Margaret coming toward them.

"Wait for me," she called.

After not having spent any time with Margaret since Þingvellir National Park, Kristen could afford to be gracious. "Sure. Watch your step." Kristen winced as Margaret stepped into a slushy puddle in her lightweight tennis shoes.

"Just perfect." Margaret scowled. "But what did I expect from this trip?"

Kristen wasn't sure how to answer that, since she wondered why Margaret came on the tour in the first place. "We've seen some lovely sites, and I think these waterfalls will be the icing on the cake." As they walked closer to the falls, the noise from the rumbling water grew louder.

Between the snow on the land surrounding the falls, the partially frozen falls, and the interestingly shaped double layered falls, Kristen wasn't sure which was most impressive. Even with the white and gray tones of the sky, land, water, and ice, *Gullfoss* was spectacular.

"Are you ready to walk down the stairs to get a closer look?" Kristen hoped Margaret would watch her step on the snow- and ice-covered steps leading downward.

"I guess as long as I've made it this far." Margaret gave the falls a passing glance. "Thank goodness this is the last stop on this wretched tour. One quick look at the falls, and I'm heading to the gift shop."

Kristen couldn't blame the woman for being bitter, but she really didn't appreciate her raining on their parade. "Well, let's have a look, then." She walked toward the stair entrance and carefully started down the stairs, gripping the railing as she went. Glancing back, she was pleased to see Brett helping Margaret on the stairs. *Then again, shouldn't Brett be helping me?* This was their honeymoon. Even if Kristen didn't need any help, holding on to your husband's arm was always welcome. She brushed aside her thoughts. Margaret had been through a lot, and if she needed an arm to lean on—or a shoulder to cry on—that was fine.

Kristen looked toward the falls as she walked, as the thundering noise and pressure from the cascading falls made it hard to ignore them. Besides, she wanted to soak up as much of the view as possible. Once they reached the bottom, they were lined up directly downstream of the falls for a perfect view.

As soon as Brett and Margaret arrived a minute or two later, Kristen turned to them. "Isn't this fabulous?"

"I've never seen anything like them," Brett agreed. "Say, Margaret, would you mind taking a couple of pictures of us?"

After a quick lesson in how to use Kristen's camera, Margaret snapped several shots.

"Thanks." Kristen took her camera back from Margaret, then took several more shots and a video of the waterfalls. She wanted to capture the beauty forever. "Shall we walk around the perimeter?"

"Not me. I've seen what I need to see, so I'm out of here," Margaret said.

Kristen felt sorry for the woman but was secretly glad she and Brett would have time to continue exploring on their own. "Do you want some help back up the stairs?"

"I'm not some pathetic old woman," Margaret spat, her earlier true colors once again showing. "Sorry, that was rude. I'll manage just fine and will get a cup of hot chocolate in the café in the visitor's center."

"Sure, see you there in a few minutes." Kristen would love to have a chance to talk to Margaret, to see what she could find out about Lewis and his past, but now wasn't the time.

Once Margaret was a safe distance away, Brett grabbed hold of Kristen's hand. "Finally, just the two of us."

"At least she was able to take some pictures of us, which is better than trying to maneuver a selfie." Kristen grinned. "I wouldn't want one of us to slip and fall." She paused for a moment, a sudden thought popping into her head. "Why do you think Lewis was murdered in the middle of Reykjavik, right next to the church? Wouldn't it make more sense to shove him into a mud volcano or over the edge of the waterfalls?"

"Wow, maybe I don't want to stand too close to you," Brett teased.

"Seriously, though. It could be passed off as an accident, rather than a murder. They might even have a tough time retrieving a body—at least one intact."

"Well, as gruesome at that sounds, it does make more sense."

"Why kill him in a crowded city square where it would be hard to make it look like an accident, unless someone may have thought he slipped on the ice."

"It's crowded, or relatively crowded here, too, but it would be much easier to make a casual push turn fatal without anyone noticing."

"Exactly. These falls are so spellbinding that we aren't even paying attention to the other tourists around us. We wouldn't notice if anything were amiss until it was too late." Kristen gazed out at the thundering falls. "Let's postpone our discussion for now, shall we?"

For once, Brett wanted to continue their conversation on murder. "Maybe they chose a spot in the middle of town to prove a point."

Kristen chewed on that for a minute. "*You* may have a point. But still. Why? Even though the number of winter tourists is less than the number of summer tourists, there were still plenty of people hanging around the church. Besides, it only takes one person to notice something."

"It would help if we knew how Lewis had died."

Kristen nodded. "That's why I'm holding on to hope that the police will tell us. They don't have to know we're going to take that information to help them solve a murder case. Maybe we could somehow convince them to tell us for our peace of mind or something. "

"Or you could get Margaret to spill the beans when they give her the cause of death."

"That's a good idea. I plan to ask her some questions anyway, and that one will go to the top of my list."

"Okay, now we need to take a break from sleuthing to check out these amazing waterfalls." Brett put his arm around Kristen's shoulder and drew her close. "Under normal circumstances, wouldn't this be romantic?"

Kristen snuggled against Brett's strong arm. "I think it's romantic now."

"Only you could switch from talk of murder to romance in a matter of minutes."

"Sometimes mood swings are a good thing." Kristen gazed out at the waterfalls, content once again. Even though she loved the partially frozen falls in the ice and snow, she wondered what they would look like during greener months. Since *Gullfoss* translated to Golden Falls, Kristen was sure the waterfalls were just as majestic in the warmer months. *If* gull *means golden, I wonder if the Gull beer we drank last night is named for its golden color.* The thought of the tasty brew made Kristen want to try another glass when they were done for the day. She glanced at her watch.

"Maybe we can walk around the rest of the viewing area, then head on up to the gift shop."

"Sounds fine to me."

As they walked Kristen noticed others on the tour ahead of them. Doug and Betty were off to the side, leaning on the railing, their heads together, as if they were in deep conversation. Their backs were to the thundering falls. Kristen thought it odd they weren't facing the falls. After all, they could talk all they wanted on the bus during the two-hour drive back to Reykjavik. Besides, how could you even have an intelligent conversation with the noise of the waterfalls behind them drowning out everything else? As they came closer to the couple, Kristen could hear their raised voices. Betty was gesturing with her hands, as if upset about something. She knew some older couples who bickered constantly after living together for decades, but between their loud voices—though Kristen couldn't make out their words with the water from the falls crashing to the riverbed below—hand gestures, and Betty's flushed face, Kristen knew something more serious was wrong.

As they came closer, Kristen cleared her throat loudly, not wanting Doug and Betty to think anyone had overheard them. She made a point to try to act natural, though if Doug and Betty had actually been paying attention to them, they would think it was all an act. Kristen grabbed on to Brett's arm. "Look, the view is even more amazing from here." By now Doug and Betty had paused their conversation. Kristen gave them a minute to regain their composure before she spoke. "I can see why you two picked this spot to hang out."

Betty pulled her stocking cap down over her ears. "Why, yes. It's beautiful here." She turned back toward the falls to emphasize the fact.

"We were just admiring this amazing scenery, but I'm sure it's time we start back," Doug said. "We don't want to hold up the rest of the group. You know how there's always that one annoying person in the group who's always late, and you just want to kill him."

Betty's eyes almost bugged out at Doug's comment. "You mean like that poor man, Lewis Sawyer?"

CHAPTER 14

Kristen's jaw dropped at Betty and Doug's comments. She wasn't sure what to say. She had a feeling that whatever they had just been arguing about led to their unexplained outburst. Were they trying to tell her something about Lewis' death? Did one of them know something—or worse yet—had one of them *done* something to Lewis?

Kristen quickly regained her composure. "Would one of you like to explain that?"

Betty jabbed Doug in the side with her elbow. "Do you want to tell them, or should I?"

Kristen was becoming more curious by the minute, but she wasn't sure she wanted to hear whatever the older couple had to say. "Is it something you should be telling the police?"

Betty shook her head. "We didn't mention it earlier."

"Did the police actually question you?" Brett asked.

"They asked the people who were gathered around the body if any of us had seen anything," Betty said. "But we didn't, so we didn't say anything."

Kristen wasn't sure where they were going with their babbling. "Why don't you just spit it out. We need to be boarding the bus pretty soon."

After another glance between themselves, Betty began to talk. "We didn't see anything, which is the truth."

Kristen knew there was more to the story and had a feeling she knew where Betty was going. "But you know the Sawyers, is that right?"

Betty threw her a shrewd glance. "Are you sure you don't work undercover for the police or something?"

Kristen smiled, her eyes wide with innocence. "Of course not. I think I already told you I'm a naturalist." She nodded toward Brett. "And he's a forester with IDNR."

"But you seem to know a lot about Lewis' death," Doug said, also giving her a shrewd look.

Kristen wished she knew more about how and why Lewis had died, but she supposed she knew more than the Schmidts knew. "I don't know a thing about it. We just stepped in to try to help, which seems to have gotten us involved."

Betty and Doug seemed satisfied with her explanation.

"Why don't you tell me how you know the Sawyers." Kristen figured the more they knew about Lewis and Margaret, the easier it would be to figure out who had killed him. From her experience, she'd spent as much time digging up dirt on the deceased as on the suspects.

Doug and Betty exchanged another look. This time Doug did the talking. "We were next door neighbors to the Sawyers at one time."

Kristen couldn't have been more surprised. Even though these days neighbors didn't always behave neighborly or even speak to each other, she felt sure people in the Schmidts' generation were used to being neighborly. She couldn't believe the couple had pretended not to know the Sawyers. Were they pretending about anything else? She remembered the hostile words exchanged between Margaret and Betty while they were waiting for the shuttle. Was there more to their past than Betty being annoyed about Margaret cutting to the front of the line?

Kristen finally sputtered, "How long ago were you neighbors?"

"More importantly," chimed in Brett, "why didn't you say something earlier—to the police?"

Doug held up his hand to ward off their questions. "Slow down. We didn't do anything wrong."

"But you let us—and the police—believe you didn't know the Sawyers," Kristen said. "Don't you think the police would want to know that?"

Betty glared at her husband. "That's what I told him, but he wouldn't listen."

"Just because we knew them thirty odd years ago doesn't mean a thing." Doug sounded defensive.

"But you might be able to give the police some insight into the Sawyers' backgrounds that could help the investigation. Especially since they don't seem to have much to go on," Kristen said.

"Much to go on?" asked Doug. "Was Lewis murdered?"

Kristen's face reddened. She didn't want to be the one to leak that information.

"It's okay," Betty said. "That's the word on the street, and Doug was trying to get you to confirm it. I'm sure the police told you not to mention it, but we heard the news anyway."

Interesting. Kristen wondered who was spreading that rumor—which was actually fact. "That's right. The police don't want us discussing the case and urged anyone to come forward if they have information about Lewis." She gave the older couple a look. "That includes you." Kristen thought the Schmidts probably knew more about the case—not to mention the Sawyers—than they were letting on.

Betty sighed. "All right. We'll check in with the police when we return to Reykjavik this evening."

"But we'll miss the Northern Lights tour we booked." Doug didn't look happy.

"We can go another night," Betty insisted.

Kristen glanced up at the sky, which was already losing what little light there was. "With all the clouds, they'll probably postpone the tour until another night."

"Good thing we don't have dinner plans," Doug mumbled.

"You're welcome to join us for dinner." Brett glanced at Kristen, who gave a slight nod.

Betty answered for them. "Why, we'd enjoy that very much. Maybe we can tell you what we know about the Sawyers, and you can give us guidance on what to tell the police."

Kristen thought this was exactly what Brett had in mind when he invited Doug and Betty to dinner. She could kiss him for making the offer. "We'd be happy to."

"We'd better head back to the visitors' center," Brett said, after checking the time. "We're due to board the bus soon."

Kristen waited until Doug and Betty started toward the flight of stairs leading them back toward the visitors' center, then turned to Brett. "That was quick thinking."

"I figured you'd want to question them further, and we're running out of time to do it here."

"Good idea. Now, I want one last look at the falls before we leave." She snuggled into the arm Brett put around her. She was glad for the bus ride back to Reykjavik. Not only would she enjoy the warmth of the bus after a long day of sightseeing in the Golden Circle, but she would use the time to think of questions for Doug and Betty. One thing was for sure, she'd make the most of the opportunity. She only hoped the couple wouldn't spend the bus ride comparing notes and getting their story straight.

CHAPTER 15

Once they arrived back at the hotel Kristen waved to Betty and Doug, then walked over to them. "Shall we meet for dinner in an hour?"

"Sounds good to us," Betty said. "We'll check at the front desk to see if the tour is still scheduled for tonight."

Kristen bet it would be cancelled. She couldn't see any stars on the cloudy night; weather conditions hadn't improved when they arrived at Reykjavik, but it would be good to know for sure. For all she knew, the clouds would clear before the tour. "Perfect. Let's meet in the lobby."

Once Kristen and Brett arrived in their room she flopped on the bed. "I'm worn out. What do you think about going to the same place we ate at last night?"

"Sounds fine to me. They had traditional Icelandic fare for reasonable prices, and it's in a great location. We can walk there and even explore the area at night."

"Hopefully I'll have more energy by then. The Hallgrímskirkja should be beautiful at night."

"Are you sure you want to go back there?" Brett asked.

"You know I like to return to the 'scene of the crime,' as they say." Kristen knew odds were slim they'd find a clue. *Besides, that only happened in detective novels, right?* But she could get a better feel for the place. Maybe seeing how things were laid out would help spark an idea as to how Lewis could have been murdered in broad daylight in the middle of a city.

"As long as you're feeling up to it."

"I'll have my strong and handsome husband with me to make sure I'm safe." If Kristen had more energy, she'd get off the bed and walk over to where he was still standing by the door and kiss him to show him how she felt. But who knew where that may lead, and they had a dinner date. "If you need the bathroom, go ahead. I'll rest here for a few minutes before I freshen up."

Kristen shut her eyes to rest, but she couldn't shut off her brain. She didn't have enough information to come up with any theories, let alone draw any conclusions, but she still sifted through what they did know. Lewis had been murdered, but the cause was yet unknown. Kristen would check in with Margaret in the morning to see if she knew the cause of death yet. She vowed to ask her other questions as well.

She also knew Lewis was a professor at the University of Illinois, and four students from U of I happened to be on this trip, as were Doug and Betty, his past neighbors. Surely all this couldn't just be a coincidence, could it? That was the big question, and Kristen hoped to find out some answers tonight.

* * *

The night was still cloudy, so their Northern Lights tour was postponed until the next evening. Kristen hoped the weather would cooperate at least one of the nights they were in Iceland, since seeing the lights was at the top of her bucket list. Still, it was a beautiful evening, with the city lights casting a subtle glow against the cloudy sky. Tiny snowflakes fell as they walked toward the café with Doug and Betty. Kristen hoped they would be able to ditch the couple to check out the Hallgrímskirkja after dinner. Even if they didn't make any discoveries at the church, Kristen would prefer to have a romantic walk back to their hotel alone with her husband, rather than spending the entire evening with Doug and Betty. Walking to the café, plus having dinner together, would be enough time with them.

"I hope you like this place," Kristen said, as they neared the café. "We had a lovely dinner there last night." Kristen didn't tell them they'd also spent part of the afternoon there being questioned by the police.

"I'm sure it will be nice," Betty said, as she walked alongside Kristen. The men were walking and talking behind them. "We're trying to take in as much of this country as possible. This is our dream trip."

"I think it's great that your dream is coming true. I'm sorry a murder had to mar such an otherwise perfect trip."

"Well, if you two aren't letting it ruin your honeymoon—and you're more involved than we are—we aren't going to let it ruin our trip."

"Once you've talked to the police, you'll feel much better," Kristen said, wanting to emphasize the need for the Schmidts to turn their information over to help with the investigation. Kristen couldn't wait to get seated, so they could hear what the older couple had to say. Then they could just enjoy their dinner.

"Oh, I know, but I feel nervous about speaking to them."

Kristen wondered why Betty should feel nervous if they didn't have important information to share or anything to hide. "The officers who spoke to us are very nice and professional, so you shouldn't worry about it." Of course, not everyone had experience dealing with the police during a murder investigation.

Betty must have been thinking the same thing. "You act like you've been through this before."

Kristen tried to shrug it off. "My best friend's husband is a deputy with our sheriff's department, so I'm familiar with the procedure." *Which was sort of the truth.* "It doesn't seem that much different in Iceland than it does at home."

"I'm sure when you thought about your honeymoon, you didn't think you'd become embroiled in a police investigation."

Don't be so sure of that. "No, I had no idea." Kristen saw the Hallgrímskirkja looming ahead of them, the lights surrounding it giving the church an eerie glow. It looked like their destination was just beyond it. She turned around to the men behind them. "I think the café is up ahead."

"Yeah, that's it," Brett came closer to walk next to her the rest of the way. "Let's hope we don't have to wait long for a table."

"It wasn't very busy last night, although I guess we were there for an early dinner." Kristen was hungry, and she thought a Gull beer and bread would help make the conversation they were about to have with the Schmidts go more smoothly.

Brett held the door for them as they entered the café. As they waited for a table, Kristen glanced into the dining room. She was pleased to see their waiter from last night. She caught Gunnar's eye and waved. He smiled in return and headed their way.

"I'm so glad you returned to dine with us this evening and have brought some friends along as well. " Gunnar bowed slightly toward Doug and Betty. "Velkominn."

He turned toward the dining area. "Now, if you'll follow me, I will find the perfect table for you."

Soon they were seated at a table in a cozy corner of the restaurant that granted them a view of the Hallgrímskirkja while they scanned their menus.

"What's good here?" Doug asked.

"I had some delicious grilled haddock last night," Kristen said. "Gunnar was kind enough to bring us beer and bread first, and both were much appreciated." Kristen returned to her own menu. She was having trouble deciding between *plokkfiskur*, a type of fish and potato stew, and the *kjötsupa*, a hearty and rich meat soup. Deciding to try the soup, since she had fish the night before, she snapped her menu shut just as Gunnar was bringing a basket full of fresh breads and rolls to their table.

"Can I get you anything to drink?" Gunnar glanced questioningly at Kristen and Brett. "I think you enjoyed the Gull beers?"

Brett nodded. "Of course. I'd like to order another one tonight."

"I'll take one as well," Kristen added, then Betty and Doug ordered their drinks.

While they waited for the drinks to arrive, they munched on bread and butter. Once Gunnar brought their drinks, Kristen planned to pounce. With luck they could discuss Margaret and Lewis before their main dishes arrived.

Minutes later, Gunnar arrived with a round tray bearing frosty glasses of Gull. Kristen savored her first sip, then got down to the business at hand. "Let's talk about Lewis and Margaret Sawyer. What do you know about them?"

"You mean other than the obvious?" Betty asked.

Kristen thought Betty was probably referring to her grudge against Margaret—a well-deserved one, considering Margaret's rude behavior earlier on the trip. "Why don't you tell us about the time you lived near each other, and then we can talk about more recent dealings."

Betty took a small sip of beer. "Boy, that's nice, and I'm not much of a beer drinker. But years ago, when we lived near the Sawyers, Doug and Lewis would often enjoy a brew together."

Interesting. Kristen merely nodded in encouragement, wanting Betty to get rolling with her story before their food arrived. No sense ruining a good meal with talk of murder—or the murder victim's past.

"In fact, they were close friends." Doug nodded in confirmation.

Kristen wondered why Doug wasn't doing the talking if he and Lewis had once been good friends.

"As for Margaret and I, well …" Betty looked toward the window, staring into the darkness. "We were never close, but at least we were polite. Our kids are about the same age, so we knew each other from living so close, but also ran into each other at school events and around the neighborhood. She always seemed to feel she was better than the rest of us, and from how she appears now, I wouldn't say she's changed much."

"Maybe she's just standoffish or shy," Kristen said.

"Standoffish because she looked down her nose at the rest of us," Betty said. "We lived in a neighborhood with lots of families with young children. Most of the women stayed home to raise their children, and we got to form a close network of helping each other out when needed. Swapping recipes and housekeeping tips, where to get the best products for the cheapest prices, watching each other's kids, and having kids run through our house and yard to play with our own kids were common practices for most of us. But Margaret worked outside the home, so she was already different from us. When she was at home, she didn't have time to hang out with the likes of us, and she hired someone to care for her children and take care of the house while she was at work. I realize this is commonplace today, but it wasn't as common in those days."

"Times have changed quite a bit since then," Brett agreed.

"It wasn't like they needed the money. Lewis was a professor at a private college at the time, and they did okay. They moved from the suburbs when Lewis got a job at the University of Illinois, and needless to say, we didn't keep in touch."

"Even though Doug and Lewis were friends?" Kristen glanced at Doug, wondering how close of friends he was with Lewis.

"We might have a beer after we were both done working in the yard," Doug explained. "We didn't live right next to each other, but our back yards butted up against one another's. When I heard Lewis fire up his mower, I knew I'd better get my yard mowed as well. In those days our lots weren't separated by fences like many houses are today. Things were much more open, which allowed kids to run back and forth to play and neighbors to get to know each other better."

Just how well did the Schmidts know the Sawyers? "So you would shoot the breeze over a beer when finished with yard work?"

"Yeah, it wasn't a weekly event, but quite a few times over the years."

"How long did the Sawyers live in your neighborhood?" Brett asked.

Betty glanced at Doug. "I think they moved before their kids started high school. I don't think their kids graduated with our kids."

"So you lived near each other for ten or fifteen years?" Kristen asked.

Betty nodded. "Something like that."

Wouldn't they have gotten to know each other better in that amount of time? Kristen felt like the Schmidts were holding something back. "Doug, it sounds like you knew Lewis better than Betty knew Margaret. Can you think of anything that may have led to Lewis' murder?"

"That's quite a stretch—of your imagination—and years between when we lived near each other and when Lewis was killed," Doug said. "I can't think of anything that happened back then that would have been a factor in his murder."

Kristen tried not to let her frustration show. "I realize it's a stretch, but sometimes you have to dig deep to figure out why someone was killed and who did it."

"Why are you the one doing the digging?" Doug shot back. "Who appointed you to be the detective on this case?"

"I thought we were getting together over dinner to talk about the Sawyers, to see if you knew anything of merit to pass on to the police," Brett intervened. He put his arm around Kristen. "My wife's curiosity oftentimes gets the better of her, so don't take it personally."

Kristen was thankful for Brett's intervention. It gave her a minute to calm down and switch tactics. "So, even if you can't think of anyone who would have wanted to hurt Lewis or anything in his past that may have prompted his murder, it's still good background information. The police will want to hear what you have to say." Kristen took a healthy swig of her beer, then turned to Betty. "Let's talk about Margaret for a minute. You said she was standoffish, and you didn't particularly like her. Did the other women in the neighborhood feel the same way?"

"You've seen her in action. She's only gotten more stuck on herself over the years, but most of the other women didn't care for her behavior. Plus, she was too busy working to have much spare time to get chummy with a bunch of neighborhood housewives."

Kristen wondered if Betty was resentful of Margaret's career. "Where did Margaret work?" If the family didn't need the money, it wouldn't make sense for Margaret to work at a lower paying job if it meant spending time away from her family and money on a housekeeper.

"She worked at her family's business, but I'm not sure what all she did."

Kristen was even more curious. Oftentimes there was some flexibility when working at a family business— especially if it was a woman trying to raise a young family. "Do you remember what kind of business?" Maybe it was something high tech, or she was in an upper management position that didn't allow Margaret to come and go as she pleased.

Betty shook her head. "I'm not sure I even knew at the time. If I liked her more, I probably would have asked, but since we didn't go out of our way to be friendly, I didn't ask many personal questions."

Kristen hid a grin. Betty was likable, but she could picture the woman nosing around about her neighbors—especially if they gave her the cold shoulder. It was probably more of a matter of Margaret keeping things to herself. It made sense that if she didn't spend much time hanging out with her neighbors, she wouldn't feel the need to go into details when they bumped into each other.

"Were your children friends with the Sawyer kids?" Kristen remembered Margaret mentioning her children and wondered if one of them would be flying to Iceland to assist with arrangements and be with Margaret. Was it possible the children resented Margaret not giving them her full attention when they were younger? But even if they did, it wouldn't have any bearing on the case.

"Our daughters were in the same grade, so they played together," Betty said. "With our backyards butting up against each other, it only made sense."

"Getting back to Lewis. Was he well liked in the community?" Kristen still couldn't fathom how a man who appeared to be a decent guy ended up dead on his vacation in Iceland. Maybe it was a random killing. *It would help if we knew how he died.*

"He was easygoing and a good neighbor," Doug said. "Most of us liked Doug, even if we didn't care for his wife as much."

"If Margaret was the one who was murdered, I wouldn't have been shocked," Betty said. "But Lewis?" She shook her head. "None of it makes sense."

Kristen couldn't agree more. "Maybe whoever killed Lewis intended to kill Margaret."

"It's hard to believe someone could have mistaken Lewis for Margaret in broad daylight," Doug said. "Margaret does stand out in a crowd."

Betty giggled. "That she does." She quickly sobered. "Margaret was always put together, and she's aged well. Lewis and Margaret should have had many more years together, but now that's not possible."

Doug nodded. "We'll do whatever we can to help bring Lewis' killer to justice. If you think telling the Reykjavik police what little we know about the Sawyers, it's worth a shot."

"It's definitely a start." Kristen casually picked up a hard roll and peeled the foil wrapping off a pat of butter. "Maybe you can also tell them the rest of the story."

CHAPTER 16

Betty looked at Doug, obviously flustered. "Whatever do you mean?" Her eyes were wide with innocence.

"Come on, Betty. I can tell you're not being totally straight with us." Kristen glanced at Brett, wondering if he had the same take on the older couple.

"I think what Kristen means to say is that while we're sure you're telling us the truth, we think you're leaving out a few important parts." Brett leaned back in his chair after taking a sip of Gull, as if he had all the time in the world.

Kristen suspected he was pulling a police move she'd read about in the dozens of detective novels that lined her bookshelves. He waited for them to speak, saying nothing and even mimicking Kristen's earlier move as he leaned toward the table to take bread out of the basket and spread butter on it, then took a bite of it and leaned back in his chair again. Kristen held her breath, not daring to say a word. In order for their ploy to work, the Schmidts needed to feel uncomfortable in the silence that ensued—uncomfortable enough to finish their watered-down story.

Kristen hid a grin. She knew the normally chatty Betty would probably be squirming about now. Most people would feel the urge to break the awkward silence. Kristen concentrated on the background noises in the café. The clink of silverware on dishes, the low murmur of conversations, and even the sound of clean glasses being lined up on shelves by the waiter manning the bar. Even though time seemed to be dragging by, Kristen knew it was probably less than a minute before Doug finally spoke.

"Okay, you got us." He eyed Kristen and Brett shrewdly. "Where'd you two learn to drag information out of people? Aren't you a couple of tree huggers back home?"

Kristen tried not to flinch at the tree hugger reference. What was wrong with enjoying nature and trying to protect it for future generations? "Brett is a forester with IDNR, and I own my own business, the Nature Station, but I don't think either one of us has ever actually hugged a tree."

"I'm sure Doug didn't mean anything by that." Betty jabbed her husband in the ribs. "But you're right. We aren't being totally upfront with you."

Shocking. Kristen couldn't wait to hear what they had to say, but she forced herself to be patient and remain silent—a method that seemed to be working well so far. "Why don't you get us up to speed on what you know about the Sawyers." She glanced toward the kitchen. "They'll be bringing our food out soon, and it would be nice to put this talk of murder behind us while we eat."

Doug sighed. "Okay. Everything we already discussed is true. We didn't share the rest because frankly, we don't think it has anything to do with Lewis' death."

Reading between the lines, Kristen suspected it was more of a matter of something the Schmidts didn't want revealed. Maybe the longer she was involved in murder investigations, the more cynical she became. "When it comes to tracking down a murderer, there are several factors and variables. No one knows for sure how they fit together or if they are relevant until the murder is solved."

"If you'd prefer to wait and tell the police, I'm sure someone's at the station who will be happy to listen to what you have to say," Brett said, once again taking the casual route, as if he didn't care one way or another whether the Schmidts fessed up. Kristen resisted the urge to kick him underneath the table.

"No, I think we'd rather run it by you two first," Betty said. "As long as you promise not to tell anyone."

"Your secrets are safe with us." Kristen's interest was peaked. What could this cute couple have to hide? "Besides, who would we tell?"

"Sorry, that's just me being paranoid, I guess." Betty sighed. "There's a reason the Sawyers left our neighborhood all those years ago."

"Lewis got a job at U of I, right?" Kristen took a sip of beer, waiting for Betty to continue.

"That's only part of the reason, though it was very fortunate that Lewis landed a cushy professorship at U of I." Doug said.

Kristen didn't consider a geology professor position to be cushy, if their research and field trips were anything like what she'd experienced as a biology major. "That's probably a dream job for many in academia."

"I'm sure it is, if you're into that sort of thing. Unfortunately, Lewis seemed to be into many sorts of things." Doug's face was red.

"What Doug is trying to tell you is that Lewis made a pass at me. It wasn't a big deal. *I* wasn't interested in that sort of thing, even though I have to admit I was a little flattered Lewis found me attractive." Betty pursed her lips and fluffed her snow-white hair. "After all, I was trying to keep up the house and raise the kids. Some days I was lucky to take a shower before I started cooking dinner."

"From what I gather," Doug said, "he tried to put the moves on several women in our subdivision."

"Did he make any progress?" Kristen asked. She wasn't really surprised. She couldn't believe how many affairs she'd learned about while digging up dirt during murder investigations.

Doug nodded. "With our neighbor to the north. Eventually her husband found out, and the Sawyers up and moved."

"Was this purely gossip, or do you know for sure?" Brett asked, ever practical. "We come from a small town, where tongues are always wagging, and it's probably the same thing in larger cities."

"I agree with you about gossip," Betty said. "There was plenty of that going around about Lewis. But we were in a perfect position to see the comings and goings next door. Let's just say it wasn't coincidental that Lewis would stop by the neighbor's house several times a week—usually right after the neighbor's husband left for work."

"Didn't Lewis have to go to work himself?" *How in the world did the man land a prime job at a state university if he was late for work all the time?*

Betty shrugged. "I have no idea. He must have had later classes."

And perhaps kept late office hours. "I'm assuming Lewis waited until Margaret left for work as well, but didn't the

Sawyer's housekeeper notice something was amiss?" Kristen wondered aloud.

"What was she supposed to do if she did?" Doug asked. "Tell on him?"

"Oh, he was a smart cookie," Betty said. "He drove his car around the corner from where they lived to the house to the north of us. If the housekeeper was busy with morning chores, she probably didn't pay any attention to what was happening in the rest of the neighborhood."

Kristen wasn't so sure about that. Betty was busy, and she found time to notice what her neighbor—and Lewis—were up to. Even if the housekeeper was busy, she probably knew the ins and outs of the neighborhood just as well as anyone who lived there. "Did Margaret find out?" If Margaret was bitter over Lewis' affair—perhaps one of several—did that give her a motive for murder? If he'd been unfaithful over the years, maybe she couldn't take it anymore. That would explain why no one noticed a murderer lurking around the Hallgrímskirkja.

"I'm not sure if Margaret knew about the affair with our neighbor or not, but doesn't the spouse usually suspect something is wrong?" Doug looked at Betty. "Not that we had to worry about one of us cheating on each other."

"Of course not." Kristen smiled at the couple, who seemed to be enjoying their trip together. She hoped she and Brett would be like that when they were that age. "Is there anything else you want to tell us about the Sawyers?"

"No, that's all. But we honestly don't see how it could help track down Lewis' killer," Betty said. "It's unpleasant to drag up all that and discuss it, so let's change the subject."

Kristen looked up to see Gunnar carrying a large tray and headed toward their table. Kristen couldn't wait to sink her teeth into her dinner, and had a feeling they were starting to sink their teeth into factors that could have contributed to Lewis' murder.

* * *

Kristen tucked her arm through Brett's as they left the café and walked toward the beautifully lit Hallgrímskirkja. They had seen Doug and Betty off in a taxi before they started walking back to the hotel. The air was brisk, but Kristen was glad for the fresh air. She wanted to think about what they'd learned and discuss it with Brett while they walked.

"I can see two motives for murder after learning about Lewis being unfaithful—at least once—to Margaret."

"And those are?" Brett looked amused.

"First of all, Margaret could have killed him. Maybe she got tired of Lewis' cheating ways."

Brett nodded. "What's the second motive?"

"Maybe the husband of a woman he cheated on killed him."

"That could be a possibility if we were in the Sawyers' hometown and not on a different continent."

"Technically, are we on a different continent? Is Reykjavik located on the North American or European tectonic plate?"

Brett grinned. "I hadn't thought of it that way, but if Lewis were alive, I'm sure he could tell you for sure.

Either way, we're too far from home to have a jealous husband decide to kill Lewis."

"But what if they just happened to be on the same trip?" Kristen asked.

"What are the odds of that happening?"

"Normally I would agree, but we already have the Sawyers' ex-neighbors on this trip, plus some students from the college where he taught."

"Then it would be a real coincidence if someone else they knew was on the trip."

What Brett said made sense, but it wouldn't hurt to ask Margaret. Kristen added it to the list of things she wanted to discuss with her tomorrow. "I know it seems farfetched, but stranger things have happened. The world is a smaller place these days, and ironically, the Land of Ice is the new hot spot."

"And not just because this island is a geothermal hotbed," Brett agreed, then changed the subject. "Wow, I can't believe the sights we visited today. What's on the schedule for tomorrow?"

"We're heading north to see the ocean and fjords. It's supposed to be a pretty drive with several volcanic mountains as well."

"Sounds cool."

"It should be more low-key than today—more looking at scenery than visiting actual tourist destinations."

"Since we aren't the ones driving, we can relax and enjoy the view, which is perfect for a honeymoon."

And ask a few questions of the other passengers. Kristen hoped their "persons of interest" would be on the same trip. Since they kept bumping into others in their group, she thought it likely. Kristen looked up, pleased to see their hotel was only a block away. "Come on. I can think of a few other things perfect for a honeymoon."

CHAPTER 17

Kristen and Brett were walking down the hall on the way to the dining area for breakfast when Kristen heard someone calling her name. She turned around to see Margaret walking toward them, so they waited for her to catch up. *Perfect. Just the woman I want to talk to.*

"How are you holding up?" Kristen asked.

Margaret shrugged, her already thin shoulders appearing to be even thinner. "At least I got out of bed today and am about to have breakfast with the closest things to friends I have on this trip."

Kristen supposed Margaret was trying to pay them a compliment, even if it was a backhanded one. She would have preferred to wait until they were seated—with a steaming cup of coffee in front of her—to start badgering Margaret, but she took advantage of the opportunity now. "Are you sure you don't know anyone else?"

Margaret looked away as she mumbled, "I guess that depends on your definition of *knowing* someone."

"Let me clarify, is there anyone on the trip you may have lived near in the past?" Kristen knew full well Margaret had once lived near the Schmidts, but she was interested in hearing what Margaret had to say. Kristen thought both the Schmidts and Margaret were being cagey about their past association. She still suspected Doug and Betty still hadn't told them the full story last night. It was wishful thinking to think they would be totally honest with the police officers—assuming they went to talk to them today, as they'd promised.

Margaret whipped her head around. "Why would you ask that? What are the odds I'd know someone on this trip, other than poor Lewis, of course?"

Kristen stopped walking just outside the entrance to the dining area. "I know the years pass quickly, and we all age, but don't you recognize the Schmidts? Doug and Betty had dinner with us last night and mentioned you were once neighbors."

Kristen watched Margaret's face. "The Schmidts? I had no idea. I didn't recognize them."

Kristen sensed Margaret wasn't being straight with her and found it hard to believe Margaret didn't recognize the older couple. Even though Betty was aging gracefully and didn't get hung up on fashion or trying to look younger than she was, and perhaps Doug had gained a few pounds and lost a little hair, and both had gray hair, but did they look so different than when they were neighbors? Kristen could understand not realizing who they were at first, but after they ran into each other around the hotel and when sightseeing, Margaret should have figured out who the Schmidts were, even in her bereaved state. But was Margaret truly bereaved, or was that an act?

"Well, it sounds like it's been years since you lived near each other, and a lot has happened since then," Brett chimed in, probably realizing Kristen wanted to grill Margaret on the subject. "Why don't we have some breakfast?" He gestured for the women to lead the way into the dining room.

Once they were seated, Brett offered to get them coffee. Kristen knew he was giving her a chance to talk alone with Margaret. She decided not to question Margaret further about the Schmidts. What would be the point? "What are your plans for the day?"

"I'm staying in town today. The police want to talk to me. They mentioned reviewing the autopsy results with me, and I'm sure they'll have more questions. Hopefully they'll be ready to release Lewis' body soon, so I'll need to move forward with preparations to take him home."

Even though Kristen noticed Margaret's teary eyes, she didn't want to lose the chance. "I'm there for you if you want someone to talk to after you've talked to the police."

"Oh, Kristen, that would be great. Are you going out today?"

Kristen nodded, glad to see Brett carrying coffee cups and headed toward their table. "We're booked for an excursion to see the ocean and a fjord, but we should be back later this afternoon."

"Maybe we can have a drink before you go to dinner." Margaret smiled wryly. "I have a feeling I'll need one by then."

"Let's plan on it. But first, coffee." Kristen accepted the cup Brett offered her and took a sip of the hot brew.

* * *

As they were leaving Reykjavik, the sun was starting to rise, casting beautiful lighting over the scenery they were passing. As they left the city behind them. Kristen gazed out the window of the minibus that would be taking them north to *Hvalfjörður*, which their guide told them meant "whale fjord." Kristen didn't attempt to say the name aloud, knowing she would mangle its pronunciation. Kristen wasn't sure if it was named for what could possibly be construed as a whale shaped outline of the fjord, whale sightings in the area, or the fact Iceland's only operating whaling station was located there. Regardless of the name's origin, Kristen was excited about seeing the fjord. At 19 miles long, the fjord was surrounded by volcanic mountains and other snow-covered terrain. Not only would they be able to drive around the perimeter of the fjord via Route 47, but they would also be taking the tunnel below it on the return trip. Kristen wasn't thrilled about driving below the water and hoped it would be a short and sweet trip. She had read the tunnel was approximately three and a half miles long. That was a long time to drive underwater, but it probably saved about an hour of driving back around the fjord road, which was snow and ice covered at this time of the year, making it a treacherous drive around the curves that traced the outline of the fjord. *At least the tunnel is a shortcut, which gives us more time to look at scenery.*

She tried to focus on the landscape and not let thoughts of the Sawyers or the Schmidts invade the beautiful drive along Iceland's Route 1. They had about an hour before they reached the road that would take them around the fjord, so Kristen settled back in her seat, glad she was seated on the left-hand side and would be able to see the Atlantic Ocean from her window when it came into view.

Brett took her hand and squeezed it. "Let's hope the weather holds. The sun shining on the snow is amazing."

"I think the weather can change pretty quickly in this area, but for now I'm enjoying the sunshine." Kristen turned away from the window to look at her husband. "This country seems to be beautiful no matter what the weather's like."

"I agree with you, but I'd like to see the Northern Lights tonight, so let's hope that if it changes to snow and clouds, it changes back to clear skies by tonight."

"At least we have the next several nights to view the lights, even if tonight turns cloudy." Kristen, cozy in her seat, yawned. "After another day on the road, I'll be tired tonight."

"We should get back to the hotel for a quick nap before dinner, and we can sleep late in the morning."

"Don't forget that I'm supposed to meet Margaret for a drink before dinner."

Brett sighed. "Whatever you find out from Margaret will lead to more questions. I just hope you don't get carried away."

Kristen grinned. "When have you ever known me to get carried away?"

"Since we're still in the honeymoon phase, I'd prefer not to answer a question I know will get me in trouble with my new wife."

"Good answer," Kristen said. If only they could find more answers to put Lewis' murder behind them.

CHAPTER 18

Kristen stared in awe out the window. The sun hitting the dark blue water of the long fjord contrasted with the snowy landscape around the *Hvalfjörður*. Route 47 wove around the perimeter of the fjord, the narrow road affording them an excellent view of the water and surrounding scenery. Kristen was glad they were riding in a small bus; she couldn't imagine a regular tour-sized bus navigating the curves and hills, especially on the slick road. She was also glad someone else was doing the driving. All they had to do was sit back, relax, and enjoy the ride.

She wished they could visit *Glymur*, a 650 foot tall waterfall—the second tallest in Iceland. She was sure it was an awesome sight, with its water from Botnsá River cascading down the side of Hvalfell mountain into a steep canyon. Even though there was supposed to be a parking area off Route 47 that led to a hiking path to take visitors to a viewpoint distinguished by a large rock resembling an anvil, Kristen assumed it was more of a summer hike. She glanced at the other passengers on the bus, ranging in age anywhere from the foursome of U of I students to herself and Brett, all the way up to Doug and Betty and others in their age group. All had seemed to fare well on the Golden Circle tour, but the almost five-mile hike to the falls would be long, strenuous, and potentially dangerous in the snow and ice. She was glad *Gullfoss,* the waterfalls they visited yesterday, was so easily accessible. *That will just give us reason to come back in the summer one of these days!*

The trip around the fjord took close to an hour. Once done, they headed north and west toward Borgarnes, where they would cross a bridge spanning Borgarfjörður, another fjord. They would stop for lunch in Borgarnes. In the meantime, Kristen did more sightseeing from the cozy confines of the minibus. Volcanic mountains covered with white snow, while blending in with the snowy landscape, also stood out with their height and texture a contrast to the flatter ground. The lighting had changed once they'd finished the circuit around the *Hvalfjörður.* Now, dark gray clouds swooshed across the tops of the volcanic mounds. The sun peeked through occasionally, and as the bus rounded a curve, sometimes the lighting and clouds would change again. Between the changes in scenery and the dramatic weather differences, Kristen's eyes were glued to the bus window, everything else forgotten.

Kristen could feel the bus slowing down. Wondering why they were coming to a stop, Kristen looked out the window across the aisle to the east. She could see several small but sturdy Icelandic horses congregated in a fenced flatland pasture. "Oh, look," Kristen said to Brett and pointed to the window.

A smile crossed Brett's features, and he stretched. "It looks like we might be able to get off the bus to see the horses close-up."

"I could use some fresh air, and if the horses are tame enough maybe I can get some good pictures of them."

"From the looks of them they're used to people stopping. The side of the road even has a small parking spot big enough for this bus."

"That's good news for us, then. We saw horses as we drove yesterday, but they were definitely not in areas where the bus could pull over and stop." As Kristen put on her coat, she could see a few horses standing near the gate. Several more milled in the background. It only took a couple of minutes to deboard the bus; everyone wanted some time to stretch their legs, even if they weren't as excited about seeing the adorable Icelandic horses as Kristen was. Though from the looks of their small crowd of travelers standing at the gate, everyone else was as enthralled as Kristen and Brett. Luckily their small group wasn't enough to spook the horses, and the horses seemed to enjoy the attention they were receiving.

Kristen walked to the gate, holding out her hand to pet a brown horse with a white mane. The horse nuzzled against Kristen's gloved hand, its mane blowing in the gentle winter breeze. She was charmed. She stepped back to snap some pictures of the horse and its friends, then took one of Brett as he stepped forward to pet the horse.

"I'm not even a horse person, but these are amazing," Kristen said, walking closer to pet the horse again. Other horses came toward them, as if sensing two animal lovers were there, ready to shower them with attention. Kristen took more pictures before petting them each in turn.

"Isn't this something?" Betty asked, with Doug standing next to her.

"I'll say," Kristen turned to greet them, then turned back to the horses. They were only making a brief stop, and she wanted to make the most of it.

133

"They're so much shorter than horses in our area, but they're sturdily built and adapted to Iceland's rough terrain," Brett said. "I remember reading that Icelandic horses walk, trot, canter, pace and *tölt*."

Kristen raised her eyebrows. "I'm impressed you did some research. You usually tease me about reading up on the places we're visiting. Please explain what *tölt* is."

"I'm glad you're prepared. It makes our honeymoon even more pleasant," Brett said with a wink. Brett opened the rolled-up travel booklet he pulled from his inner coat pocket. He cleared his throat and began to read. "Descended from Viking horses brought to Iceland between 860 and 935, the Icelandic Horse is the only breed in the world that can perform five gaits, while other breeds can only perform three or four."

"Wow, that's pretty cool," Kristen said, even more excited to have time to visit the horses up-close and personal.

"Well, all that's well and good, but I just think they're cute." Betty chuckled loudly. The horses stared at her, briefly startled by her outburst. Then they walked closer to be petted.

"They sure do take your mind off things," Kristen agreed, finding it hard not to listen in on their conversation after Betty's lively laugh.

"Things like murder?" Betty's eyes were wide with innocence. "I saw you talking with Margaret at breakfast. What's the scoop?"

Kristen didn't have the heart to tell Betty that Margaret supposedly didn't recognize her. Besides, Kristen was certain Margaret wasn't being honest with them. The question was why?

"She wasn't looking forward to meeting with the police today." Kristen decided to be as vague as possible.

"I'd imagine she would be on edge—especially if she was the one who killed her husband."

Kristen was a little shocked by Betty's outburst. "Is that what you think happened?"

"I wouldn't have put up with his philandering all those years."

"Maybe he wasn't like that anymore." Kristen wasn't naïve enough to think Lewis had totally reformed, but if Margaret had known about his past affairs all this time, why would she wait until now to kill him? And why come all the way to Iceland to finish off Lewis, especially in such a public area? *Maybe to give herself an alibi.* But that didn't make sense either. Then again, none of it did.

"If you knew Lewis like we did, you'd know odds were slim he'd changed his ways," Doug spoke up. "But that doesn't mean Margaret killed him."

"Then who did?" Betty asked.

Betty's rhetorical question deserved an answer, but it wasn't one Kristen could provide—at least not yet. "What do you guys think of today's trip?" Kristen asked, trying to change the subject.

"Totally awesome!" Betty sounded more like the U of I college students headed their way than a sixty-something grandmother. "Between the volcanos, fjord, ocean views, and these adorable creatures, there's a lot to see."

"We couldn't agree more," Sam said, with his friends joining him. Nora and Alicia smiled at them, then turned toward the fence to pet this batch of horses.

"This is why we came to Iceland." Trevor spread his arms wide to indicate the snowy mountains in the background. "Some of our other friends thought we were crazy for going to Iceland in the winter, but the weather is better than at home, and the scenery is amazing."

Sam nodded in agreement. "Between the stuff we saw yesterday, plus all this today, it's hard to believe we've only covered a small portion of the island so far."

"For such a tiny country, there sure is a lot to see and do." Kristen grinned at the boys' enthusiasm. She felt the same way. She couldn't believe the breathtaking sights they'd visited so far that day, and it wasn't even lunchtime. Just then, the bus driver announced they would be boarding in five minutes. She turned back to the horses once more for some final pets. Snapping a few more photos, she wished Nora and Alicia weren't standing so close to the horses, but she could try to crop them out later. Sighing wistfully as she turned back toward the bus, she vowed to try to catch a glimpse of the horses when they headed back this direction later that afternoon. There was something about them that drew her to them—not just the horses, but how they looked against the dramatic Icelandic landscape.

Brett was smiling as he waited for Kristen to join him to board the bus. "That was a nice diversion, wasn't it?"

"Diversion from the perfect scenery …" Kristen lowered her voice. "Or from thinking about murder?"

"Well, I meant it as a lighthearted question. We've seen so much beautiful scenery that the horses were a nice change of pace." He paused and lowered his own voice as they lined up for the bus. "But it seems you can't shake this murder business from your mind."

Kristen shook her head. "No, you're right, but I'll try to do better." She squeezed his hand. "I promise not to mention it again—at least until it's time to have a drink with Margaret."

Now it was Brett's turn to shake his head, and he rolled his eyes for good measure. "But that doesn't mean you won't be thinking about it, and that's almost as bad."

Kristen snuggled closer to Brett as they edged closer to the bus entrance. "If I've been neglecting you, I'm sorry. I'll be sure to make it up to you later." She kissed him quickly on the cheek, then scooted ahead of him to board the bus and find their seats.

"How do you plan to make it up to me?" Brett asked once they sat down.

"You'll just have to wait and see," Kristen enjoyed their playful banter, but she knew Brett was right. Her mind was on Lewis' murder, and she'd most likely continue to concentrate on it until the case was solved. She only hoped it would be solved soon, so they could salvage the rest of what was supposed to have been a romantic and peaceful honeymoon.

CHAPTER 19

Kristen sat across the table from Brett, sipping her coffee as they scanned their menu for lunch. The café where they were eating in Borgarnes had tables in front of large windows that overlooked the Borgarfjörður Fjord. Even though it was only early afternoon, the sun was already heading westward, but for now, the sun shone brightly on the ice-cold water. Kristen was glad the clouds had dissipated earlier. She crossed her fingers the skies would remain clear, making a Northern Lights tour possible that evening.

She closed her menu and set it on the table, then quickly opened it again, squinting at the menu items. It was hard to remember Icelandic words. "I'll have the salmon and egg Brauðterta, which is an Icelandic style sandwich loaf."

Brett's eyes were twinkling. "Are you sure you pronounced that correctly?"

Kristen closed the menu and swatted him playfully. "Since I haven't heard you utter one Icelandic word since we arrived in Iceland, we're going to assume my pronunciation—while not being quite correct—sure beats yours."

Brett closed his own menu. "That settles it. I'll have the same thing, and you can order for both of us."

"I think you just played me." Kristen grinned. "What if I was planning to order something you don't even like?"

"Since I'm not known for being a picky eater, that wouldn't really be an issue."

Kristen was saved from thinking up a retort by the arrival of Doug and Betty at the small table next to them. "You're welcome to scoot your table closer to ours."

After a glance at Betty, Doug nodded. "Don't mind if we do."

"We're a little late getting inside, since we stopped to take a few pictures," Betty explained. "But with these windows we could have just taken them from inside."

"Boy, what a view," Doug agreed. "It wouldn't matter what they served us for lunch, as long as I can look out the window and stare at the landscape—or actually, seascape."

Betty was already scanning the menu. "We probably should figure out what we're going to eat since we don't want the bus to leave without us."

"Why not?" asked Doug. "I wouldn't mind being stranded here."

Kristen chuckled at the older couple. It appeared they were thoroughly enjoying their vacation. Any lingering thoughts of murder must have been pushed aside. She figured if she hadn't been prodding them to talk to the police, they probably wouldn't have given Lewis' murder a second thought. There didn't appear to be much love lost between the couples. Was there something more to the story? Did Doug and Betty hold a grudge because of Lewis' behavior? Did they dislike him enough to kill him?

Kristen hated to do it, but once they'd placed their orders, she broached the topic of Lewis' murder once more. "I'm meeting with Margaret when we return from sightseeing."

She was silent, merely watching the expressions on the others' faces. Brett was blatantly disgusted, rolling his eyes, then bugging them out at her, as if to remind her of their agreement not to mention the case again until it was time to meet Margaret. Doug's expression registered a little shock, but Kristen attributed it to her quick change of subjects. She wondered if she should have broached the topic more gradually. A flush crept over Betty's features. *What's that all about?*

Betty gathered her wits enough to ask, "What's the point of that?"

"Not only does she need someone to lean on at the moment, but since she's talking to the police today, she may have more information about the case."

"What's that have to do with you?" Doug asked.

"Aren't you the least bit curious to know who killed Lewis?" Did Doug's lack of interest signify something of importance, or did he just wonder why Kristen kept wanting to discuss the murder? Or was he the one to kill his old neighbor—perhaps over an old grudge?

"I'm honestly getting fed up with the entire situation." Doug drank from his water glass before continuing, then set it back on the table with a bang, causing the remaining water to slosh over the sides. "Our entire trip has revolved around that blasted pair. First of all, Margaret was making a spectacle of herself, acting like a high and mighty nasty piece of work. Then, her husband gets himself killed—a nasty piece of work, himself, and now, we're being grilled continuously about his death. We haven't associated with them in years—and didn't part ways on the best of terms, so why on earth would we care what happens to either one of them? To top things off, Margaret, who wouldn't normally have any use for us, wants everyone to feel sorry for her loss and help her through it. Why does she deserve any courtesy when you consider the way she treats people?"

Betty was staring open mouthed at her husband. "Doug, that's enough. Right now, you're the one making a spectacle of yourself. Even though I feel the same way you do, that's no excuse to voice your thoughts in such a manner." She looked at Kristen, as if gauging her mood after Doug's outburst.

Kristen wasn't in the least bit shocked or offended at his behavior. After all, she'd brought the topic up out of the blue to get a reaction out of the couple. However, she wondered why Doug was so upset at the mention of Margaret. Was he in the same boat as Brett, who was sick of the murder encroaching into their trip, or was it something deeper? She couldn't believe a pass Lewis supposedly made at Betty all those years ago would provoke such a response.

Kristen felt Brett grab her hand. Not sure if he was offering it in support or to help her remain calm, she spoke up, after letting Doug and Betty's words hang in the air for a few more seconds. "I didn't mean to stir up a hornet's nest."

"I apologize for Doug's outburst," Betty said, glaring at her husband.

Kristen bit the sides of her mouth to keep from grinning. It was just a short time ago that she envied the couple's closeness and love for each other. Apparently their second honeymoon was over. "I'm sorry if I ruffled any feathers. I obviously don't have the past you both have with the Sawyers. I also witnessed Margaret's appalling behavior early in the trip and don't blame you for not wanting to help her. But, the truth of the matter is, she's kind of attached herself to Brett and me, since we're the ones who arrived on the scene and tried to help Lewis and then Margaret. She's hanging onto us like a lifeline. Fortunately, she's been behaving much better than before Lewis was killed."

"Kristen is a one-of-a-kind woman," Brett said, snaking his arm around Kristen's shoulder. "She'd do anything for anyone, if they really need help."

Kristen glanced at him, a loving smile plastered on her face, but wondering what Brett was up to.

"Add that to the fact that she's just plain curious about the case since we're the ones who were there on the scene right after it happened, and you can see why she's befriended Margaret." Brett grinned widely. "Don't take it personally if she wants to talk about Lewis' murder all the time. After all, look at what I have to deal with. We're on our honeymoon, and we've talked about this murder way more than we should—when we have better things to do, if you know what I mean." Brett winked at them.

Doug laughed heartily and clapped Brett on the back. "Yeah, I see what you mean."

Kristen decided to chime in while everyone was in good spirits. That was probably Brett's motive all along. "So, obviously, we want to see Lewis' killer brought to justice as soon as possible—not just for Margaret's sake but because we're on our honeymoon, and murder doesn't mix well with what's supposed to be a romantic trip for us."

Everyone chuckled at Kristen's remarks, then sobered as Betty spoke. "Nothing mixes well with murder, and since lunch is on the way, let's speak of other things."

Kristen gave the older woman a sidelong glance. Although she agreed murder was not dinner time conversation, nonetheless, she'd spoken of murder multiple times over breakfast, lunch, and dinner. She wondered again if the Schmidts' aversion to discussing Lewis' murder or the Sawyers in general, was rooted more deeply than a long ago disagreement. Doug's earlier outburst was fresh in her mind. Even though she'd mentioned the topic to prod for a reaction or more information, she was still surprised at Doug's tirade. Kristen would bet 1,000 Króna that Doug and Betty were withholding something that could be important to the case, and she vowed to keep digging until she unearthed whatever it was.

CHAPTER 20

Kristen and Brett held hands as they gazed at the sun, already setting low in the sky at two o'clock in the afternoon. The sun reflected off the frigid Atlantic Ocean water in a small bay—or was it the mouth of the fjord?—tucked between two mountains. The restaurant where they had just eaten had lovely views of this spot. Kristen could look at it until the sun would start to sink further but knew they were due back on the bus in a few more minutes. Even though their view from indoors was similar, there was nothing quite like viewing it outdoors. Not only was Kristen standing closer to the water than from their snug table inside, but there was something to be said about being able to experience the full effect of not only the beautiful scene, but also the cool temperatures and brisk breeze.

Kristen needed the view and the sharp winter weather to give her energy after a tasty and cozy lunch with the Schmidts. Once they'd begun eating, their conversation had switched to lighter subjects, but that didn't stop Kristen's mind from working. Kristen pondered Doug's earlier anger. Even though she knew the couple was probably sick of her questions, they seemed to be overly sensitive to the subject of Lewis and Margaret. Whatever the pair had done to the Schmidts in the past probably wasn't even relevant when it came to

Lewis' murder, but Kristen wasn't one to judge what was important and what wasn't. *Unless Doug or Betty had been the one to kill Lewis.* If that were the case, the couple must have been trying to cover for each other.

Kristen tried to brush aside the thought that kept occurring to her. She forced herself to be objective. Just because she liked Doug and Betty didn't mean she could afford to overlook anything that might point to one of them as being Lewis' killer. Kristen had a feeling if she could get Betty to herself the woman might open up to her more. Despite Doug's usually jovial manner, he seemed to be leery of Betty saying too much about the Sawyers. Having a grudge against them was one thing, but knowing something about Lewis' murder was another.

"I can't get enough of this view." Brett gave Kristen's hand a squeeze. Even through their gloves, Kristen enjoyed his touch.

Kristen shook her head to clear thoughts of the Schmidts and Sawyers from it, focusing on her husband and the beautiful scene before them. If Brett knew how Kristen's mind had been wandering, he didn't let on, and Kristen had no intention of letting him guess she'd been thinking of murder again.

"It's definitely one of the high points of the day," Kristen agreed. "And there have been several."

"Maybe the tunnel we'll be driving through soon will be another one?"

Brett knew Kristen wasn't looking forward to driving underneath the sea, but that didn't mean he needed to keep mentioning it. "Since the sun will be setting in a couple of hours, it's good we're able to shave an hour off our return trip," Kristen said, trying to be positive.

"It will save some time, and just think …" Brett turned to face Kristen. "We can tell our kids about how we drove underneath the ocean on our honeymoon."

Kristen's stomach did a flip-flop, thinking about the two of them having children together. "I'm sure it will be a memorable moment."

"Hey, you two lovebirds, you'd better head back to the bus," Sam said, walking toward them with his friends behind him. "We don't want to keep the bus waiting." Sam grinned.

"You don't have to worry about that," Kristen said, hating to have their last few minutes interrupted by a bunch of college kids—even if they did seem nice. She decided to make the most of it. "It's such a lovely scene. I almost feel guilty about enjoying it so much when we still don't know what happened to Lewis Sawyer, and I'm meeting his wife Margaret tonight when we return."

Did Kristen imagine it, or did Sam's red-haired complexion flush a little? Maybe it was only the brisk temperatures and the wind coming off the bay.

Sam seemed to gather his composure—if he'd actually lost it. "That's nice of you. I'm sure she could use a friend right now." Sam looked at his friends. "We all feel pretty bad about it. Even if we weren't all U of I students where he was a professor, it sucks to have a murder put a damper on our trip."

"I'm sure it's not much fun for him or his survivors either." Kristen felt unsettled by Sam's careless remark. She supposed he didn't mean much by it. She tried to put herself in their shoes. This may have been their first trip out of the country, and they'd saved money for it and been looking forward to it for a long time. *Then again, poor Brett has to put up with his new wife preoccupied with a stranger's murder while on his first trip overseas on his honeymoon.*

"Oh, relax," Nora said. "He wasn't even that great of a teacher, and I've heard stories about him chasing his grad students around the lab."

Now, this was interesting. "I thought you didn't know him," Kristen said, trying not to sound accusing, even though she was irritated at Nora's tone.

"I didn't say I knew him," Nora said in a snarky manner. "But it sounds like others did, if you know what I mean."

Trevor put a restraining hand on Nora's arm. "Come on, hon. You know it's not nice to speak ill of the dead."

"I'm only relaying what I've heard about him."

"You didn't mention this when we were talking about him yesterday," Kristen said, trying to refrain from sounding accusing.

"To be honest, I didn't even make the connection until afterwards." Nora said, sounding friendlier. "I don't get to that part of campus much to know one professor from another."

Fair enough, Kristen reasoned. U of I was a big school, and there could have even been more than one Dr. or Professor Sawyer. It was a common name. The bottom line was, Lewis had kept up his pattern of womanizing, which wouldn't sit well with several people. Margaret wouldn't be happy—if she knew about it. But who else would be unhappy about it? Were his advances welcome? Were the co-eds egging him on, or did they want nothing to do with him? The biggest question of all was, did Lewis' affairs have anything to do with his demise?

Kristen glanced up from her thoughts to see their driver standing outside their minibus. She checked the time. "Looks like we should be boarding right about now."

"We'd better get a move on," Brett said with a grin. "We'll catch you guys later."

Once settled in their seats, Kristen leaned in and kept her voice low. "I wanted to follow up more on Nora's remarks. It's a shame we had to get moving."

"You mean it's a shame we get to head back to the hotel and see more beautiful scenery along the way?"

"You know what I mean." Kristen took off her hat and gloves. "I feel like everyone we talk to is holding something back."

"You're probably right, but who's to say whatever it is they may not be telling us has anything to do with the case? Nora even admitted what she'd heard was a rumor. You know how those can fly around a campus—or small town, like Eklund—and not have a shred of truth to them."

"Do you really think that with what Betty told us that there's nothing to the rumors Nora mentioned?"

"I'm sure there's something to them, but I don't know that one of his past students was lurking around Reykjavik, waiting to pounce on an unsuspecting Lewis to do him in."

Kristen grinned at the mental image. "I guess when you put it like that …"

"You're just trying to make sense of the situation—no harm there." Brett reached over to grab Kristen's hand. "Except for the fact that Lewis' murder is interfering with our vacation."

Kristen knew Brett was right. In a few hours she was supposed to meet Margaret for a drink and possibly receive new information. Would she be able to control the urge to explore new leads? *Highly doubtful*, Kristen thought with a sigh. Right now, she wished their honeymoon itinerary included sipping margaritas on a white sandy beach rather than journeying through a white winter wonderland, trying to figure out who killed Lewis Sawyer.

CHAPTER 21

Nervous out of her mind, Kristen held Brett's hand with a death grip. "What if we don't come out of this alive?"

"Stop it. You're being overly dramatic," he said with a chuckle. "Haven't you been through a tunnel before?"

"Of course, I have, but none of them have been this long or underneath the Atlantic Ocean," she said through gritted teeth.

"To be fair, I think the tunnel goes underneath a fairly shallow fjord."

"Considering we're from the landlocked Midwest, that's still a lot of water to me."

"I just meant that it's not like we're out in the open ocean." Brett patted her arm. "It will be over before you know it, and then you can check it off your bucket list."

"Unfortunately, this tunnel was never anywhere close to being on my bucket list." Kristen gripped Brett's hand even harder as they began to see signs for the approaching tunnel.

"Just lean back and close your eyes."

"Didn't you listen to the guide?" Kristen mimicked the guide's voice as she recited the facts she'd just been reminded of. "The Hvalfjörður Tunnel is a road tunnel under the Hvalfjörður fjord that is18,930 feet long and reaches a depth of 541 feet below sea level."

Kristen stopped talking as the bus edged closer to the entrance, pausing to flash what she assumed was a pass to drive into the tunnel. Soon they started the drive downward—541 feet to be exact—before they would start the ascent up the ramp to the other side. It was just like any other tunnel she'd driven through or taken a train through. She'd never experienced any issues in tunnels, caves, or other enclosed areas, but the thought of all that water surrounding the tunnel made her freak out and feel claustrophobic. Was it possible the tunnel could spring a leak? Would the heavy-duty sides burst and allow billions of gallons to enter? What would happen to their minibus and its occupants if the worst-case scenario played out? Kristen tried to ignore her negative thoughts and began taking consistent, regular breaths to stave off the panicky breathing issues she was beginning to experience.

Kristen did the mental math and estimated the tunnel was about three and a half miles long. She wasn't sure how fast they were travelling but thought they should be back on dry ground again in about five minutes.

She tried looking out the window to pass the time, but since there was no view, other than the claustrophobic tunnel walls that didn't help much and only served to remind her that they were driving through a tunnel twenty thousand leagues under the sea—or something like that. She had never understood what that book title meant. *Maybe if I'd read the book it would make sense.*

Brett glanced her way, a concerned look on his face. "It feels like we're starting to go back up again," Brett said, his voice soothing and encouraging. "We'll see daylight—or what's left of it—in a few more minutes."

Kristen took a deep breath. "I sure hope so."

"Fortunately, you're meeting Margaret for a drink when we get back to the hotel," Brett joked.

"A shot of something before we entered the tunnel may have been helpful. A little preventative medication, rather than treating the illness after the fact." Despite herself, Kristen could see the humor of the situation, at least now that they were getting closer to the exit with every passing second.

"Look at the bright side," Brett said. "Can you imagine taking the route around the fjord at this time of afternoon? It will be getting dark pretty soon, and that could have been dangerous."

"I'm sure the driver is more used to these roads and driving conditions than if we were to attempt it." Kristen eased her grip on Brett's hand. "Besides, I would have loved to take the scenic route again."

"Well, you'll have to sit tight for just a minute or two longer, and we'll be out of this tunnel."

"Thank goodness," Kristen said, her breathing finally starting to return to normal. Between Brett's calm voice trying to take her mind off the tunnel and knowing they were almost through it, her case of the nerves was improving.

"I've been with you when you've discovered bodies and been cornered by murderers, and I've never seen you react the way you did to a harmless tunnel." Brett spoke quietly, as not to alert their fellow passengers of Kristen's affinity with murders.

"We all have our crosses to bear," Kristen smiled. Brett was right. She'd been through a lot worse than riding through a tunnel in a beautiful country—though the view wasn't currently all that great. Still, things were looking up, and Kristen thought she could see light at the end of the tunnel—literally!

As the dim light gradually grew brighter, Kristen thought about Brett's earlier words about coming into contact with not only murder victims, but also their murderers. Have I come into contact with a murderer this round? *Have I been chatting with seemingly harmless people trying to dig up information from them when all along one of them could be the one who killed Lewis?*

Of course, that's a possibility, you idiot! The ride through the tunnel had given Kristen a jolt of reality. Why it hit her now, when it didn't sink in until it was almost too late in previous murder investigations, she did not know. *It was probably the deep breathing exercises I've been doing for the last few minutes.*

She felt another revelation as the bus surfaced from the dreary tunnel and came out into the fading afternoon sunlight with beautiful white snow covering the landscape. Even though the tunnel had been lit, it was nothing compared to the almost blinding light that surrounded them now. The sun was still hovering and bright, though low in the sky. It would probably still be light for most of the drive back to Reykjavik. *And I will make the most of the trip, planning what I want to ask Margaret.*

Brett squeezed Kristen's hand. "Feel better?"

"Much!"

"If you're sure, I'm going to take a nap. I want to be fully awake for the Northern Lights, and from the looks of it, the sky should be clear enough to see them tonight."

"Get some rest. I'll entertain myself. Hopefully the sky will stay clear." Brett snuggled closer, leaning his head on Kristen's shoulder.

Kristen, enjoying the warmth of Brett's closeness, probably should have napped herself, but she had other plans. Besides wanting to see another view of the scenery en route to Reykjavik, she would outline what she would ask Margaret. She stared out the window, trying to soak up the gorgeous view while her mind whirled away. She assumed Margaret would lead off with the official cause of Lewis' death. At least she hoped Margaret would share that information. It was hard to know which direction to pursue when she didn't know all the details.

Depending on the outcome of that conversation, Kristen would keep probing to see if the police told Margaret anything else—and what the police asked Margaret. She also needed to ask Margaret if she knew of any enemies Lewis had. Like everyone she'd talked to lately, Margaret seemed to be withholding information. She felt sure there was more to the story. If necessary, she would inquire into their marital relationship. Did Margaret know the extent of Lewis' affairs? Had she finally had enough? *Must tread lightly*. Not only was Margaret grieving—at least outwardly—but if she had killed her husband, she wouldn't welcome Kristen badgering her. *Then again, she's the one who has been seeking me out, wanting to confide in me.* Why would she do that if she was a killer? Wouldn't she stick to herself and not be reaching out to relative strangers?

Depending on what all Kristen learned from Margaret, she decided to squeeze in some time searching online for information. She knew the internet was oftentimes more forthcoming with information than grieving family members or suspects—who sometimes were one and the same. It also wouldn't hurt to search for the Schmidts. What were they holding back? She doubted their secret could be found online, but hard telling what else might pop up in a search engine.

Wondering when she would find the time to search for information online, Kristen remembered they didn't have plans tomorrow morning. They would be heading out to the Blue Lagoon in the afternoon, so there would be time. Kristen would tell Brett she wanted to view and edit the hundreds of pictures she'd taken so far. She hated stretching the truth—especially since they hadn't even been married a week. But she knew he would give her a hard time for spending precious honeymoon time getting too wrapped up in yet another murder investigation.

Feeling better now that she had a rough plan for the evening and tomorrow, she slouched down in her seat, snuggled up with the man of her dreams as she watched the snowy countryside pass by. Looking at Brett's peaceful face as he dozed, she wondered what he was dreaming about. One thing was sure; it wasn't murder.

CHAPTER 22

Once Kristen and Brett arrived back at the hotel, Kristen tapped into the hotel's Wi-Fi to catch up on messages that had come through while they were away. Sure enough, a text from Margaret was waiting.

Let me know when you return, and I'll buy you a drink.

Kristen tapped out a reply. **Just got back.** She checked the time. Four o'clock. **Is four-thirty okay?**

Her phone buzzed seconds later. **Sure. Meet you at the hotel bar.**

Brett looked at her questioningly. "Was that from your buddy?"

"If you mean Margaret, she's your buddy, too." Kristen punched the elevator button. "I'm sure she wouldn't mind if you tagged along."

"No, thanks. I'll do some checking to see if tonight's tour is a go, and if you don't mind, I can scout out somewhere to go for dinner."

"Sounds perfect." She leaned closer for a quick kiss just as the elevator arrived. She was lucky to have a man like Brett. Once in their room, she freshened up, then sat down to wait until it was time to meet Margaret.

"What sounds good for dinner?" he asked.

"Maybe somewhere close by, since we hope to go on the tour tonight."

"That's a good thought. I'll see what I can do while you and Margaret do your thing."

Kristen was glad Brett would be taking care of their evening plans while she was meeting Margaret. He was less apt to be upset with her for deserting him if he was occupied. She yawned, thinking if she didn't get up soon, she wouldn't want to leave their cozy hotel room. "If you don't mind, I'm going to go on down to the hotel lobby a little early. I might check out the gift shop while I'm waiting for Margaret. If I stay here, I'll be tempted to stay."

"Well, it *is* our honeymoon, you know." Brett wiggled his eyebrows.

"I know. I know," Kristen said with a grin. "I'll get my meeting over with Margaret and look forward to whatever you have planned for the rest of the evening. How's that?"

"Sounds like a deal."

Kristen gathered her things, gave Brett a quick kiss, then left the room. Deciding to take the stairs since she'd been riding on the bus for much of the day, she located the stairwell. With a grimace, she opened the door, trying to block out the image of being chased by a murderer down a hotel staircase in Wisconsin on their first Nature Station bus trip to visit Lake Michigan. *If I can make it through a tunnel underneath the sea, I can handle a few flights of stairs—at least going down. Going up may be another matter.*

Having safely arrived in the lobby, Kristen made a beeline for the gift shop. It wasn't large, but she'd eyed a few things from the window when passing through earlier. She needed to take time to pick out a few souvenirs to take home to her close family and Hope. Picking up a Icelandic wool stocking cap she turned it over, admiring the earthy colors of the wool as well as the craftsmanship. She sucked in her breath when she noticed the price. Things were definitely more expensive in Iceland, and maybe a hotel gift shop wasn't the best place to find a good deal. Still, there were some lovely things, so she continued browsing.

She was fingering delicate Icelandic lava earrings when she spotted Sam and his friends headed her way— or at least entering the small shop. She doubted they were stopping by to chat with her. She grinned as the foursome began lifting up items and exclaiming over the prices. *Talk about sticker shock*, she thought. *At least I'm out of college and earning my way in the world. Well, sort of.* At least the Nature Station was in the black, even if she didn't make a six-figure salary with all the paid benefits. *But there's something to be said for doing what you love and having flexibility.*

"Hey, look at this cute Icelandic horse stuffed animal," Nora said.

Kristen looked up from the jewelry and smiled, thinking the animal would be cute to take home to her niece, Chloe.

"Hi, Kristen," Trevor said. "Checking out the merchandise?"

"You could say that. But most of it is way out of my price range, I'm afraid."

"Tell me about it," Sam chimed in as he walked over with Alicia.

"Hotel gift shops aren't known for their bargains," Kristen said. "But there are some nice things here. I'd like to take home something made from Icelandic wool, and some of this lava jewelry is cool."

"Give me a t-shirt, and I'm good to go," Sam said, ever jovial.

"I try to pick up something that the country or state I'm visiting is known for," Kristen said, realizing she probably sounded snotty to the student travelers. Still, you could buy a t-shirt anywhere, and they were probably all made in the same country and printed with different destination names.

"How about some Gull beer then?" Trevor asked, his voice carrying throughout the shop and probably half the hotel lobby as well.

Kristen wasn't sure if he was asking his friends if they wanted to drink a beer or if he meant he wanted to take beer home as a souvenir, and she supposed it didn't matter. She checked her watch. "Speaking of beer, I need to meet ..." Her voice trailed off. She wasn't sure why she didn't want to tell the kids she was meeting Margaret for a drink. After all, anyone could see them if they happened to walk by the bar. But she didn't want to call attention to their meeting, or remind Sam of it, since she'd let it slip when talking to him earlier.

"Yeah, you gotta meet your new hubby, don't you?" Sam asked.

Kristen was glad he'd assumed she meant to say Brett. She picked up a couple of postcards. "Yes, I am meeting him in a while, so I think I'll pay for these and see you later—maybe at tonight's Northern Lights tour?"

"Sure will, if they have it tonight," Alicia said. She put down the wool scarf she'd been looking at. "Although this is pretty, I'm not as worried about keeping warm as I am about keeping safe."

Kristen threw her a questioning look. "What do you mean?"

"Well, there's a murderer on the loose, right?"

"I think we'll be safe on a sightseeing tour, even it if is at night."

"But Dr. Sawyer was killed in broad daylight in the middle of the afternoon in a high traffic location." Alicia shrugged dramatically.

"Don't worry, honey. I'll keep you safe." Sam put his arm around her.

Kristen had to admit Alicia had a point she kept ignoring. If one of their travel mates was the killer, she really should be more careful when talking to them. If they hadn't figured out Kristen was asking so many questions for a reason, it was only a matter of time before they did.

"We've been on other sightseeing tours since Lewis was killed," Kristen said, wondering what the difference was.

"Oh, so you're on a first name basis with the deceased?" Nora asked.

Kristen was getting tired of everyone seeming to have an attitude. She was ready to go and meet Margaret, who was probably in her own funk. But who could blame her? Her husband had just died.

Kristen shrugged. "Even though I didn't know him, what else am I supposed to call him?"

"It doesn't matter what his name is, there's still a murderer out there, and we're headed out to the great outdoors tonight." Alicia shivered.

"Strength in numbers," Kristen said. "We'll be fine. They take hundreds of these tours every year."

"But how many murders can there possibly be in a country like this?" Alicia asked.

"Probably not that many, which means the police are working diligently to catch the killer." *With a little help from me, perhaps.*

"I'm not that excited about standing outside in the cold, hoping to see some creepy looking light show, while trying not to get murdered," Alicia said.

Creepy looking light show? "Most people are amazed by the Northern Lights, and I hope to be one of them later tonight." Kristen fumbled in her purse for the correct coins to pay for her postcards. She didn't want to keep Margaret waiting.

"I think I can safely say that the rest of us are looking forward to the tour," Sam said. "Alicia will be fine once she sees the lights. She won't have time to worry about a murderer."

"Exactly, which means he—or she—could catch us unawares." Alicia shook her head.

"But why would the murderer want to kill one of us?" Kristen asked, puzzled by Alicia's behavior.

"Why would anyone want to kill Dr. Sawyer?" The normally jovial Sam was serious as he spoke. "And yet it happened. He may have been a jerk, but did he deserve to die?

Kristen was thoughtful as she took the paper bag of postcards from the shop clerk, who was probably eavesdropping on their conversation with interest. She felt sure news of Lewis' murder had reached the hotel staff. "No one deserves to be murdered." But had Lewis gotten his just desserts?

CHAPTER 23

Kristen left the gift shop and walked down the hallway to the lounge, where she figured Margaret was probably already waiting. Sure enough, she spied Margaret settled at a table in the far corner, her back to the wall. Margaret, apparently on the lookout for Kristen, lifted her glass as a wave.

Kristen made her way toward Margaret, thankful none of the others from their trip were in the dimly lit lounge. After the conversation she'd had in the gift shop, she wanted to steer clear of the others for a while. She didn't want to provoke questions from her fellow travelers if they saw her hanging out with Margaret.

Margaret smiled weakly as Kristen pulled out a chair and sat down, glad they didn't have to hold their conversation at a crowded bar, teetering on a bar stool. "What are you having? My treat." Margaret held up her hand in an attempt to wave the bartender over to their table. "Although, if we need more than one drink for this conversation, I'll be broke before I know it."

Kristen wasn't sure if Margaret was serious or just making a joke about how expensive food and drinks were in Iceland. "No problem. I can get the next round." Kristen tried not to grimace. If she was going to stick around for a second drink, she'd prefer to enjoy it with Brett. She thought Margaret could cough up the cost of a draft beer for the woman who was giving up precious honeymoon time to be her sounding board. To be fair, Margaret probably didn't realize Kristen was snooping around, trying to figure out who had killed Lewis. If she did, maybe she would have been more appreciative. *Then again, maybe not*, thought Kristen, remembering back to the first few times she'd seen Margaret in action.

When the bartender arrived, Kristen ordered a draft of Gull beer, then turned back to Margaret. "We had a busy day sightseeing, but I bet you're more worn out after talking to the police."

Even in the dim light, Kristen could see Margaret roll her eyes. "It was quite an ordeal, even if it didn't last long."

Kristen was curious to hear what had happened but told herself to be patient. "*Takk,*" she said to the bartender who sat her beer on the table. Taking a sip, she looked encouragingly at Margaret. Hopefully she would get on with it, now that they didn't have to worry about an interruption from waitstaff.

Another moment or two of awkward silence passed before Margaret finally began to speak. "As you know, I met with the police today."

Kristen nodded. She supposed stating the obvious was Margaret's way of getting the conversation rolling.

"They told me how Lewis died." Margaret used her cocktail napkin to wipe her eyes.

Again, Kristen nodded, then patted Margaret's hand, but growing impatient. After all, the point of their meeting was to discuss the cause of death and whatever else the police told her. "What did the police say?"

Margaret sniffed. "They think he died of arsenic poisoning."

Kristen was taken aback at this news and almost spit out the beer she'd just sipped. Even though she'd read dozens of mystery books where arsenic was used, wasn't that more of a Victorian or early 20th century murder method? "Are they sure?" *Because I didn't realize things like this happened in real, modern-day murders.*

"I'm afraid so," Margaret said. "In fact, the paramedics must have realized it right away, and that's what pointed to Lewis' death as being suspicious. I would have assumed he had a stroke or heart attack—even if he'd never had any issues before. Why would I jump to the conclusion he'd been killed?"

Why, indeed? "How could they tell?" Kristen decided to play dumb and not tell Margaret about the scent she'd noticed on Lewis' body—or about her vast experience of solving murders in the mystery books she read, much less the real-life ones.

Margaret dropped her gaze downward, as if afraid to meet Kristen's eyes. "He had some of the symptoms of arsenic poisoning before we left our room, but I didn't realize it at the time. He complained of stomach cramps and diarrhea, but I thought it was just from traveling. I didn't think much about it, and he said he felt okay enough to do some sightseeing."

"But you didn't mention these symptoms to the paramedics at the time, so how did they realize it was arsenic poisoning?"

"First of all, let me clarify that I had no idea his earlier stomach issues had anything to do with his murder. I thought his digestive system was off kilter from traveling across the time zones, very little sleep, and not eating at his normal time." Margaret was starting to gain more confidence as she spoke. "I did mention Lewis' symptoms after the police asked if he had displayed any of them when we talked today."

"That's all understandable. Please go on." Kristen tried her best to reassure Margaret and keep her talking. Kristen remembered the foul smelling odor she'd sniffed when trying to help Lewis. Maybe the paramedics or police had also smelled it, and that was one of the things that made them think he was poisoned. She didn't want to mention what she realized now was probably the excrement smell to Margaret. The poor woman had been through enough without knowing her husband had lost control of his bodily functions as the effects of the poison worsened.

"Apparently, the paramedics or police noticed some skin irregularities and lesions on Lewis's ..." Margaret gulped. "... body."

"But why would they assume he was murdered just from seeing some sores?" Kristen immediately regretted blurting out something so crude and insensitive.

Fortunately, Margaret didn't seem to mind. "That's what I said. I wasn't following them. And to be honest, I felt horrible not noticing them earlier, but it's winter, and he's been wearing long sleeves."

"If he'd just been poisoned lately, it makes sense that the sores just showed up recently." But would a skin irritation show up immediately after poisoning, or would it happen over time? Kristen tried to remember what she'd read about arsenic poisoning. Even if most of what she knew about it came from fiction novels, she knew authors researched and fact checked that type of thing, so she assumed most of the information could be counted on to be correct. "I think arsenic poisoning can occur in small doses over a long period, or it can happen with a large dose and do more damage in a short period of time." *Which really narrows down the suspect list.*

"Well, it did the ultimate damage in Lewis' case."

"Do you or the police have any ideas as to how it happened?" Kristen's mind reeled through the possibilities. Did rat poison still contain arsenic?

Margaret shook her head. "Do you mean besides me?"

It made sense that the police suspected the wife in this case. After all, the Sawyers were in a foreign country where they didn't know anyone. But that didn't make it any easier on Margaret—especially if she was innocent, which Kristen felt was the case. Why would Margaret and Lewis go on a trip to Iceland if she were going to kill him? Why not just murder him at home? *Maybe she thinks there will be less press in Iceland.* But for all Kristen knew, the story had already broken in the U.S. Between everything available online, camera phones, instant publication of news, and other modern technology, the world was a smaller place.

"You have to admit that the police need to start with the person closest to Lewis, especially since you are so far from home and don't know people over here. Or do you?"

"Know anyone, you mean?"

"Yeah, the police have to look at you if no one else is around to blame."

"As much as I hate to admit it, you're right." Margaret took a sip of beer and looked Kristen straight in the eyes. "But I didn't do it. You have to believe me."

"I happen to believe you, but it's not up to me." Kristen decided it was time to get down to business. "Could it have been an accident? How on earth did Lewis ingest enough arsenic to die?"

Margaret shrugged. "I have no idea. We ate the same things. The police already asked me that."

"I find it hard to believe that this was long term arsenic exposure, which I think can also kill you. What are the odds Lewis would have reached the maximum threshold for exposure the minute you started sightseeing?"

"So you think someone poisoned him in Iceland? I would have guessed that, since I didn't even realize someone could die from arsenic poisoning over time."

"I'm only speculating and thinking out loud, but it makes sense to me." Kristen searched for arsenic poisoning symptoms on her phone, then scanned the list that popped up. "Had Lewis experienced any of the stomach issues before you arrived?"

"The police asked me that as well. I told them he hadn't complained of any upset stomach or irregularities." Margaret smiled wryly. "Then again, that's not something we often discussed."

Kristen wondered at what point a couple started talking openly about such issues as diarrhea, vomiting, and such. She would think Margaret would have noticed a change in Lewis' appetite or energy level, even if she didn't know he was having digestive issues that were getting progressively worse.

Margaret sighed. "If one of us had the stomach flu, it was quite obvious. Reactions to arsenic poisoning over a long time period would have probably been more gradual is what I gathered from the police."

"Which leads us back to the fact that he was probably poisoned in Iceland." Kristen took a sip of beer, thoughtful for a moment. "Are the police sure it wasn't accidental?"

"They aren't ruling it out, but since no one else has been poisoned—including me—they are assuming it was intentional poisoning."

Kristen hated to ask the next question forming in her mind but decided to ask anyway. "Is there any indication Lewis could have wanted to harm himself?"

"Suicide? No way. Lewis loved life way too much."

Did Kristen imagine the look that crossed Margaret's features? Was she referring to Lewis' dalliances with other women? Kristen also wondered if it had gotten to be too much to be married to a woman like Margaret. Had her poor behavior at the start of the trip pushed him over the edge?

"I find it interesting that you're asking so many of the same questions the police asked." Margaret smiled grimly. "Are you sure you're not in the law enforcement field back home?"

"No, way. I'm a naturalist. But my co-worker is married to a sheriff's deputy, so I've probably picked up a lot of information from her over the years." Kristen was proud she'd answered Margaret's question without actually stretching the truth. "I also read a lot of mystery novels," Kristen joked, trying to take the spotlight off her crime solving adventures in the past that had added to her current knowledge.

"You seem to have a keen interest in this investigation," Margaret said. "I would normally not want to share so many details with someone I just met, but in this case, I'm glad to have you to talk to."

"Happy to be of service," Kristen wanted to change the subject to get back on track and get her back to Brett. "Did the police say what other leads they're pursuing?"

"I'm not sure if there are any other leads."

That didn't bode well for Margaret. "So, how did you leave things?"

"Well, I'm here, aren't I? Not locked up in a cold Icelandic jail cell, waiting for the rats to find me."

Kristen suspected an Icelandic jail was about as clean, warm, and modern as possible, but she wouldn't want to be locked in one, so she couldn't blame Margaret for being so dramatic. "Do they want to question you again?"

"I'm sure they do, but they just told me to stay put while they continue gathering information—whatever that means."

"I'm sure they are checking into Lewis' background, yours, and probably other travelers in our group." Kristen didn't have the heart to tell Margaret that she was doing the same thing. Although, it might actually improve Margaret's spirits.

Margaret's eyes widened. "Our backgrounds. Oh, dear."

Kristen wondered if Margaret was worried about the police finding out about Lewis' affairs or something else. "Is everything okay?"

"Of course not," Margaret snapped. "I'm sorry, that wasn't fair. You're just trying to help, and I'm cutting into your personal time."

"If you're holding anything back from the police, you may as well tell them. Let them hear it straight from you instead of having them dig it up. It will be better in the long run." Kristen wanted to tell Margaret that if she could find out about Lewis' affairs, then anyone could, and that went for whatever else Margaret may be trying to hide.

"I hate to run to them to air our dirty laundry when it might not be pertinent to the case."

Kristen felt like she'd just had this conversation with the Schmidts—which she had. "Everyone has things they'd rather not have known to the police or public. But if it's something that could help them figure out who killed Lewis, then it's worth it."

"I'm sure you're right, but I want to sleep on it."

Kristen thought Margaret had already had plenty of time and opportunities to tell the police whatever they wanted or needed to hear. "You'd better not wait too long. Don't you want this wrapped up soon?"

"Of course, I do, but it's not as simple as that."

"I can only imagine. I doubt murder investigations are ever simple." Kristen knew that firsthand. "And there's probably always muck that's dredged up that's better left buried, but sometimes it has to be done to get to the bottom of things."

Margaret sighed. "Unfortunately, there's plenty of muck to dredge."

"Look, if you want to talk about anything, I'm here for you. I won't judge you for anything you tell me, and it won't go any further. But you have to be the one to tell the police if there's anything relevant to the case you haven't already told them."

"I told you, I need to sleep on it—before I tell the police who all Lewis slept with and the results of his sleeping habits."

CHAPTER 24

Even though Kristen already had an indication of what Margaret was hinting at, she still felt her jaw drop in surprise. At least Kristen didn't have to feign her shock, after already hearing from multiple sources that Lewis had been quite the lady's man. "Are you saying Lewis cheated on you?" Kristen stammered. She knew all about Lewis' womanizing, but she was surprised Margaret could be so offhand about it.

Margaret laughed, but it wasn't a pleasant sound. She signaled for another drink. "Unfortunately, he had a string of affairs, starting from right after we married—maybe even before that—to the day he died."

Kristen sucked in her breath at the bitterness of not only Margaret's words, but also her tone. If they weren't already in Iceland, Kristen would have felt the icy chill of Margaret's words even more. She couldn't blame Margaret for feeling the way she did, but if the police heard the way she was talking, it would be another story. Still, it was a relief to have Lewis' infidelity out in the open. Kristen wouldn't have to tiptoe around and pretend she didn't already know about it from the other travelers.

Not sure what else to say, but knowing Margaret expected some kind of reaction from her revelation, Kristen stammered. "I'm sorry. I had no idea." Crossing her fingers under the table, Kristen told herself a white lie was fine in certain situations. What good would it do to let Margaret know she and her dead husband were the talk of the city of Reykjavik—at least among the American visitors staying at the same hotel?

"Oh, come on, don't tell me you haven't heard rumors."

"I didn't set eyes on the two of you until I noticed you—and dozens of others—at the airport. How would I hear rumors?"

"Don't play dumb—you're much too smart for that. Don't you think I don't know your precious friends the Schmidts have probably filled you in on everything?"

Kristen was surprised to hear this, after Margaret told her earlier she didn't recognize the couple. Had Kristen underestimated the grieving widow? Was she actually grieving? "They seem like a nice couple, but other than telling me they lived in the same neighborhood as you at one time, they haven't mentioned much else."

Margaret scoffed at that remark. "Oh, please. Why do you think I pretended not to know them? Hard telling what kind of stuff they would tell you—or worse yet, the police."

Kristen didn't want to let on she knew about Margaret and Lewis' past. "I don't know why you're getting so excited. The Schmidts appear to be decent, harmless people."

"Appearances aren't everything, and I ought to know that firsthand." Margaret stared into her empty glass. "Lewis and I weren't as we seemed."

How could they be worse than they appeared? Kristen swirled the beer in her glass. "What do you mean?"

"Like I started telling you earlier. Not only did Lewis have several affairs throughout our marriage, but there were at least two women I know about who came forward to accuse him of fathering children."

Accuse him? Was there any doubt? "Did he have a blood test to prove his paternity?"

Margaret shook her head. "No, he managed to weasel out of it somehow. He didn't want to acknowledge children other than our own—that was plenty."

Kristen didn't know what to say about a man who not only didn't want to claim children he'd fathered, but who also probably didn't offer to pay child support either.

"I can see what you're thinking. He did offer the women one-time cash settlements, but he didn't want to be chained to monthly payments, and he didn't want our children to know they had half brothers and sisters. He wanted no further involvement."

Kristen couldn't believe how much Lewis had gotten around, let alone how he'd behaved when approached by women later who carried his children. "What was to stop the women from wanting child support down the road?"

Margaret shrugged. "Probably nothing, which is why one of his spurned women probably killed him."

Kristen's eyes widened. "If that's the case, why don't you let the police know? Why are you hesitating to tell them?" Didn't Margaret want the killer to be caught to remove the spotlight from herself?

"All this digging into Lewis'—and my—life is starting to get to me. We were supposed to have a nice trip together. Maybe we could have put the past behind us, but now we'll never know."

Kristen wasn't sure they could have ever moved past Lewis' chronic infidelity. She didn't think Margaret was the type to ignore it for long. Maybe she had taken matters into her own hands. "But don't you want Lewis' killer brought to justice?"

"Not so sure anymore. Maybe he got what he deserved."

Dying an awful death from arsenic poisoning? "But if you tell the police about Lewis' other women, they should start looking into them and leave you alone."

"What are the odds that one of them is in Iceland?"

"That would be easy enough to check through the airlines and passport control." Kristen was thoughtful. "Besides, have they pinpointed when the poison was actually administered? Or even whether it was one large dose or several smaller doses over a longer time period?"

"My, you have a lot of questions. I'm not sure they know exactly."

Kristen chose to ignore Margaret's remark. Did the woman want Kristen's help, or not? "But don't you see? The poison could have been administered before we even left the U.S."

"That sheds a whole new light on things," Margaret agreed. "But it also opens up a whole new suspect list."

"Exactly. Which can be good—or bad." Kristen glanced at her watch, knowing she needed to wrap up her conversation soon. "How did you leave things with the police?"

"Didn't I answer that in your earlier barrage of questions?"

Kristen rolled her eyes, hoping Margaret wouldn't notice in the low light. "I'm sorry if my questions offend you, but I thought you wanted someone to help you?" Kristen didn't wait for Margaret to apologize, since she was confident she wouldn't receive an apology. "I meant, do the police want to talk to you again tomorrow?"

"We didn't set a date and time. They used the standard police statement and told me to be available if they had more questions or uncovered pertinent information."

"So, no plans for tomorrow? Any word on when Lewis' body will be released?"

Margaret shook her head. "After hearing what you had to say, I'm assuming they're running further tests to better pinpoint when and how the poison was administered."

"That makes sense." Kristen wasn't about to volunteer to let Margaret tag along with them tomorrow. "Just let me know if you hear any more news." Kristen stood. "Thanks for the drink."

"No problem. It's the least I could do after you've taken the time to talk to me and put up with my moods the past few days."

"You have a right to be moody after everything that's happened recently."

"The past several years, is more like it," Margaret muttered, just loud enough for Kristen to hear.

Kristen ignored the comment, not wanting to prolong their conversation, even if she was curious to know if any of Margaret and Lewis' past history had come back to haunt them.

"I'll probably see you tomorrow," Kristen said, and then headed for the door, relieved to be on her way to meet Brett.

She headed to the lobby and found an empty chair. Pulling out her phone, she texted Brett. **I'm done and waiting in the lobby.**

It wasn't long before Brett replied. **Be there in five.**

Kristen smiled, glad they could chill for the rest of the evening. She took a moment to mentally review what she'd learned from Margaret. Arsenic poisoning was the cause of death, and Lewis' affairs may have been more numerous and more complicated than originally thought. If he'd left unacknowledged children in his wake, had one of the children—or a mother—killed Lewis?

Kristen heard the elevator bell and looked up, happy to see Brett exiting the elevator and walking toward her.

"That seemed like less than five minutes."

Brett grinned. "Well, you don't normally say that you'll meet someone in 2.7 minutes, do you?"

"I guess not." Kristen laughed. "What do you have planned for the evening?

"The weather is right for the Northern Lights tour tonight, and we're booked to meet in the lobby at eight-thirty. So, we can either eat at the hotel restaurant, or there's a café around the corner that looks nice."

As much as Kristen would have preferred to keep it simple and eat at the hotel, she wanted to put some distance between herself and their fellow travelers. "Let's try the café."

Brett grabbed Kristen's hand. "Let's get out of here before Margaret tracks you down for another therapy session."

"Aren't you the least bit curious to hear what we discussed?"

"I am, but not enough to delay our dinner."

They left the hotel to walk the short distance to the café. The cool air felt refreshing—just what Kristen needed after a busy day of sightseeing and a long conversation with Margaret.

Brett held the door for Kristen, and she gave the cozy dining area a quick glance while they waited to be seated. She breathed a sigh of relief when she didn't recognize anyone from their hotel.

They were soon seated at a table looking at their menus. Kristen's stomach grumbled as she picked up the menu. "I should order something pretty filling if we're going to be taking the tour tonight."

"Great idea." Brett shut his menu.

Kristen looked at him questioningly. "You already know what you want to order?"

"While you were chatting away with Margaret, I was researching dining options. Since I'd already seen the menu, it didn't take me long to decide." He grinned impishly. "I was glad you chose to eat here, since I had my heart set on trying the traditional Icelandic lamb stew."

If Brett is that good at research, maybe I should try to recruit him to help dig up dirt on the players in Lewis' murder. "I'll have the same then. Normally I'm not fond of lamb meat—except in gyros, of course. But since lamb is so common in Iceland, I'm willing to give it a try." Kristen shut her own menu and glanced around the dining area, eyeing its warm and cozy décor. Contemporary, simple furniture and dinnerware were softened by Icelandic wool wall hangings and centerpieces and glowing candles on each table. The restaurant smelled of fresh baked bread and cold weather comfort foods.

"The reviews said this dish is one of their most popular specialties," Brett assured her. "Besides, I know you want to try as many traditional dishes as possible while we're here."

"That's true," Kristen said, glad Brett knew her so well.

"Once the waiter takes our orders, I want to hear everything."

Kristen grinned. "You seem to read my mind. I found out a couple of things from Margaret, but that woman can be exhausting." Kristen stopped talking as the waiter came their way.

Orders placed, Kristen filled Brett in on what she'd learned from Margaret. "Arsenic poisoning? In this day and age?" he asked.

"Apparently so. It's tricky, since that type of poisoning can occur over a long or short time period, depending on the dose."

"Between arsenic being used as a cause of death, making it harder to determine where and when he was poisoned, and Lewis making lady friends wherever he went, the suspect list has increased drastically."

"My thoughts exactly."

"Which may make it easier—or harder, depending on how you look at it—to figure out who killed him."

"Again, I agree," Kristen said. "I'm not sure how the police are handling things. Margaret thinks the police are out to get her."

"That makes sense. She had motive, opportunity, and she certainly seems capable of it."

Kristen thought of Margaret's cold attitude, but she couldn't blame the woman for feeling bitter about a cheating husband—killing him was another story. "More than capable, in my opinion."

"Since you've been talking to her so much lately—more so than your new husband, I might add—what do you think?"

"I think I've given you plenty of attention—that's what I think!" Kristen teased, knowing Brett was only kidding—to a point.

"I can see you've set the stage to be a neglectful wife."

"You poor thing," Kristen cooed. "Seriously, I know Margaret has a lot of motive and probably more opportunity than anyone else we know about, not to mention being bitter about the women and children he's left in his wake, but I don't think she killed him."

"Why are you so willing to give her the benefit of the doubt?"

"I'm not sure, but I'm just not getting any 'killer vibes' from her."

"That's a relief, since she could have easily poisoned your drink if she were the killer." Brett sobered. "Seriously, honey, you need to be careful, even if your gut instincts don't think she did it. The matter remains that someone did it, and they could be in Iceland."

"Since this country is not all that big or very populated, the odds are good we could bump into the killer." *And that's what I'm counting on.* Even though Kristen had no intention of actually confronting the killer, as she had in the past, she did want to help Margaret and the police round up the killer. The tricky part was bumping into the killer without getting bumped off in the process.

CHAPTER 25

Nestled in the small bus that was transporting Kristen, Brett, and their fellow travelers north out of Reykjavik, away from the city's lights in the hopes of watching the Northern Lights work their magic, Kristen couldn't believe the day she'd had. Although happy at the prospect of seeing the famed lights, Kristen would be glad when it was time to head back to the hotel where her warm and comfortable bed was awaiting. *If only the Northern Lights were visible during the day when I'm more awake.*

Kristen could feel the bus slowing down, and it soon turned into a parking lot, where other small buses were parked. "This must be it—not just for our group but for others as well," she said to Brett.

Brett squinted out the window into the dark night. "It looks like we're in the middle of nowhere, so we should have a great view."

Kristen caught a glimpse of a green flash of light. "There," she said, pointing out the window. "I think the lightshow may already be starting."

"Then let's make sure we have our things and be one of the first ones off the bus."

Kristen put on her hat and gloves as they stood in the aisle, ready to go once the doors opened. She adjusted her camera strap around her neck. "I hope I get some decent shots."

"I'm sure you will, and you can add them to the hundreds of pictures you've already taken on this trip."

Kristen giggled. "Who knows when we'll have a chance to return."

"That's a good point."

"Besides, I can always delete the duplicates or the ones that don't turn out well." Kristen remembered her plan to review her pictures tomorrow. "I'll take a peek at them in the morning."

Kristen was planning to check her pictures, but she also wanted to look online for more information on Lewis, Margaret, and it wouldn't hurt to run quick searches on the rest of their traveling companions. Even if someone not on the trip or in Iceland was the culprit, what harm could it do to research the others? *Besides wasting valuable time on my honeymoon*. Kristen knew Brett wouldn't be pleased if he knew, unless he had plans of his own.

"While you're doing that, I'll try to scout out places to eat and do some souvenir shopping."

Kristen was not only glad Brett had something to entertain himself while she was busy, but it was nice to have someone make plans. She was happy he was getting into the spirit of things.

Kristen's thoughts were interrupted by the guide giving last-minute instructions. Kristen followed Brett off the bus, where they stood to the side, waiting for the others to disembark. "I'm sure you'll have fun doing some looking around on your own."

"It's nice to have a free morning."

"Then we can relax at the spa afterwards," Kristen finished for him.

"I'm not sure I'm into having a 'spa day,' but if you insist."

"I'm with you on that, buddy!" Doug spoke up from behind them and clapped Brett on the back. "But the ladies are excited about the Blue Lagoon excursion, and we do our best to make them happy."

"It's hard to believe it's the most popular tourist destination in Iceland, when there are so many natural wonders," Kristen said, looking to the sky beyond the parking lot. "Like the amazing Northern Lights."

"I know how much you're looking forward to them," Brett said, "so let's get a move on it."

They walked the short distance to one of the observation decks surrounding the parking area. Kristen held on to Brett's hand as she walked, her eyes glued to the lights. "I don't really want to take my eyes away from the lights to watch where I'm going."

"Don't worry, I have your back." Brett gave Kristen's hand a squeeze.

Kristen was amazed how the lights and colors changed with every passing moment. The sky was dominated with the almost iridescent green, but other colors were visible as well. "Even though I'm tired and would have loved to have an early evening, I wouldn't have missed this spectacular display for anything."

"Now that we're here, I don't want to leave," Brett said. "We'll probably want to do this again tomorrow night."

"I certainly wouldn't mind. In fact, wouldn't it be cool to see the lights every night we're in Iceland? I just wish we could have seen them before now." Kristen walked ahead on the dimly lit pathway, eager to get to one of the observation areas, where they could lean against a railing and stare at the sky.

"They're even more special, since we had to wait a few nights."

"Well worth the wait," Kristen agreed, walking over to the railing of one of the observation areas. She took the lens cover off her camera, leaned on the railing, and started snapping pictures. She blocked out everyone—except for Brett—and stared through the lens as she framed the everchanging lights in her camera, mesmerized by the colors, shapes, and dimensions of the famous lights.

After shooting several pictures, Kristen paused and put the cover back on her camera. She leaned against Brett, just enjoying the moment. She started at voices behind them.

"Hey, it looks pretty quiet here. Far away from the nosy people on our trip."

Kristen shrunk against Brett, recognizing Alicia's voice.

"Oh, they're not so bad," Sam said. "What do you think you're going to be like when you get old?" he joked.

Kristen wanted to say something to let them know she was standing within hearing distance—if, in fact, they were actually talking about her. *Then again, ignore them, and enjoy yourself.*

"I don't necessarily think she's that old—just annoyingly curious," Alicia said.

What did I ever do to her? Kristen wondered, then remembered her plan to ignore them. Of course, it wasn't a realistic plan when she was within hearing distance.

"Why's she bugging us with questions, anyway?" Nora asked. "We would have told the police if we'd seen anything, which we didn't."

"She probably thinks we knew the poor stiff," Trevor said. "Since we're all at the U of I."

"I guess that makes sense, but so what if we knew him?" Alicia asked.

"Police always want to know as much background about the victim as possible," Sam said.

"But she's not a policeman, so it's downright strange," Nora said. "Why does she need to know details about the dead guy?"

"Who's to say she's not a policeman?" Trevor asked.

"Even if she is, she's obviously out of her jurisdiction here in Iceland," Alicia said.

"We're here to watch the lights, not get into it with a bunch of college punks," Brett murmured into her ear. "Let's walk the other direction and find a spot by ourselves."

"But they'll notice us as we leave."

"So? Who cares?"

Brett had a point. They hadn't done anything wrong. "Okay. Let's get outta here," she said, using her best gangster voice.

They began to walk to another corner of the deck, but unfortunately in doing so, they had to pass in front of the college students. "Hey, we didn't realize you guys were there," Trevor yelled out.

"Hopefully we weren't being too noisy for you two lovebirds," Sam chimed in.

"No problem. We're a little hard of hearing in our old age," Kristen couldn't resist saying, as she sashayed away.

"That was smooth," Brett said once they were out of earshot. "So much for ignoring them. Plus, can you blame them? I'm sure they wonder why a woman supposedly on her honeymoon is snooping around and asking a bunch of questions."

"I'm not supposedly on my honeymoon; I *am* on my honeymoon." Kristen slid her arm through Brett's. "Now, let's enjoy the lights."

"Whatever you say, dear."

"Hey, I don't need an attitude from you, too." Kristen pulled her hat down over her ears. "Besides, I don't think I asked them that many questions."

"You're so used to asking questions that you probably don't even realize you're doing it."

Brett had a point. "Maybe you're right, but I just want to figure out who killed Lewis. What's wrong with that?"

"Probably nothing, but it can wait until morning."

Kristen snuggled against Brett, watching in awe as vivid colors splashed across the night sky. Was she imagining it, or did Brett just give her the okay to proceed with investigating? *Good thing, because that's what's on my schedule for tomorrow anyway.* Kristen planned to see what she could dig up on the college buddies. If they didn't have anything to hide, then why would they care so much about her asking questions?

CHAPTER 26

As much as Kristen was enjoying her first time viewing the Northern Lights show—and she hoped it wouldn't be the last for this trip—she was starting to get cold. She checked her watch and couldn't believe they'd been standing there for almost an hour. No wonder she was practically frozen, even though she was adequately dressed for the weather. "I think I've been standing in one place for too long. I need to walk around a little."

"You're not going anywhere alone," Brett said, his voice low. "You haven't forgotten a murderer is on the loose."

"As if I could forget." Kristen took Brett's hand. "Although it was nice to push it to the back of my mind for a while." They began walking back toward the parking lot to pick another observation deck.

"Hopefully you can push it away for the rest of the evening. If the lights can't help you with that, I don't know what else to try." Brett chuckled. "Well, maybe I can think of a few things."

"Oh, no, the honeymooners are at it again!"

Kristen almost cringed at Betty's loud voice and the chortle that followed, shattering the peace and quiet of the beautiful evening. "Hi, guys." Why couldn't the well-meaning couple leave them alone?

"Are you enjoying the lights?" Betty asked.

Of course, we are. We'd have to be blind not to. Kristen stopped herself from blurting out her thoughts just in time. She tried not to let her irritation with the couple show. "We sure are. They are beyond anything I could have even imagined."

"Then what are you doing wandering around?" Doug asked. "You don't want to miss a minute of the lights."

What are they doing wandering around? Kristen wondered.

"I'm sure you don't want to either, so we'll leave you two alone to enjoy them," Brett said, his voice as smooth as silk. Kristen grabbed onto the arm Brett crooked, and they started walking.

Kristen gave the couple a wave as they headed away. She was grateful for Brett's fast thinking. She wasn't sure why, but she felt unsettled by the brief exchange. Doug and Betty, nice as they were, were not only getting on her nerves, but they were acting oddly. *Brett and I were minding our own business. Maybe I'm just ticked they interrupted us.*

They began walking toward the observation decks to the opposite side of the parking lot. Several cars, vans, and minibuses like their own were parked there, but there was still plenty of room for more vehicles. Kristen was thankful they weren't at full capacity for their first Northern Lights outing.

She spotted a row of portable toilets. Realizing the cold was doing more than making her toes and fingers chilly, she said, "Hey, I'm going to pop in and use the facilities, as they say, before we watch more lights."

"Sounds like a good idea to me," Brett said. "I'll meet you by the sign over there. No sense me hanging out by the toilets any longer than needed."

"I won't be long." But it took longer than she anticipated, maneuvering through the many layers of warm clothing. She was almost finished when she heard a loud banging on the fiberglass door. "Hurry up in there," bellowed a man's voice.

"I am hurrying, but I think the rest of the toilets are pretty much deserted, so find another one."

The man pounded on the door again. It was then Kristen realized just how deserted the area was, and Brett was either still in his own toilet or waiting for her by the sign. "Keep your pants on," she called out, as she struggled with her own pants. Even though she tried to sound calm and confident, she was starting to shake, and not just from the cold temperatures that were beginning to seep into her warm clothing. Then she felt herself heat up from the rage she was starting to feel, which intensified even more when she felt the lightweight toilet's side walls begin to shake.

As the seconds passed, rage turned into frightened panic. *Where on earth is Brett?* Multiple layers made getting dressed in a hurry challenging. She finished dressing as quickly as possible, despite the loud banging on the sides. Just as she started toward the door to pull the latch, she felt the toilet lurch to the left, and she lurched with it, landing on the floor. Breathing heavily, she picked herself off the floor, bracing herself against the sides as best she could. Trying not to think of the germs and other things she may touch as she groped her way to stand, she shot the latch to the right and shoved open the door. Not sure what she would find when she came out the door, and not caring at this point, she stepped out, half disappointed then relieved to see the person who had accosted her was nowhere in sight. Since the area was only dimly lit—enough to see where you were going if trying to find the restrooms, but not enough to detract from the Northern Lights—it would be easy for someone to run a few yards away and blend in with the night.

Still, she scanned the area, her heart racing. She squinted over toward the signpost where Brett was supposed to be. Not seeing him, she felt panic rise again. Before she could go into full blown terror, she heard banging—similar to the sound she'd heard from someone banging on the outer toilet walls, but this time the sound was coming from the inside. "Brett? Is that you?"

"It's about time," he said. She could hear the laughter in his voice. "I'm not sure why I can't get this darned thing unlocked."

She noticed a walking stick wedged in tightly underneath the door latch. It wouldn't have been enough to keep Brett in there forever, but apparently long enough. She wasn't sure whether to be mad or scared. Probably a little of both would be normal emotions under normal circumstances. *This is not normal.*

"No worries," she said, trying to push aside her own worry. If Brett knew how upset she'd been, he would come unglued. "I'm right here." She shoved the walking stick out from underneath the door latch. "Give it a try now."

Brett pushed open the door. "Thank goodness you came along." He gathered her in his arms. "Don't worry, I used hand sanitizer."

"I wasn't worried about that." *Not when my whole body is covered with germs.* "Let me get a squirt of that. I

189

didn't see a dispenser in mine." *Or maybe it was the fact that someone was trying to rattle my cage—literally!*

As she stepped inside, her mind was racing. She didn't want to tell Brett what had happened until they were safe back in their room. *Hard telling who may be lurking close by, listening.*

She pumped hand sanitizer on her hands. She normally hated the stuff and would prefer to wipe her hands in the snow in lieu of a proper sink with running water, but she needed a minute to collect her thoughts. Taking a deep breath, trying to ignore the chemical cleaners and other lingering odors, she stepped outside again.

"I'm glad you found me," Brett said. "I wouldn't like to be stranded out here alone at night—at least not without having a view of the lights. I would have tried to call you but doubt we have any reception out this way. Besides, I knew you'd eventually come looking for me."

"Of course. It's not as if I'd leave you behind." She picked up the walking stick, glad she was wearing gloves. Then again, whoever had shoved the walking stick underneath the latch probably was as well. Still, it wouldn't hurt to show it to the police. She turned it upside down and held it on the bottom end. No sense smudging any prints that might be lingering.

Brett smiled, then looked at the stick. "Where'd you get that?"

Nothing got by Brett, but Kristen was glad Brett didn't automatically assume that's what had been used to trap him inside. Since he had no idea what Kristen had just gone through, he didn't jump to the conclusion that he'd been locked in and still thought it was the latch not working properly.

Even in the low light, Kristen tried to smile naturally. "I found it on the ground outside my portable toilet. Someone must have set it there and forgot it when they came out. If someone mentions missing their stick, I'll be able to give it back to them." Although Kristen knew the person missing their walking stick wouldn't claim it as their own because that would give away their identity. Though, she supposed, whoever locked Brett in could have found the stick lying nearby and taken the opportunity. *They must have been following us, waiting for the right opportunity to get me alone.* But she found it hard to believe someone would have left the whole thing to chance. For someone to lie in wait for the right opportunity, it would have taken some fast thinking to lock Brett in so quickly, then go down the row of toilets to accost Kristen. *How did Brett not hear anything?* Maybe he had heard something but wasn't expecting someone to attack his wife. He could have attributed whatever noise carried his way to sounds echoing in the fiberglass stalls. He could have just thought someone was using a neighboring toilet. Between a light breeze blowing, the cold fiberglass shifting in the wind, and the echoes of even the smallest sound, she could more easily understand why Brett hadn't heard any noise, let alone come to her rescue. Then again, did she want her husband to come face to face with a killer on a dark night in the middle of the Iceland countryside? Probably not.

Kristen would have giggled aloud at all her thoughts concerning portable toilets if she weren't still upset and didn't want Brett to think she was a lunatic. *I can't believe I'm spending this much time thinking about what we call Porta-potties at home.*

By now they'd returned to the viewing area. "Why don't we try seeing the lights from here," Brett said.

"Sure." Gathering her wits, Kristen tried to sound cheerful. She could think about what had happened and what she would tell Brett on the drive back to the hotel. "I think the lights will look amazing no matter where we stand, but we may as well see how they look from this angle." Which was what they had intended to do before the whole toilet incident. She glanced up at the fiery lights. Even though they were one of the most beautiful natural wonders she'd ever seen as they danced across the dark, clear sky, Kristen couldn't fully focus on them. She was worried that the murderer was trying to scare her away, and no lights—no matter how vivid and spectacular they were—could take her thoughts away from the fact the killer was roaming free among them.

CHAPTER 27

Kristen and Brett were worn out after not only a long day, but also a long night of viewing lights, not to mention the bathroom incident. Kristen had tried dozing in the minibus on the way back to the hotel, but she couldn't stop thinking about what had happened. Still, she kept her eyes closed, so Brett wouldn't ask her any questions she couldn't answer.

After returning to the hotel and finally safe and sound back in the room, Brett took off his jacket. "Okay, what gives? You've been moody since the whole bathroom incident. Look, I'm sorry I upset you by getting locked in the bathroom. You were probably worried about where I was."

Kristen hung up her jacket, then turned to Brett. "No, it's not that, silly." She propped up the walking stick inside the closet as well.

"Say, no one claimed the walking stick, so I guess it's ours to use for the trip."

Kristen hated to burst Brett's excitement. Who knew a forester wouldn't be able to find his own wooden walking stick? "Actually, I brought it back with us so we can take it to the police station tomorrow."

Brett's dark brows shot upward. "What are you talking about?" He sat on the bed, patting the spot beside him. "Sit down and tell me everything. I knew something happened. Why didn't you want to talk about it earlier?"

Kristen heaved a sigh as she sunk onto the bed next to Brett, taking off her boots. "I didn't want anyone to hear us." She fluffed a pillow behind her, then snuggled closer to Brett. "I'm not sure who to trust anymore."

"Just start from the beginning. I can't wait to hear why you want to haul a perfectly good walking stick to the police station."

Kristen hid a grin as she made a mental note to get Brett a walking stick for his birthday. "For starters, that stick was wedged under your bathroom's door latch to keep you locked inside."

"What are you talking about? Why would someone do that?" he asked. "Come on. I'm sure it was just one of the kids playing a prank on us."

Kristen shook her head. "Even if it were someone playing a prank, it wouldn't have been funny. Besides, the reason they wanted you locked in was so they could scare the crap out of me—almost literally." Kristen chuckled at her own crude joke, trying to lighten the mood.

"Care to explain what you mean by that?" he asked. "And I'm not taking any crap from you." Brett smiled at his own pun.

Kristen relayed the whole story but didn't go into detail about how frightened she was. She didn't want to fire Brett up any more than he already was. But she was sure Brett understood without hearing the actual words. When she thought about it, she would have panicked if she'd been in Brett's shoes. Locked in a cold and smelly portable toilet on a dark night with a murderer on the loose wouldn't have been fun. However, since the murderer was probably banging on her own door at the exact time Brett was trying to open his door, she wasn't as sympathetic as she might have been.

"The murderer is obviously trying to scare you off. You must have asked the right person the wrong question, just like you always do. You need to back off, Kristen."

"I'm taking this threat very seriously, even if it could be someone random playing tricks on us."

"You don't really think that, do you? No one in their right mind would lie in wait for a couple to use the bathroom, then lock one in while he tried to scare the other."

"You're right. We aren't dealing with someone in their right mind," Kristen reminded him. "We're dealing with a murderer. She had a sudden thought. "I think this means the murderer is here in Iceland. Even if the murderer had started poisoning Lewis in Illinois, it's someone who is here in Iceland.

Brett nodded. "I thought it was a stretch to think they gave him enough of a dose to finally kill him in Iceland."

"They could have administered poison before he left, and the travel and flight were the final straw, and he died on Iceland soil."

"Since we now think the murderer is in Iceland, it doesn't really matter how it could have been done from Illinois."

"I guess not," Kristen agreed.

"Do you think it was a man or woman's voice?"

Kristen thought for a moment before speaking. "It sounded like a man, but I think he was trying to disguise his voice, so in theory, it could have been either one."

"That sounds pretty cloak and dagger. I'm guessing you would have been able to tell if it was a woman trying to sound like a man."

"This coming from the man who didn't hear any of this taking place?" Kristen chided him. "You know how the fiberglass distorts sounds. It could have been anyone."

Brett nodded, then switched gears. "So you think there could be fingerprints on the stick?" he asked. "What are the odds of that, since everyone had gloves on since we stepped off the plane?"

"Probably pretty slim, but we have to try, don't we?"

Brett sighed. "I guess. We have a free morning, but I thought it would be nice to sleep in a little, have a leisurely breakfast, and walk around downtown."

"I was planning to sort through my pictures, remember?" Kristen felt researching their travel companions was even more important after what had happened on the lights tour.

"Can't that wait until we return from the spa?"

"I'd like to at least glance through them quickly, but I can do that while you're in the shower." Kristen knew she wouldn't have much time for research anyway. She'd have to run quick searches on the main players and follow up later that afternoon. After all, Brett was a low maintenance guy who didn't usually spend long in the shower. *Maybe I can talk him into going into the lobby to bring me back some coffee.*

Then Kristen's plan ran into a snag. *Wait a minute. I don't even know the students' last names.* Kristen tried to think of a way to snag a roster of those who had booked through Land of Ice Tours. Then she had an idea. She got off the bed, her limbs stiff from a long and stressful day, and walked over to the shelf where she'd stashed her backpack. Rummaging through the various travel brochures, she found what she was looking for—a roster of those who were travelling together using the same Land of Ice trip package. Even though they weren't on a formal tour, most of them were following the same rough itinerary with add on excursions. The tour guide from the Golden Circle Tour had written information for Kristen on the back of it and given it to her. She was glad the guide didn't have qualms about turning over personal information to her, though it wasn't anything other than a list of those from the hotel who were taking the same tour that day. She ran through the names. Sure enough, she found the four students with their last names listed.

Brett who had remained on the bed, watching her curiously, finally spoke. "What on earth are you doing now? Haven't you done enough for one day?"

Kristen tried to remain casual. She didn't want to hide anything from Brett, but she knew he would disapprove of using their honeymoon to check into their travel mates' backgrounds. "I was looking for something."

Brett chuckled. "You obviously found it."

Kristen tried to brush it off. "It's just a list." *Which was true.* "It's been bugging me that I couldn't remember where I'd stashed it, and while we were talking, I remembered I'd put it in my guidebook to look at later." Kristen lay the book on the nightstand.

"You can look at it tomorrow. Let's get ready for bed. The lights were amazing and worth the night out, but it's pretty late."

Kristen smiled smugly. She had Brett's blessing to look at it tomorrow. While he had no idea what was listed on the paper, it was good enough for her.

CHAPTER 28

Even after Brett got up and began hunting around for something to wear, Kristen enjoyed the warmth of the bed the next morning. She wasn't being lazy; she was plotting her next move. Her laptop and travel roster were within easy reach. She had every intention of running the most basic of searches on the Sawyers, Schmidts, and the four students before breakfast. For now, she casually picked up her guidebook and took out the folded roster, scanning it for the students' first name. *Bingo!* Sam Hartley, Nora Taylor, Trevor Munsing, and Alicia Cassidy.

She pulled up her pictures first since she'd already told Brett her plan to take a look at them. At least that way, she wouldn't be lying to him. She cruised through them quickly, glad to have captured some lovely scenes on her camera. She paused at the wild horse photos, taking extra time to view the adorable animals. She couldn't wait to view her pictures again when she had more time to do some cropping and adjust the lighting if needed, but first, she was itching to get going on some internet research. One of the last horse pictures contained Nora and Alicia in them. *It's a shame they're in the way, but I should be able to crop most of them out of the picture.* She squinted at it closely, not sure why it had caught her eye, other than it stood out as being the only one with people in it, with the exception of the ones she'd taken of Brett nuzzling the horses. *That's not it, then.* She mentally shrugged and clicked through to the end of the pictures, marveling at how well the Northern Lights shots had turned out. *At least something from last night turned out well.*

"I'm hopping in the shower," Brett said.

Whatever had caught Kristen's attention in the photos was now gone. But at least now she could open up her browser and start plugging in names without Brett peeking over her shoulder. She started off with the victim. Entering Lewis Sawyer's name into the search engine, she watched as multiple entries popped up. Many of the recent entries were related to his work as a professor and researcher at the University of Illinois. She only had time for a quick scan, so she scrolled through the dozens of hits, pausing at one on his research topic—arsenic in Illinois groundwater systems. *You've got to be kidding me. How ironic.* But was it ironic? Had he poisoned himself through prolonged research with a toxic substance? *But why would someone be trying to scare me away from digging up information, if that were the case?* She shook her head. But it could be he was poisoned by someone who didn't like his research, or maybe from a rival researcher. The fact he came into contact with arsenic through his research could explain why Lewis had skin irritations and lesions on him. She wouldn't have thought they would have occurred so quickly or from a single, but lethal, dose.

She continued scanning the entries. There were pictures of him and Margaret. They looked like a loving couple, but she knew that wasn't true. She heard the shower turn off. Brett would be out of the bathroom soon, and she'd only just begun.

She hastily plugged in Margaret's name and began scrolling through the list of hits. Some of the same pictures she'd just seen of the loving couple were there, as well as several work-related pictures. She remembered Margaret had been a career woman back in the days when it was less common for a woman to work outside the home when her children were young. She remembered Betty saying Margaret worked at her family business when they were neighbors. So, at some point, Margaret must have broken away when Lewis took the position at U of I. The more recent pictures of Margaret showed her retirement reception, where she'd been the marketing and promotions manager at a hospital. Wouldn't she have recognized Lewis was ill if she'd had some health care background? Even if she wasn't involved in treating patients, she had to know enough about the basic processes to effectively do the marketing for the hospital. She heard the bathroom door open and looked up to smile at Brett.

"I'm going to run down to get some coffee while you're in the shower. Want me to bring you back a cup?"

"Of course, I do." Kristen closed out of the web browser and shut her laptop. She walked over to Brett and hugged him. "What kind of question is that?"

"Hey, I was just offering to do something nice for my woman."

Kristen raised her brows. "Your woman?"

"Well, we are married, and you're Kristen Stevenson now, so …"

She knew Brett was only teasing her. They were equal partners in their marriage. "Just go get me some coffee, mister."

"It's obvious you can use some." Brett grabbed his key and ducked out of the room before she could swat at him. "I'll be back soon."

Kristen would have loved to use the time to continuing surfing the net, but she needed to shower. While she let the hot water spray over her body, she let her mind and body relax, hoping some ideas would come to her. She wondered again if Lewis' arsenic poisoning was related to his research. Could someone have chosen that murder method for vengeance related to his research? She knew enough about academia to know how competitive researchers were for grant dollars and publication slots. It wasn't easy to attain either one of those, so professors had to stay on top of things. Maybe he had cheated the system to obtain funding for his research. But would another researcher kill him because of that?

As she rinsed shampoo out of her hair, she contemplated Margaret. Working in the marketing department, Margaret would know how to put a positive spin on things and promote the programs and services to the community it served. After witnessing Margaret's abrasive and snobbish behavior, Kristen wouldn't have pictured the woman being overly effective at public relations and the other things her job entailed. Still, Betty hinted that Margaret was a driven career woman. In Kristen's experience those driven the most were usually excellent at their jobs, even if they were hard to get along with at times.

As she worked conditioner through her hair, she thought about the others she wanted to check into. As quickly as she'd been able to look up information on

Margaret and Lewis, the others probably won't take too long to at least be able to dig up the basics.

Rushing through the rest of her routine, she was soon back at her laptop, ready to look into the others on the trip. Deciding to check on Doug and Betty Schmidt, she typed in Doug's name first. His name brought up several entries. Kristen cruised quickly, knowing her time was limited. She paused at one that appeared to be work related. Clicking for more information, she found a picture of Doug in a suit, being presented an award for being a top insurance salesman. Nodding to herself, she could picture Doug selling insurance. He could be friendly and helpful, which would be good traits to have in the insurance business, even if he was loud and a hothead at other times. Hopefully he kept those traits to himself while with clients, Kristen thought. She continued scanning through the rest of the hits, landing on one of Doug about five years ago. It appeared he was retiring and passing his business on to a younger agent. She found one more picture of him in a bowling alley. He looked much younger and was holding a large trophy in one hand. Sharing the trophy and holding the handle on the other side was … Kristen squinted at the grainy picture. Her eyes widened in surprise, for also pictured holding the trophy was none other than Lewis Sawyer.

Even though Kristen knew they could have just been on the same team by chance, she thought it unlikely. From the looks of the other jovial team members, they were all friendly, and if Doug and Lewis were on the same team, their teammates may have been others who lived in the neighborhood. *So why would Doug say they weren't close friends?*

Kristen knew the couple wanted to distance themselves from the Sawyers as much as possible, but it seemed they did share a lot of history, whether they admitted it or not. Kristen wondered what else they hadn't told the police.

She plugged in Betty's name next. Betty's name was linked to several community organizations—everything from church fundraisers to the Parent Teacher Organization. Kristen could picture Betty keeping busy after her kids were all in school and probably even more so once she was an empty nester. She seemed like a high energy woman who liked to be around other people. Kristen thought Betty had a big heart who would enjoy helping others. She was about to move on to the next person on the list when she saw a hit that sounded interesting. Clicking on it, she was again surprised to see the Schmidts and Sawyers linked together again—this time at a charity golf event. From the looks of things, they played as a foursome. This reaffirmed the fact the couple was much closer than either Margaret or Doug and Betty let on. In fact, Margaret didn't even act like she knew the couple. What on earth happened to cause such a rift, Kristen wondered.

Then she remembered that supposedly Lewis had made a pass at Betty. She could understand that not being kosher, but with Lewis' reputation was that enough to fully sever the friendship they shared? Lewis seemed to be the type to try to make a pass at every attractive woman. It was his way. If the woman wasn't receptive, he probably moved on to the next victim. Kristen was thoughtful as she heard Brett unlocking their door.

"Hey, honey," Brett said, as he juggled two steaming paper cups of coffee to shut the door.

Kristen leapt up to take a cup from his hands. "Thanks. Just what I need—a good cup of coffee."

"Find out anything interesting in your research?" Brett asked, an innocent smile on his face. "Did I give you enough time to find out anything useful?"

Kristen took a sip of the delicious brew before giving him a playful smack on the arm. "Why would you think I was looking for something?"

"Because I know you. You've been itching to get your hands on your laptop to dig up some dirt on our fellow travelers. The question is ..." Brett scrutinized Kristen's face. "Have you been successful?"

Kristen finally gave in. "Halfway. Which means I'm only half done." Since Brett was already on to her, she didn't think it would hurt to ask. "If I can have another hour, I can finish checking out the U of I group." While they sipped their coffee, Kristen relayed what she'd found out about the two couples.

"Interesting," Brett said. "I'll tell you what. Why don't we grab some breakfast? It's only eight-thirty, so it's not even light yet. After breakfast there should be time to finish your research. I'll find something to do while I wait. Then, we can drop by the police station to deliver the walking stick and have a little time to explore, grab an early lunch, then be back and ready to leave by one o'clock as planned."

"Oh, that sounds like a great plan." Kristen was glad Brett was flexible enough to let her do her thing. "I'd love to be able to tell the police anything else interesting I find."

"You realize the police are doing their own research?" he asked.

"Of course, but we've had the opportunity to get to know the people of interest a little and make our own observations that you can't find online."

"Just don't go overboard, okay?"

Kristen smiled as she took another sip of coffee. "When have you ever known me to get myself in over my head?" She only hoped the words she now said in jest wouldn't come back later to haunt her.

CHAPTER 29

Kristen sat at a table sipping a cup of coffee while Brett got his breakfast. Kristen used the time to scan the dining room, looking for her fellow travelers. *Maybe I should try to chat with everyone who was on the Northern Lights tour to see if anyone's acting oddly.* If someone was, she would assume they were the one who'd threatened her in the portable toilet. Even though it was no laughing matter, just thinking about her experience made her grin. The whole experience was outrageous!

She spied Doug and Betty in the doorway. They looked around for a table. Kristen caught Betty's eye and waved. The couple strolled over.

"Mind if we sit with you?" Betty asked.

"Not at all." Kristen watched as Betty sat down.

"I'll go get us some coffee," Doug offered.

Kristen made use of her time alone with Betty. "Sleep well last night?"

Betty's sweet face broke into a smile. "Sure did. After a long day and the tour last night, I was glad for the chance to sleep a little later this morning."

"Same here." Kristen didn't notice Betty behaving any differently than usual, but she didn't honestly think the sixty-something grandmother was capable of rattling the porta potty—not to mention the person inside it.

"Do you have plans for the morning?" asked Betty.

Kristen nodded. "I want to scan through my pictures when we get back to the room. Then, we're planning to take a look at some shops downtown and have an early lunch before our Blue Lagoon trip this afternoon."

"Are you excited about visiting the spa?"

"Yes, but I'd prefer to see more scenery." Kristen shrugged. "I guess we'll see some along the way."

Betty nodded. "Plus, it seems like a fun thing to do on your honeymoon."

"That's true. And something we'd never do at home."

"That's what we thought." Betty chuckled. "Then there's also the hope that the thermal mineral waters will help some of our old peoples' aches and pains."

"I'm sure they will. At least it's a chance to relax after the past few hectic days." Kristen looked at Betty thoughtfully. Was she imagining it, or was Betty more subdued than usual? She didn't seem quite as peppy, and their chitchat wasn't as lively as usual. Betty usually had something humorous to say. Maybe she was just tired, and a cup of coffee would give her some energy.

Kristen saw Brett headed their way with Doug walking behind him. Brett sat his plate down, and Doug handed Betty and Kristen cups of coffee. Kristen looked up to see the students entering. As usual, they were a lively bunch. Kristen took a fortifying swig of coffee, pushed back her chair, and stood. "I'm going to get something to eat." She didn't care she'd left so abruptly and so soon after Doug had delivered their coffee. She didn't want to miss the chance to gauge the students' reactions. She walked slowly, trying to time it so she was filling her plate while they were getting their food and make it seem like she just happened to bump into them.

She had just picked up a whole grain roll and some butter when someone brushed up against her. "Hey, Kristen." She looked up to see Sam standing next to her, reaching in front of her to snag some eggs and tomatoes.

"Hi, Sam. Did you guys recover after last night's tour?"

Sam had the grace to look sheepish. "Yeah, we're good. Say, I don't know if you heard us talking, but we were just being stupid. None of what we said had anything to do with you."

While it was nice of Sam to try to smooth things over, Kristen wasn't buying it. However, she chose to play along. "No problem. Brett and I were in our own world. Star gazing—and Northern Lights gazing—is pretty romantic."

Sam laughed. "Yeah, I know what you mean. Alicia and I thought it was really cool. The other guys did as well."

"Did you stay in the same spot the entire time, or did you check out some of the other areas?" Kristen was curious to know whether Sam and his buddies migrated over to the portable toilet area. Then again, she remembered talking to Doug and Betty on their way there. She supposed any of them could have followed them.

Kristen had a thought. Maybe it was a dual effort. *What if Betty locked Brett in, while Doug tried to scare me?* It made total sense to Kristen. Otherwise, there wouldn't have been much time for one person to do both. However, she thought it was unlikely those two were the culprits. Then again, how likely was it that any of the people they had gotten to know over the past few days was a murderer? But someone had to have done it.

"Did you try the muesli?" Sam asked, interrupting Kristen's musings.

"Not today." She pointed to her plate. "I'm having the ham and cheeses instead."

"Well, I'll see you later then."

"Yeah, sure." Kristen finished piling food on her plate, then went over to the drinks area. She grabbed a clean glass and stood in line for milk. Kristen saw Nora take a sip of her full glass, as she walked away from the dispenser.

"Hi, Nora."

"Oh, hi." Nora gave her a half smile. "Sorry, I'm not much of a morning person."

Kristen wondered what time of day Nora preferred, as she didn't seem overly friendly any time Kristen had seen her. "Maybe some coffee will help. Especially on a cold and still dark day."

"I'm not really into coffee, so I'll take your word for it."

Kristen had had enough of their awkward conversation. "Well, I'd better let you eat your breakfast."

"Catch you later."

Kristen watched as Nora walked back to her table and sat next to Trevor. Nora said something to Trevor, and they both looked in Kristen's direction. Kristen quickly averted her eyes, not wanting them to catch her staring at them. They already thought she was a nosy old woman. Then again, they were watching her, so what difference did it make? Still, she wondered what they were discussing.

Kristen poured milk into her glass, picked up her plate and headed back to her table. She couldn't help but notice all four students watching her as she walked.

What's up with them? Were they the ones involved with the bathroom incident—or some combination of the foursome? Or maybe they were just looking at her because she was an old busybody.

Kristen made it to the table without spilling anything and was relieved to sit down. Doug and Betty must have been getting their food, so she was glad to have a moment alone with Brett.

"You were gone a while. I was starting to wonder about you," he said. "It was a lot of fun making small talk with Doug and Betty."

"With those two, you don't have to do much to hold up your end of the conversation. Try talking to the know-it-all college students. Sam and Trevor are okay, but their lady friends don't have much going on in the personality department."

"Aren't you a ray of sunshine today?"

Kristen was about to explain further, but she saw Doug and Betty headed back to the table. "Don't mind me. I guess I'm just tired."

"As long as you didn't irritate the murderer," Brett murmured just as Doug and Betty set down their plates.

"Goodness, it's hard to decide what to eat when they're so many delicious things to choose from," Betty said, her perkiness seeming to return.

Maybe she wasn't a coldblooded killer after all and just needed some coffee and breakfast, Kristen thought. "What did you guys think of the Northern Lights?"

"Eh, they were okay," Doug said.

Kristen glanced up from the roll she was buttering. "Just okay?"

Betty elbowed Doug in the ribs. "He's just kidding. We thought they were amazing—even more than we thought they'd be."

Was Doug really kidding? Did he grow bored from watching them and decide to accost Kristen in the bathroom? "We couldn't get enough of them. We watched them from a couple of different areas."

"That's right, we saw you when you were on the way to the toilets," Betty said.

Red flag. When they had bumped into each other last night, Kristen couldn't remember telling the couple where they were going. Did Betty just assume they were going to the bathroom, or had she followed them? Kristen chided herself. *You're just being paranoid. Not everyone is a villain. But someone is …*

"You know how it is when you get cold," Kristen said, hoping not to go into too many details over breakfast.

"Even so, I don't do porta potties." Betty bit into her toast.

Well, someone sure did. "I can't blame you for that," Kristen agreed. "It's a shame they don't have more permanent structures. I could have really used a hand dryer to warm up my hands."

"And you'd be able to wash them properly," Betty said.

Kristen took a big bite from her bun, considering their conversation. Had the couple been tailing them? "Right. I prefer warm soapy water, for sure."

"Enough of this talk about toilets at breakfast," Brett said, trying to sound jovial while, giving Kristen a shrewd look.

She bugged her eyes at him in return. It wasn't her fault. Betty was the one who'd brought up the topic. "My thoughts exactly. I'm ready to dig in." Kristen was referring to breakfast, but she knew they still had more digging to do before the killer was caught.

CHAPTER 30

Back in the room, Kristen was propped up against the bed pillows, her laptop open. She was ready to make the most of her small window of time to look up the four students. Her breakfast encounters with them had done little to dissuade her from checking into their pasts. Deciding to start with Sam first since he seemed to be the group's ringleader, she typed Sam Hartley's name into the search bar. Several articles on his high school activities popped up, including basketball and track awards and game stats. Kristen could see the tall, lean, and highly energetic boy being an athlete. She didn't see any mention of him being in college sports, other than intramural basketball. It appeared he was a junior at U of I and was majoring in accounting. There was also an article about him doing volunteer work at the local hospital when he was in high school.

Hmm. I wonder if he knows anything about arsenic poisoning. Or for that matter, did he volunteer at the same hospital where Margaret worked? Kristen was thoughtful for a moment, trying to put together what she knew about the jovial guy. If he—or any of the students--had killed Lewis, then what was their connection? They were all students at the college where Lewis had taught, but none of them claimed to have known him. She thought back to the search she'd performed on Margaret. Even if Sam had volunteered at the hospital where she worked, Margaret had retired a few years ago, probably before Sam arrived on campus.

Since Sam was an accounting major, Kristen could understand Sam never taking one of Lewis' geology classes, unless he just wanted to satisfy a science requirement. *But wouldn't most people just take a general biology or chemistry class if they weren't majoring in a science field?* She cruised through the listings, not seeing much else of interest. Then, she landed on an article about one of the university's fraternity houses. Clicking on it, she saw a photo of both Sam and Trevor. The fraternity was featured as helping out at a hospital fund raising event. Maybe it was a requirement of fraternity members to volunteer there, which would explain Sam's work at the hospital. It probably offsets some of what goes on at wild fraternity parties, Kristen thought cynically. At least the two men belonging to the same fraternity explained how Sam and Trevor knew each other. Kristen had no idea if Nora and Alicia knew each other before becoming Trevor's and Sam's girlfriends.

It probably didn't matter if the girls knew each other or not before they started dating Trevor and Sam. Whatever the case, they were friendly enough to travel together to Iceland. Kristen was just trying to figure out the link one of them may have had to Lewis and if that connection ended up getting Lewis killed by one of them.

Kristen scrolled back to listings from Sam's high school days. She looked more closely at the name of the high school he'd attended. Not recognizing its name, she searched its location and found it was located in one of the northern Chicago suburbs. Not remembering which suburb the Sawyers once lived in, Kristen realized it wouldn't matter, since the Sawyers would have moved long before Sam was even born.

Entering Trevor's name next, Kristen's fingers raced over the keyboard, hoping to finish before Brett returned. She felt her informal research was important, but it was more important to have time to deliver the walking stick to the police and tell them about what happened on the Northern Lights tour the previous evening. She paused for a minute, wondering how to phrase her explanation to the police. They would want to know what Kristen had been doing that led up to the warning she'd received. How could she tell them she'd been bugging her travel mates with questions the past few days? She knew the police would also frown on her morning's worth of research. While the police were doing some digging of their own, she doubted they'd be willing to share any information, which was why she needed to do her own. It made perfect sense to her, but the police would probably not agree. *I'm sure I'll think of something to satisfy them. Besides, what are they going to do, lock me up?*

Turning back to the computer, she skimmed through the entries. Like Sam, Trevor was an athlete, though he played baseball in high school. He was pictured in one article at bat, and during that game he'd hit a home run, which allowed their team to win and advance to the playoffs his senior year. Peering closely at the name of the high school he'd attended, she saw it was a school in Bloomington. Depending which side of town he was from, it was about an hour's drive from Bloomington to Urbana, where he went to college. Chances were slim they knew each other before Trevor began attending U of I. Both Bloomington and Urbana were decent sized cities—at least compared to Eklund, Kristen thought.

She checked out the rest of the listings for Trevor. He'd been involved in various activities and organizations from church youth group to the National Honor Society. Nothing stood out that made him appear to be a killer.

Kristen let the laptop rest on her bed while she got up and stretched, then paced around their hotel room. Sitting back down on her bed, she decided to give the research a rest and switched back to the photos she'd viewed earlier. Sorting through them until she came to the Icelandic horse pictures, she stared at the final ones she'd taken while visiting the furry creatures. Both contained portions of Alicia and Nora. Staring at the pictures and wondering what was prompting her to look twice at the pictures when she was on tight deadline to finish her research, she zeroed in on the backpack in one of the pictures. Sticking out of the main outer pocket was a book. It didn't look like a traditional travel guide but more like a field guide. She zoomed in on the photo in question. Peering at it closely, she was surprised to see it was a Geology of Iceland book.

What on earth? Literally. Maybe Kristen assumed no one was interested in science because they supposedly didn't know Lewis or have him for classes, but she was surprised to see the field guide. Though the book was proof of nothing bad, most people with only a passing interest in the basics of Iceland geology would read what they wanted to know in a regular travel guide. Kristen's own guide covered Iceland's many geological wonders— she'd seen several of them already and had more on her to-do list. Many people interested in geology—Lewis included—visited Iceland for that reason. Others appreciated the rugged scenery that could in part be related back to its geology. But to someone who studied geology as a major or worked in the geological field, Iceland was a dream trip. Whatever Kristen may or may not have assumed about the students, she had a feeling they weren't being totally honest with her.

In fact, no one on the trip seemed to be totally honest—or at least they liked to hold things back. Kristen could understand the other travelers not wanting to confide their personal details to her. Why would they when they thought she was just another tourist. They probably didn't know she'd had the misfortune to have been involved in other murder investigations and already knew the ropes. But it was important they tell the police anything that could be helpful to the investigation.

Kristen, still pondering her latest discovery, was about to plug the girls' names into the search engine when Brett unlocked the door and entered their room. "Are you about ready?"

Kristen checked the time. "Wow, I didn't realize it was that late already. I'm not quite finished, but I suppose we'd better get moving."

Brett nodded. "Right. The police will probably wonder why you didn't get in touch with them right away." Throwing Kristen a curious glance, he said. "Why *didn't* we contact the police last night?"

Kristen sighed. "For starters, it was late, and we were exhausted. Besides, what could they have done once we were back safe in our hotel in Reykjavik? We would have sent them on a wild goose chase if we'd been able to reach them while on the Northern Lights tour."

"Maybe so, but it would have let whoever did it know we were taking the threat seriously." Brett shrugged. "Besides, you never know. The police could have found some clues we didn't."

"I think the walking stick is a pretty major clue," Kristen argued. "One we want to hand directly to the policemen on the case, Officers Grímsson and Helgason. I'm sure they weren't working that late last night."

"Whatever you say, dear," Brett joked.

Kristen closed her laptop, hoping to search for the two remaining students if she could tap into Wi-Fi later with her phone. "I'm going to ignore your tone." She stood and got her jacket out of the small closet and carefully picked up the walking stick. "Come on." She grinned at Brett. "Don't make me use this on you again."

He smiled in return. "No way. I'm sure whatever you have in mind would be worse than being stuck in a porta potty on a cold January night."

"I doubt that." But Kristen's mind shot back to last night. Whoever they were dealing with wasn't monkeying around like they were—they meant serious business. *And I'm making it our business to track them down and bring them to justice.*

CHAPTER 31

As they walked through the lobby on the way to the police station, Kristen heard her name being called.

"Kristen!"

She looked around and spotted Doug and Betty across the lobby, sitting on a cozy couch in front of the fireplace. Groaning inwardly, she waved. Betty waved in return, beckoning Kristen and Brett toward them.

Kristen tried to shuffle the walking stick out of view but doubted it was possible to fully hide it. She wasn't in the mood for questions and just wanted to get to the police station. "What are you guys up to?" Kristen asked in what she hoped was a friendly tone. Unless the couple had decided to open up about whatever they were holding back, Kristen didn't have time for chitchat. She doubted much had changed since they'd seen each other at breakfast.

"We're just hanging out before this afternoon's Blue Lagoon outing," Betty eyed Kristen's arm. "Are you okay? You're holding your arm a little awkwardly. You didn't hurt yourself, did you?"

Kristen shook her head. "No, of course not."

"She's fine. She's just holding a walking stick," Doug said, then squinted. "Wait a minute. I think that's mine. I haven't noticed you with a walking stick any other time on this trip, so what are you doing with one now?"

Oh, wow. This could get awkward. "I've never noticed you with one either," Kristen said, trying to keep things light.

"I had it last night. Didn't want to trip in the snow in low lights," Doug said.

Kristen wasn't sure how to handle this new development. "Are you sure it's yours? Don't they all look alike?" *Was Doug the one who locked Brett in and harassed me?*

"Of course they aren't all the same." Doug looked at Kristen as if she were crazy. He stepped closer as if to get a better look at the stick. "Let me see that."

"Hold on," Brett interjected, holding off his hand to prevent Doug from moving closer to Kristen. "We didn't take your stick. We found it last night and were going to turn it in to the front desk in case the person who left it behind is staying at this hotel."

"But it looked like you were headed straight for the front doors," Betty said, ever helpful. She eyed Kristen's gloves. "You're even dressed to go outside."

Actually, I'm wearing these to prevent more fingerprints from interfering with whatever other prints were on the stick. "I guess we got a little ahead of ourselves," Kristen chuckled. "So much to see and do in such a short amount of time."

Now it was Betty's turn to look at Kristen as if she were crazy. "How did you get hold of Doug's walking stick?"

Since the couple was so observant, Kristen was glad Doug and Betty didn't spot Doug's stick last night while riding back on the bus and call them out on it. Even if someone had borrowed Doug's stick to use and Doug wasn't the one who had accosted Kristen and locked Brett inside the portable toilet, it would have drawn attention to the fact that they had a stick—one the killer had used to warn them off. Had the killer noticed them carry the walking stick onto the bus and to their room? Did the killer know what they intended to do with it? Kristen stared at the older couple, trying to form her thoughts into a plausible explanation.

"Listen, it's not a big deal. We found it by the portable toilets last night." Kristen wanted to keep it simple. She didn't fully trust the Schmidts, but why would Doug comment on the walking stick if he'd been the one to use it last night? "We had a little fright last night and wanted to take it to the police."

At Betty and Doug's matching astounding looks, Kristen continued. "No worries. We're fine, but we think the killer may have wanted to warn us off."

Betty's snow-white eyebrows shot upward. "Warn you off? From what?"

"Good question," Brett said, keeping his voice low. "That's what we hope to find out. We'll make sure Doug gets his walking stick back, but right now, we're off to the police station to let the police have a look at it."

"Do you think it has something to do with Lewis Sawyer's murder?" Doug asked.

"We're not sure, but we aren't taking any chances," Kristen checked the time. "We need to get moving, since we're stopping for a quick bite to eat afterwards."

"We'll see you on the bus for the Blue Lagoon." Before Doug and Betty could say anything else, Brett took Kristen's arm and steered her toward the hotel doors.

"Wow, that was close," Kristen said as soon as they were out of earshot.

"We did a good job of giving them an explanation without actually explaining what happened."

"I doubt they're the ones who killed Lewis, but I do think they know more than they are telling. Then there's the fact Betty assumed we'd used the bathrooms last night, though we didn't actually tell her that."

"It's not much of a stretch to think someone's going to have to use the bathroom when outdoors in the cold for an extended amount of time," Brett said. "But I agree it's better to keep things simple and only tell them the bare essentials."

Kristen nodded. "By the way, I didn't get a chance to tell you what I discovered about Sam and Trevor." She filled Brett in on everything she'd researched that morning, including noticing the geology field guide.

"But that could have been any of theirs." Brett argued. "They could have been sharing a backpack between the couples."

"But from what I could tell, the guys aren't studying geology."

Brett shrugged. "Anyone can have an interest in geology without actually majoring in it."

Kristen knew Brett was right, but she had a feeling the field guide was an important clue. She had to admit she didn't know how it related to the case, but from past experience, she knew she'd figure it out eventually— hopefully before things came to a head. At the rate things were going, it was only a matter of time before all the facts came to light. At least, she hoped they would.

"But someone was more interested in geology than what they originally claimed to us. That's the point."

"Just because they may be interested in geology doesn't mean they killed Lewis Sawyer."

Kristen hated to admit it, but what Brett said made sense. She thought perhaps she was grasping at straws to try to find a connection between one of the students and Lewis when there may not be one. She didn't particularly care for the two young ladies, but that didn't mean one of them was a killer.

They were silent as they walked the rest of the way to the police station, both lost in their own thoughts. Even though Brett would never admit it, Kristen thought he was almost as wrapped up in the case as she was. Maybe his calm, levelheaded common sense would shed some light on matters.

When they arrived at the police station, Brett held the door. "Ladies first."

Kristen went ahead, not sure where to go. Once inside the inner set of doors, she spotted a reception counter ahead. She spoke in English, too nervous to recall her limited Icelandic vocabulary that didn't stretch far enough to include translations for walking stick and portable toilet.

"May we please speak to Officers Grímsson and Helgason?"

"What is your name?" the man asked. "I will call to see if they are available."

Kristen gave them their names. "We have something we think could be a clue to the Lewis Sawyer murder case."

The man nodded, then picked up the phone. He rattled off several sentences in Icelandic, hung up, then turned back to Brett and Kristen. "Please follow me."

They followed the man down a long hallway to a small conference room where the officers were already seated.

"Please, sit down," Officer Helgason said. Officer Grímsson nodded at them but didn't say anything. "We understand you wanted to talk to us about the Sawyer case?" Officer Helgason looked questioningly at the walking stick Kristen held in front of her.

Since the officers didn't seem too interested in asking questions, Kristen plunged ahead, figuring they would have plenty of questions once she was done. "We just wanted to bring something to your attention." She held up the stick, still wearing the gloves. "This walking stick was most likely used by the killer to lock my husband in a portable toilet while we were on last night's Northern Lights tour." Not getting much of a reaction, Kristen continued. "I was in a toilet several feet away, and we think after locking Brett in his, the killer came to mine and proceeded to frighten me."

Officer Grímsson raised his eyebrows. "How did he frighten you?"

Kristen couldn't believe the officers weren't showing more of a response. She supposed they just wanted her to tell the story, so she tried to explain the best she could without their prompting. "While I was, uh … using the facilities, someone started shouting and pounding on the door."

"Perhaps we aren't understanding you correctly," Officer Helgason said. "Maybe whoever was outside the door merely wanted to know if someone was in there."

"Then why would he lock my husband in?" Kristen was starting to get irritated and impatient with the officers, who she thought were being too laid back about the entire situation. *Maybe that's why the killer hasn't yet been caught.* "They spoke in unaccented English, so there was no communication barrier. You don't seem to be taking this very seriously."

Officer Grímsson leaned forward in his chair. "Oh, we're taking it very seriously, indeed."

"But you don't seem to be very concerned about what I'm telling you. Have you had other complaints from tourists about being locked in or accosted while using the portable toilets on a Northern Lights tour? Perhaps this is a normal occurrence?"

Officer Helgason managed to bite back a grin before Kristen noticed it. "I'm afraid you misunderstand us. We're just letting you tell your story—one we find very intriguing."

This time, Kristen saw the beginnings of a smirk on Officer Grímsson's face. "But you seem to be laughing at us."

"Of course not," Officer Helgason said. "But contrary to popular beliefs—if I used that expression correctly—we don't normally have people march into the police station holding a walking stick and tell us how it was used to scare them."

Kristen sighed. Since she remembered how ludicrous it had sounded to herself when she was reviewing the events in her own mind, she supposed it did sound ridiculous to the police. "Okay, I see what you mean, but I am serious."

For the first time, Brett spoke. "She's telling you the truth. I didn't realize I was locked in at the time. I thought I'd done something to the latch, and it was just stuck or something. I knew Kristen was just around the corner, so I didn't get too worked up about it. At the time

I didn't know the full story. She didn't want to upset me or discuss it on the tour, so she waited until we were safely in the room before she told me the details. I knew something was troubling her on the ride back to the hotel, but since the killer could have been riding on the same bus, we didn't want to talk where someone could overhear us."

Fortunately, Brett had come to her aid. Maybe now the police would listen. "My theory is they locked Brett in so they could try to scare me."

"But why would they try to scare you?" Officer Grímsson asked. He narrowed his eyes. "Does the killer know about your crime solving abilities?"

Oh, crap. They're on to me. "I'm not sure I understand your meaning."

"We conducted background checks and researched everyone who made travel arrangements through Land of Ice Travel." Officer Helgason smiled. "You wouldn't believe all the interesting things we discovered about your past."

"Nothing bad, I hope?" Kristen asked, still playing dumb, even though the officers probably knew about every single one of the murder cases she'd helped to solve.

"You seem to find a lot of murder victims," Officer Grímsson said. "Fortunately, you've helped solve the cases—and gotten yourself into trouble while doing it. Which is why we don't want your help with this case."

Kristen thought about nicknaming the stony-faced man, "Officer Grim" but managed not to say it out loud. "You don't want our help?"

"Not if it means we have another murder to solve," Officer Helgason said, in a gentler tone than his partner's. "From what we understand about your other involvements, you managed to almost get yourself injured or killed. We don't want that to happen in this case, so please back off."

"We understand what you're saying," Brett interjected before Kristen could open her mouth, "but don't you want to hear what we have to say as long as we're already here?"

"Since we're taking time out of today's schedule to try to help, why don't you give us the opportunity to explain." Kristen was still irritated, and at this point, all she wanted to do was say her piece and get the heck out of there. If they didn't want to act on it, that was their problem.

CHAPTER 32

"Why don't we start over?" Officer Grímsson suggested. "We can tell that you're serious about wanting to help, and we want to hear your information, but we don't want you to end up getting hurt—or worse."

"He's right," Officer Helgason agreed. "Besides," he said with a grin, "we're not used to receiving help from regular citizens … how do you say it in English?"

"Civilians?" Brett offered.

"That's it," Officer Helgason said. "Now, let's hear what you have to say, but you have to understand we don't want you going any further with what you have learned."

Kristen nodded. "No worries on that. We'd like to enjoy what's left of our time in Iceland."

"We want the same for you," Officer Grímsson said. "Let's take a look at the walking stick. How was this used to lock your husband in the toilet?"

"I found it wedged underneath the latch," Kristen explained. "I doubt it would have held him in there for very long, but long enough for the murderer to harass me and get away before we could see him."

"Let me see it." Officer Helgason pulled a pair of latex gloves from his pocket.

Handing him the stick, Kristen wondered if policemen always carried gloves with them. Or had the officers assumed Kristen and Brett would be bringing potential evidence with them when the front desk clerk called to let them know the couple wanted to see them.

"I should tell you that we know who the owner of the walking stick is," Kristen said, watching surprise register on the officers' faces. She couldn't help but gloat with satisfaction.

"Whose is it, then?" Officer Grímsson asked.

"It belongs to Doug Schmidt," Kristen explained. "He saw us carrying it through the hotel lobby and wondered what we were doing with it."

"But you don't think he was the one to use it during last night's incident?"

Kristen shook her head. "I doubt it. Why would he claim it was his walking stick if he'd been the one to do it? He asked us about the stick and wanted us to return it to him."

"So, his prints will be all over it," Officer Helgason said. "But perhaps we can find some other unexplained prints."

"I doubt it. Everyone was wearing gloves last night." Brett said. "But we thought you'd still want to take a look at it."

"You thought correctly," Officer Grímsson said. "Forensics may be able to pull some useful fibers or other materials from the stick."

"I'm curious to know what you told Mr. Schmidt when he wanted the stick back." There was a hint of a smile on Officer Helgason's face.

Brett grinned, then filled the officers in on the conversation.

"Now that we have the stick situation addressed, is there anything else you want to tell us?" Officer Helgason asked.

"It is a sticky situation." Kristen couldn't help but chuckle, even though she figured the officers may not be familiar with the American expression. Even if they did understand it, they didn't seem amused. She sobered. "I took it upon myself to check into the backgrounds of some of the people who we've been traveling with, but I'm sure I haven't learned anything you don't already know."

The police officers exchanged a look. "Why don't you tell us, and we can go from there. We know you've uncovered something, or you wouldn't have the potential killer trying to threaten you," Officer Grímsson said.

"Well, for starters, I noticed a geology field guide in one of the student's backpacks. Alicia Cassidy and Nora Taylor both had backpacks, but I'm not sure whose book it is."

The officers looked puzzled. "What does a field guide have to do with Lewis Sawyer's murder?" Officer Helgason asked.

Kristen tried to explain her reasoning without making it sound like she was half crazy. "When we'd talked to the students the other day, none of them mentioned knowing Lewis, even though he was a professor at the college they all attended. No one admitted to taking one of his classes. When I saw the guide, I wondered if there was more to the story. Keep in mind that my husband and I were both science majors. He's a forester, and I'm a naturalist. Although both of us are interested in the basics of Iceland geological features, the information we can read in our travel guide is thorough enough for us. The book they had looked like it was intended for someone with more than a passing interest in geology."

Officer Helgason nodded, but Officer Grímsson looked skeptical. "You can't suspect someone of murder just because they happen to have a geology field guide in their backpack. For that matter, you're not even sure whose backpack it was, let alone who was using the book."

When he put it like that, Kristen felt silly. Still, her silly hunches usually turned out to be important factors to solving past cases. "I'm just saying there may be a link between one of the students and Lewis—one that didn't seem to exist before. The students don't seem to be very upfront about things, and neither do the Schmidts. I think they all have some things in their pasts—or even presents—they don't want to disclose. Or, they just don't want to be involved with the investigation any more than is required."

"We're used to that kind of behavior, which is why in addition to questioning witnesses and suspects, we check them out fully." Officer Grímsson grinned. "It's amazing the things we discover."

Kristen had a feeling he was referring to her. "I'm sure it is."

"You wouldn't believe what your local police ..." Officer Helgason checked his notes. "Sheriff Miller told us about you."

"What did he say?" Kristen could hardly wait to hear. "I didn't realize you actually contacted people directly." Kristen thought of her own internet searches. She supposed a lot got lost in the translation—literally—

if they totally relied on searching online and through their databases.

"In your case, an international phone call was in order." Officer Grímsson grinned. "The sheriff said you like to stick your nose into places it doesn't belong and have almost gotten yourself killed in the process. At least I think that's how it's said in English."

"Oh, your English sounds fine to me." Kristen was glad the sheriff hadn't trashed her reputation too much.

"But he did say your work was important in bringing local murder cases to a close," Officer Helgason added. "You too," he nodded at Brett. "Even if the sheriff didn't ask for your help, he did seem to appreciate it."

"On another note," Kristen said, wanting to change the topic. "I didn't have time to check into the girl students—Nora and Alicia—this morning, but I plan to later."

"It's okay. We're checking into everyone on your trip," Officer Helgason said.

But would they share the information with Kristen? *Highly doubtful. Not since they were quite clear about wanting me to butt out.* Still, Kristen wanted to run quick checks for Nora and Alicia. She didn't care what the police thought, even if they were trying to look out for her best interests. She'd come this far and wasn't going to back out now.

"If you don't have anything else to add, you're free to go," Officer Grímsson said. "We know how to get in touch with you if we have additional questions."

"And we know how to get in touch with you if we discover anything else," Kristen couldn't resist adding.

"Just don't get yourself into any trouble." Officer Helgason stood. "We don't want anything bad to happen to you. If what you say about last night is true, the murderer isn't pleased with all the questions you've been asking."

"It's all true," Brett said. "But don't worry; I'll make sure she follows your orders."

"I promise to behave." Kristen smiled good naturedly, but she was still determined to finish the research she'd started. The murderer wouldn't know she was asking questions— this time through the internet. What harm would that do?

CHAPTER 33

"Are you ready for lunch?" Brett held the door for Kristen as they exited the police station.

"You bet." Kristen glanced around. "I don't think we're too far from the café we've already eaten at a couple of times."

"That's right. Do you want to eat there?"

"It sounds great to me. We already know the place, and I just want to sit down and relax after that ordeal."

"Then let's do that. They have great food and service." Brett looked at his watch. "We have just over an hour before we need to head back to the hotel."

"We'd better get a move on it." They started walking in the direction of the café, which ended up only being a five-minute walk away.

They were pleased to see Gunnar working again. "Hello, my American friends. I'm glad you're joining us for lunch today."

Kristen looked around the charming eatery, which only had a few customers. "We're here to have an early lunch."

"Please walk this way, and I'll give you a table by the window." Gunnar grabbed two menus. "You have a perfect view of the Hallgrímskirkja from here."

Kristen had a sudden thought. Did Gunnar have a perfect view of the Hallgrímskirkja the day Lewis was killed? "Gunnar, we've enjoyed having you as our waiter when we've eaten here."

Gunnar gave a slight bow in acknowledgement, looking pleased by her compliment.

"We spent time here after another American was killed. We were questioned by the police here, since we came in here for coffee and to warm up"

"Ah, yes," he said. "And you had dinner afterwards. I remember."

"Do you remember seeing anything of interest around the time Lewis Sawyer was killed?" Kristen watched his face as he thought about it.

"When the police left the other evening after questioning you, they asked me the same thing."

Kristen nodded. Maybe Gunnar had noticed something important. He hesitated before answering. "Did you see anything unusual?" she prompted him again.

"I don't know that it was anything … out of the ordinary, I think is the expression."

Kristen was impressed with the command of the English language most Icelanders she'd encountered exhibited. She was lucky to remember a few key vocabulary words in Icelandic and definitely wasn't up to attempting slang or expressions.

"What did you see?" she asked again. "We're interested in the case since we've gotten to know his widow after trying to help her husband. It sure is a shame such a good man died."

Gunnar nodded. "It looked like he knew several people, which I found odd, since he was a tourist."

"What do you mean?" Kristen asked.

"Most people who visit Iceland—or any foreign country--probably don't know anyone unless they are planning to visit them. But I saw him and wife talking to different people. It was a nice day, and I was taking a break after lunch and before the late afternoon coffee and refreshment customers started coming. It helps me to relax if I go outside to get some fresh air. I usually sit on the bench for a few minutes between busy times."

"I'm sure it's a great place to sit," Brett said.

Gunnar nodded. "I wouldn't have thought anything about it, but after Mr. Sawyer was killed, I realized he and his wife were the ones I'd been watching on my short break."

This is getting curiouser and curiouser, Kristen thought to herself.

"I also saw both of you in the vicinity, as well as some of the other Americans talking to the couple."

"You could tell we were Americans from hundreds of feet—or meters—away?" Kristen asked. *So much for trying to blend in.*

"Oh, yes, it's quite a distinctive look with clothing and accessories, not to mention mannerisms and behavior."

Boy, maybe the police should hire Gunnar. He seems very observant. "So we stood out as being Americans?"

"That's right. It's not unusual, since there are tour groups and individual travelers of all nationalities who travel to the city of Reykjavik and the entire country of Iceland. I can spot different nationalities—not just Americans—from my bench. I've had a lot of practice after working at the café for so many years, since about half our trade is tourists." Gunnar grinned and shrugged. "People-watching is interesting, don't you think?"

Gunnar sure seemed to think so, and Kristen planned to use his skill to their advantage. Remembering how she'd entertained herself at the airports on this trip she couldn't agree more. "I do."

Brett, knowing they had a schedule to adhere to, said, "Why don't you tell us who and what you saw. I'm sure we'll find it just as interesting as you do."

"First, let me get you some water and bread. Please have a look at the lunch menu while I'm away. I'm sure you have plans this afternoon, so we can talk after I've sent your order to the kitchen."

"Sounds good to me." Kristen picked up the menu. "I don't want anything too heavy if we're going to be in the water this afternoon." She cruised through the menu. "I think I'll have a bowl of the soup of the day and the salmon *smørrebrød*."

"Smørrebrød?" Brett asked. "What is that again?"

"Nordic countries are known for their open-faced sandwiches."

"Oh, now I recognize the word for bread." He closed his menu. "You haven't led me wrong yet, so I'll follow your lead."

Gunnar set bread and water glasses on their table. "Have you decided?"he asked.

Giving Gunnar their orders, he walked back to the kitchen to place them, then returned to their table. "Mind if I sit down for a minute?"

"Not at all." Truth be told, Kristen was getting a crick in her neck from looking up at the tall man whose lineage was probably one hundred percent Viking.

"I don't have long until your order will be ready, and more customers will be coming in soon, so I'll get started. First of all, I noticed the man who was killed, Mr. Sawyer, and his wife walk by the front window when I was still inside. I remember because I saw them pause outside the door to view the menu. It's always amusing to watch tourists' expressions as they read, since not all Icelandic specialties are appealing to tourists."

Kristen nodded. She always enjoyed savoring local dishes when traveling, but she wasn't into pickled herring and other less tasty Nordic delights when at home. "I can imagine."

"So, he seemed to be feeling well enough to be thinking about lunch," Brett said.

Gunnar nodded. "But the two seemed to be arguing over something. They were talking fast and in low voices, so I didn't pick up on anything they were saying from inside. It could have been they were just tired and grouchy after an overnight flight, since I understand it was your first day in Iceland."

"That's right," Kristen said. She was thinking about how Margaret seemed to dominate Lewis and boss him around. She wondered what they'd argued about. Maybe it was nothing, just normal bickering some older couples seemed to do. Still, with a murderer on the loose, everything mattered. But Margaret didn't join them on the Northern Lights tour. She was almost one hundred percent sure the person who'd threatened her last night was the murderer. *Why else would someone pull that stunt? Unless the students decided to be funny.*

"I also saw you two walk by, but nothing you did stood out as being unusual—until later, when I saw you standing near the body. I also noticed the older couple who ate dinner with you the other night." Gunnar paused, looking at his watch. "I saw them talking as they approached the church, which made sense, since they were walking together. But then, I saw the older guy start walking toward the Sawyers. His wife tried to hold him back, but he brushed her aside."

Interesting. Kristen wondered if Doug was going to confront Lewis about making a pass at Betty. But that was ages ago. Would he still be that fired up about it? Kristen had seen Doug fired up, so maybe he was a hothead who held grudges for a long time. "What happened when he approached them?"

"He got right into their personal space," Gunnar said. "He was pointing a finger at Mr. Sawyer. Even from a distance I could see his face was red, and he was angry. Mr. Sawyer didn't seem to have much reaction from what I could see. It wasn't long before the man's wife caught up with him and pulled him away."

Kristen couldn't believe how much Gunnar noticed from his breaks on the bench out front. The café was in a prime location, just a few hundred feet from the church's main entrance. "Did you see anything else."

Gunnar nodded. "I also saw the students pass that way."

Good grief. This area was like Grand Central Station on the day Lewis died, thought Kristen. She scooted forward on her chair, literally on the edge of her seat. Maybe Gunnar could make the connection between one or all of the students and Lewis.

"How do you know they were with our group?" Kristen asked. After all, there were a lot of tourists visiting Iceland these days.

"Because I saw the police questioning them afterwards, and when they came in here one day for lunch, I noticed the Land of Ice Travel tag on one of their backpacks, just like what you have on your bag," Gunnar nodded at Kristen's backpack.

"Did they do anything unusual?" Brett asked. "Or just keep walking? Kristen says they don't admit to knowing Lewis Sawyer."

Gunnar looked at Brett, then at Kristen. "Then from my eyes, they appear to be lying."

CHAPTER 34

Even though Kristen had suspected there was some sort of link between Lewis and at least one of the students, she felt her jaw drop in amazement.

"I need to check on your food in a minute, so I'll keep it brief," Gunnar said. "It looked like the boys were the ones talking to Mr. Sawyer. The girls seemed to hang back."

"Maybe they were just being friendly," Brett suggested.

"Maybe, but it didn't look like they were smiling, and it was longer than a polite *Halló*."

Kristen was trying to process the information. "But the boys didn't seem to have any connection to Lewis, so by process of elimination, I assumed it was one or both of the girls who knew him."

"They acted like they knew him. And none of them looked very happy, if you know what I mean."

Kristen wasn't sure she did, but it was an interesting development.

Gunnar sprang up from his chair. "I must get your food."

What awful timing—just when Kristen had so many questions. Still, she could chew on what Gunnar had told them before their food arrived. Kristen and Brett exchanged a look. "What do you make of that?"

Brett shrugged. "It sounds like they bumped into the Lewises on the way to visit the church. So what?"

"But Gunnar said they didn't look happy. Sam and Trevor always seem cheerful when I've run into them, even if their girlfriends aren't always as friendly."

"No one's happy all the time."

Kristen didn't agree with Brett's nonchalant attitude. "I'm going to think on it for a moment, but first I need to text Hope. If Todd has told her the Icelandic police have been checking up on us, she must be worried."

"Yeah, you'd better touch base with her. You don't want her bugging your parents about it. No sense getting them riled up as well."

Kristen found the café's Wi-Fi and tapped into it, glad for a decent connection. She hadn't realized they would end up in the midst of a murder investigation while on their honeymoon, or she would have splurged for the international phone package for the duration of their trip. Without it, she had to rely on Wi-Fi. Brett was still on his own phone plan that had at least covered the emergency call after Lewis died.

Kristen checked the time. It wasn't even six o'clock in the morning at home. **Hey, I hope I'm not texting too early, but I wanted to tell you we're fine. A man who booked through the same travel agency we did was killed the first day of our trip.**

Kristen immediately received a reply. **Nope. I'm awake. Todd told me about the Icelandic police contacting Sheriff Miller. He only knows the basics, but it was enough to worry me. You didn't reply to my earlier text.**

Kristen checked her phone, and sure enough, she'd missed a text notification. **Sorry about that. I can only use my phone when connected to Wi-Fi.** Kristen saw Gunnar headed their way with a tray. Lunch was served. **No need to worry. The case should be wrapped up soon. Gotta run.**

Okay. Be safe, and stay out of trouble.

Kristen grinned. Hope was starting to sound like Brett.

Gunnar placed their soup and sandwiches in front of them. "I hope you enjoy your lunch!"

"Oh, we will. It smells delicious." Kristen picked up her spoon to try her soup. "And tastes delicious. "Is there anything else you can tell us about the murder? In addition to what you saw, maybe you heard people talking about it."

"Kristen, let Gunnar get back to work," Brett said. "But we appreciate everything you've told us. Do the police know?"

Gunnar nodded. "I told them what I told you—at least everything I noticed at the time. But I've had more time to think about it since they originally questioned me, which was soon after they finished talking to you both."

"Anything important?" Kristen asked.

"I doubt it—just impressions." Gunnar's normally cheerful face sobered. "In retrospect, it all seems surreal. I was sitting outside taking a break and people watching. Little did I know what I saw would play out as a murder."

"Did you see anyone get close enough to Lewis to administer poison?" Kristen wondered how on earth someone had made Lewis swallow poison in a public area.

Gunnar shrugged. "They were standing close together, but I didn't see anyone give him anything to eat or drink." He grinned. "That's what I'm here for, and I'd better get back to work."

"Thanks, Gunnar. You've been very helpful." Kristen was stumped as to not only who had given Lewis the poison, but also when and how.

"What's on your mind?" Brett asked, digging into his lunch with gusto.

"Just curious as to when Lewis was actually poisoned. It doesn't seem possible that he ate or drank something—handed to him by the murderer—in the middle of a busy tourist destination in broad daylight."

"No, that doesn't make sense. Although it sounds like Lewis interacted with all the people in question. Someone could have easily slipped him something in all the hubbub."

"But Gunnar didn't see anything." In the short amount of time she'd gotten to know Gunnar, Kristen trusted his keen observation skills.

"Then maybe the killer gave him something at the hotel." Kristen bit into her open-faced sandwich and savored the creamy dill sauce and salmon. "This tastes amazing."

"I agree." Brett slurped soup from his spoon. "This soup is hearty and tasty. Reminds me of some of yours."

Kristen smiled at Brett's compliment. "But I don't get to cook with fresh fish, unlike what's available in Iceland."

"I think I've had more fish in Iceland than in the entire past year."

"Same here." Kristen couldn't fault any meal they'd eaten in Iceland. She thought back to how the poison had been administered. "If someone gave Lewis the poison earlier, then why did they interact with him again near the church?"

"That's why I think they must have somehow slipped it to him in front of the church."

"Unless the person who gave it to him isn't even on our radar." Kristen felt they were getting close to solving Lewis' murder—if last night's scary warning was any indicator—but she still had no clue, literally, who had done it.

"We haven't noticed anyone else, but that doesn't mean someone couldn't have done Lewis in, then gotten out of here."

"That's what would normally happen." Kristen took one last spoonful of soup. "Why would the murderer stick around, waiting to be caught?" But something told her the murderer had done just that and was still in the vicinity. Since no one on their suspect list could be considered a professional killer, the killer probably thought he could get by with the murder, since at first it appeared Lewis had died of natural causes. Kristen and Brett had both assumed Lewis had died of a heart attack or stroke. Someone who wasn't familiar with sudden or suspicious deaths couldn't have known the police would investigate further. And, once the police started questioning those who were nearby when Lewis died, it would look suspicious if someone left the area. Plus, the police would have an eye on the airport if someone they'd questioned tried to leave the country—or at least be able to trace their movements through their passport use and flight manifests.

"Murderers aren't always thinking straight," Brett said. "Besides, think about the other murder cases you've been involved with. The murderers were right under your nose the entire time."

What Brett said made sense. Kristen felt certain someone in their small travel circle had killed Lewis. She was back at the beginning. "I want to look up Nora and Alicia online." She checked the time. "Maybe we'll have a few minutes before we head to the Blue Lagoon."

Brett rolled his eyes. "If it makes you feel any better, then okay. But afterwards it's time for our spa afternoon."

"I'll be able to enjoy it more once I'm finished," Kristen said. "Right after I try to figure out why Doug had a run-in with Lewis right before he died, plus Sam and Trevor. It sounds like Margaret and Lewis had a tiff as well."

"So far, the more we know, the less we know," Brett said.

"What I do know is that we will get to the bottom of things. It's only a matter of time." Kristen felt she was giving herself a pep talk as much as she was trying to be positive for Brett's sake.

"Let's just hope when the lightbulb goes on in your mind, the lights don't go out."

CHAPTER 35

As Kristen and Brett walked back to the hotel after lunch, they discussed what Gunnar had told them. "Almost everyone had a beef with Lewis," Kristen said. "While we were trying to figure out whether they even had a connection to him, they went a step farther and didn't even like the man."

"Maybe it comes down to his womanizing ways," Brett said. They'd reached the hotel, and he held the door for her.

"You could be right, and there's also the research angle. Maybe he upset someone in academia or through his geological research. Speaking of research, I want to finish mine." Kristen planned to make a beeline for their room and spend a few minutes looking up Nora and Alicia.

Once inside their room, Kristen opened her laptop and entered *Alicia Cassidy* into the search engine. Alicia's name popped up in dozens of entries, including winning a college creative writing contest. Reading the article more closely, it appeared she was majoring in English. There were a couple of photos and articles about her high school cross country meets. She had gone to school in St. Louis. Kristen couldn't see a connection that could link her with Lewis in an obvious way. *Maybe Brett's right, and it boils down to an affair.* She couldn't see any other way the two could know each other, let alone know him enough—and hate him enough—to kill him. Maybe they lived in the same neighborhood? But Kristen knew in a college town most professors tended to live in nicer neighborhoods than most of the students, so the odds were slim they'd run into each other that way.

With a sigh, Kristen plugged *Nora Taylor* into the search engine. Just as Kristen was beginning to give up hope, a photo and article showed Nora in high school as a member of the geology club at Moline High School. *Bingo!* Kristen's fingers flew over the keyboard. She figured the geology field guide she'd spotted in the backpack in the photo belonged to Nora. Closing that article, she quickly kept the cursor moving, hoping to find something that specifically linked her to Lewis. Sifting through several high school entries, she finally found some more current ones at the University of Illinois. Kristen's heart was thumping as she finally found a link that seemed like it was the "missing link." Nora's name was listed as a co-author on a paper in a scientific journal. Kristen's racing heart almost stopped when she saw who the co-author was—none other than Dr. Lewis Sawyer.

"Brett, come here quick." She pointed to the screen. "Take a look at this."

Brett read over Kristen's shoulder, as she continued reading. "How could Nora lie about knowing Lewis when she was not only a graduate student under him but also his research associate?"

Kristen nodded. "I assumed they were all undergraduates. They seem so young, but Nora, at least, must be a year or two older."

"If they worked together, maybe something soured. Maybe she's the killer, but you don't know that for sure."

"Of course not," Kristen agreed. "But it links her to him. She denied knowing him, and that in itself is suspicious."

"Let's call the police." He took a card from his wallet. "Here's the number Officer Helgason gave me."

As Kristen punched in the numbers, she felt her heart start to race again. Had they just figured out who the killer was? But Kristen knew things weren't always as simple as they appeared. Not that any of this was simple, but maybe there was a perfectly reasonable reason why Nora didn't acknowledge knowing Lewis. It seemed like an eternity, but someone finally answered.

"Halló. Helgason."

Kristen didn't realize this was a direct line to the officer, but at least she didn't have to go through a switchboard operator to track him down. "Yes, this is Kristen Matthews, I mean, Stevenson. I wanted to share something I just learned about one of the people on our trip, Nora Taylor."

Kristen could sense Officer's Helgason's normally patient demeanor was a little on edge. "Okay. Why don't you go ahead and tell me?"

Kristen relayed what she'd discovered online. Officer Helgason didn't have much to say when she was finished, making her think they had already made the connection. Maybe it was nothing to get excited about, but since the police hadn't shared any of their information, Kristen had no idea what they already knew or didn't know. *Maybe if they'd told me the basics of what they'd discovered on their end, I wouldn't potentially be wasting their time, not to mention my own time.*

"I appreciate you letting me know. We had traced the students' activities and classes through the school and found out this morning that Nora Taylor was a student of the deceased. Unfortunately, we haven't been able to track her down yet to discuss things further with her."

"I just saw her at breakfast," Kristen couldn't resist adding. But she realized she hadn't seen any of the students since then. Maybe they were napping before afternoon sightseeing. She wondered if they booked for the Blue Lagoon trip?

"Have you seen her recently?" Officer Helgason asked, echoing her thoughts.

"No, I haven't. But my husband and I are taking a trip to the Blue Lagoon this afternoon. Maybe she'll be on the same excursion. So far, we've all been on the same day trips—and evening trips." Kristen shuddered when she remembered last night's adventure. Between the four students making fun of them, and perhaps even being the ones to try to warn them off in the portable toilets, Kristen wasn't feeling warm and fuzzy about any of them today. She was concerned about doing the right thing and turning in pertinent information about a possible suspect, and she didn't feel a moment of regret about doing it. Even if Nora hadn't been the one to kill Lewis, she'd held back from telling the police about her past relationship with Lewis. That sounded fishy to Kristen— way fishier than any of the fish dishes she'd eaten on this trip. She also thought it odd that the police hadn't been able to locate or talk to the students today—specifically Nora.

"Okay. Good to know. I'm sure we'll be able to reach her soon."

"Maybe she doesn't have international cell phone capabilities unless she's hooked into Wi-Fi. That's the case with my phone."

"You could be right," Officer Helgason said. "Now, if that's all you have to tell me, I need to continue with my work on the case. I appreciate your call."

"No problem." Kristen ended the call. Somehow she felt like her problems were just beginning.

CHAPTER 36

Kristen and Brett got off the elevator and began walking through the lobby. They only had a few minutes before they needed to meet for the afternoon trip to the Blue Lagoon. Kristen wasn't sure why, but she wasn't overly excited about it. She'd prefer to get outdoors and see more of Iceland's rugged scenery than going to a spa, but since the Blue Lagoon was Iceland's most popular tourist attraction, they thought it would be a nice change of pace from the other trips they'd taken. Now that the time was here, Kristen was starting to regret committing to the trip. Giving herself a mental pep talk, she decided they would have fun once they got there. Plus, as an added benefit, she could keep an eye on the others on their trip.

Looking up, she noticed Margaret Sawyer trying to catch her eye.

Kristen waved. She couldn't believe she hadn't seen Margaret all day. She touched Brett's arm. "Give me a minute to say hello to Margaret."

"Oh, brother." Brett rolled his eyes. "We need to be outside to meet the bus in five minutes."

"No worries. I'll meet you there in three." Kristen leaned in to kiss Brett on the cheek. "See you soon."

Kristen walked toward Margaret. "Hi! How are you feeling today?"

"I'm hanging in there." She eyed Kristen's tote bag. "Are you going to the Blue Lagoon?"

"Yeah, we're leaving shortly, so I can't chat for long, but I wanted to say hello and see how you're doing."

Margaret sighed. "Oh, how I wish I could go with you—actually, Lewis and I both, but that's not possible."

That was an understatement. "I'm sorry." What else could she say? She didn't think it was wise to voice her thoughts about how she didn't even want to go. Margaret would probably scoff at her attitude.

"It's my reality these days." Another sigh.

Wow, Margaret was laying it on thick. "Have the police discovered any new information?" Kristen knew for a fact they had but didn't want to let on to Margaret she already knew.

"I haven't talked to them yet today but that's next on my list—not that I have much of one for the foreseeable future."

Kristen knew she needed to get moving. "I know it's hard. But one comfort you have is I'm sure the police will have Lewis' murder solved soon."

"What makes you say that?" Margaret looked closely at Kristen. "Have you heard anything?"

"I'm sure the police would have contacted you if they'd learned anything new." Kristen checked the time. "I must get a move on to meet Brett. I don't want him to get upset with me for being late and get into an argument on our honeymoon." Kristen had a sudden thought. She touched Margaret's arm. "Did you and Lewis argue right before he died?"

Margaret scrunched up her eyebrows. "What do you mean by that?"

"Someone told me they'd seen you and Lewis having words not long before he died."

"What are you trying to say?" Margaret glared at her.

I think it's perfectly obvious. "It's just sad if you argued right before Lewis died. I'm sure it was nothing major, but I would feel awful if I'd argued with a loved one right before they passed away." Kristen had a moment of guilt, thinking she'd gone too far in trying to extract information. "I'm sorry. I didn't mean to upset you."

"No, you're right," Margaret said grudgingly. "We did argue right before Lewis was killed. But, it was nothing major. Plus, it wasn't like I was mad enough at him to want to kill him if that's what you're thinking. Good grief, if I wanted to kill Lewis—and I've had plenty of provocation over the years—I would have done it long ago." Margaret poked Kristen's chest. "And, it wouldn't have been over whether to take the elevator to the top of the *Hallgrimskirkja*."

"That's what you were arguing about?" Kristen asked. Part of her should feel glad the couple hadn't argued over anything important before Lewis was killed, but part of her wanted Margaret to confess to killing Lewis, just so they could put this whole mess behind them, even if odds were slim Margaret would confess to the police, let alone to Kristen. Which meant a murderer was still on the loose.

Margaret nodded. "Yes, that's right. I could kick myself for getting worked up over something so ridiculous. But I don't like elevators and am not all that crazy about heights. I take the stairs as much as possible."

"Couldn't Lewis have gone by himself?" Kristen didn't understand couples who had to do everything together, especially if one of the pair was so opposed to the activity.

"He could have easily gone alone. Since it was the first day of our trip, he didn't want to leave me behind but wanted to go himself. I couldn't convince him that I was fine by myself for a few minutes. It's ironic that he didn't think I'd be safe alone in a foreign country." Margaret sniffed. "Maybe if he'd gone up in the elevator, he'd still be with me today."

"Now, Margaret, you can't be sure of that, and even if it were true, it's not your fault." Kristen felt bad about getting Margaret all riled up, but she had to get going. "I'm sorry I mentioned anything."

"It's okay and no fault of yours. None of this is. It's the murderer's fault."

Kristen glanced up to see Brett beckoning her from the front door. "I really need to go, or the bus will leave me behind, and *that* will be my fault." Kristen tried to joke, but it probably wasn't very sensitive of her to make light of the situation.

"Go, and make the most of the opportunity to visit the Blue Lagoon. I can't imagine your honeymoon has gone the way you planned with all this murder business hanging over our heads. I want you to know how much I appreciate you standing by me during this time. You and your husband were there right after Lewis was killed and tried to help. Your husband seems like a great man. You need to enjoy your time together because you never know when it may be cut short."

Kristen impulsively gave Margaret a quick hug. "Take care. I'll talk to you later." She walked quickly to the door, thinking how she'd originally thought Margaret was an uppity and snobbish woman, but Margaret had also displayed sensitivity and compassion. Kristen walked out the door and stood by Brett. Before he could say anything, she kissed him and whispered. "I missed you."

"You did? You were only gone a few minutes—longer than you said you would be gone, but surely not long enough to miss me." Brett put his arm around Kristen and drew her close while they waited for the couple in line ahead of them to board.

"A very wise woman told me to make the most out of the time I have with my husband, and I intend to follow her advice." But as much as Kristen appreciated Margaret's sentiments, were they true, or had Margaret put up with Lewis' behavior for too long and decided to do something about it? Did Kristen get taken in by Margaret's seemingly wise words? Kristen sighed and got on the bus. It wasn't for her to worry about it. Her role in this investigation was complete.

CHAPTER 37

Staring out the window on the drive to the Blue Lagoon, Kristen was mesmerized by the simple but interesting scenery before them. Lumps of hardened ancient lava was covered with snow. Weak winter sunlight hit the land, striking a subtle contrast between the snow-covered lava and the horizon.

"You know what we haven't eaten since we've been in Iceland?" Kristen asked.

"What?"

"A *pylsa*." Kristen grinned, knowing she'd probably mangled the pronunciation of yet another Icelandic word, but Brett wouldn't know the difference anyway.

"Which is?" Brett raised his eyebrows.

"An Icelandic hotdog."

"Okay, we'll have to try one before we go home." Brett gave her an odd look. "What on earth brought that on? We're on our way to visit a geothermal pool and spa, and out of the total blue you mention Icelandic hotdogs. Not that I'm opposed at the thought of trying one, even though I'm not sure how different it'll taste than a Chicago-style hotdog, or even a down-home grilled hotdog."

Kristen shrugged. "I don't know. You know I do a lot of thinking when watching beautiful scenery out the window. You have to admit it's peaceful, and the thought just popped into my head. We've been eating all kinds of other traditional Icelandic dishes, but the hotdog is one you wouldn't think of when ordering a meal at a nice restaurant. According to what I've read, they taste great and are a 'must try" when visiting Iceland."

"I agree. Maybe the Blue Lagoon will have a place to buy a hotdog."

Kristen laughed. It felt good to relax and be silly with Brett. She'd missed doing that the past few days since their fun times were limited to when they weren't asking questions about Lewis' murder. "I honestly have no idea what to expect at the Blue Lagoon, but I'm not sure hotdogs are part of their spa image."

"I think visiting the spa—even if it's not really our cup of tea—and trying an Icelandic hotdog are two requirements when visiting Iceland, but maybe not necessarily at the same time."

Kristen had to chuckle at Brett's attitude. He always had a knack for making her feel happy. It was one of the things she loved about him—his common-sense approach to life, sprinkled with a great sense of humor. "I just wanted to mention it while I was thinking about it." She grabbed his hand. "Because my thoughts have been otherwise occupied by this murder investigation."

"It's a shame Lewis Sawyer had to go and get himself killed on our honeymoon. But I knew what I was getting myself into before we had our first official date. We started hanging out together during your first experience with a murder investigation, and I know you're not going to leave it alone until the murderer is caught." He leaned in closer. "I just don't want you to get caught by the murderer."

"That's not going to happen with my strong husband around to protect me."

"I'm always there for you, but it seems like things always happen to you when I have my back turned."

"No worries on that. I'm turning in my badge and letting the police handle it."

"Sure. I believe you," Brett said with a grin. "But just in case you're not serious, you need to be careful." He looked around at the other passengers. "I don't know about you, but I get the feeling something's going to happen soon, and it's hard to know who to trust."

"I agree, and I think last night's Northern Lights adventure confirmed that things are heating up in the Land of Ice. To be honest, I wish something would happen one way or another, so we can get back to normal. The longer this uncertainty goes on, the longer we won't be able to fully enjoy ourselves."

"Let's take a break from sleuthing and do what we're supposed to do at a geothermal spa—let the waters work their magic while we recharge."

"I like the sound of that." Kristen glanced out the window and saw a road sign stating the Blue Lagoon was only a few kilometers away. "We're almost there."

Soon they reached the Blue Lagoon. The driver gave them instructions for the afternoon. Kristen still wasn't sure what to expect but was determined to have a good time during the outing, even if soaking in a pool and spa weren't her style.

Brett grabbed her hand. "Come on. Let's take a look outside before we go indoors. We have our group pass, so we're covered and don't need to stick with the group."

"Great idea. It will be dark when we leave this evening." As they walked through the outer entrance and around the grounds, Kristen glanced at the eerie, powder-blue, milky water that steamed and gurgled throughout the lava rock. The contrast was striking. "It's hard to believe the water used in this beautiful spa is supplied by a nearby geothermal power station."

Brett nodded. "I also read that the high silicon is what gives the water its milky appearance." Brett grinned as they continued walking around the outdoor pools near the main entrance. "Apparently the silica forms soft white mud on the bottom of the pools, which bathers rub on themselves."

"Which they probably also bottle up and sell for outrageous prices. Kristen had seen various products in the shops they'd visited in Reykjavik and figured there would be an even greater selection at the spa.

"Since we've taken time to research this place, it makes it an even more ideal and romantic honeymoon destination." Brett chuckled.

"Actually, it does. The geothermal waters that come from the geothermal plant are natural, as are the products that come from them, so it's the ultimate recycling process—perfect for nature lovers like us"

"Oh, sorry," Betty chortled, startling them both. "We wouldn't want to interrupt the *lovers.*"

Kristen tore her gaze away from Brett to see Doug and Betty approaching them. The older couple sure had a knack for interrupting tender and private moments, even if Kristen and Brett were talking about nature and not romance. Still, it was a special moment—one of few they'd had when touring with the other travelers."

"Hello," Kristen managed. "Are you two excited now that we've arrived?"

Betty flashed a radiant smile, while Doug scowled; his good disposition from earlier that morning had somewhat soured. Kristen could easily guess whose idea taking the Blue Lagoon excursion was.

"I'm excited, but as you can probably tell, he's not." Betty glared at Doug, who was still pouting.

Why did they have to barge in on us again? And bring their negativity with them, to boot? "Sorry to hear that, but I'm actually getting more excited about our visit," Kristen said.

"Glad someone is." Doug's attitude seemed to be heading even further south.

"Why don't you just leave us alone and go somewhere to continue your sulk." Betty spoke to Doug as she probably would have spoken to her young children back in the day.

Fortunately, Doug took Betty's advice and stomped off in a huff. Kristen had no idea where he was headed, since the bus wouldn't return for hours. She didn't care, as long as he wasn't around to ruin their day.

"Sorry about Doug's behavior," Betty said with an apologetic smile. "He's out of sorts because not only does he really not want to be here in the first place, but …"

"But what?" Kristen was curious to know what had caused Doug's poor behavior.

Betty sighed. This seemed to be the afternoon for older women to confide in Kristen. "The police questioned us again."

Kristen was even more curious now. What led the police to question the older couple again? They certainly hadn't hinted to Kristen and Brett when they'd delivered the walking stick to the police station earlier. Maybe their officers' nonchalant attitudes were just an act. *And, when had the police had time to question Doug and Betty? They must have talked to them while we were eating lunch.*

"Oh, no," Kristen said. "I'm sure that wasn't pleasant."

Betty shook her head. "Not only had the police heard about a ..." Betty rolled her eyes. "A supposed altercation Doug had with Lewis not long before he died, but they also discovered something we wanted to keep to ourselves."

"We're sorry to hear that." Kristen didn't know what else to say, and she had a feeling if she kept her comments simple, Betty would open up without any prompting.

Sure enough, Betty wanted to share—probably needing to get it off her chest. "The police somehow discovered that Lewis and I had an affair."

Kristen wasn't expecting that—definitely not put so bluntly. At least her hunch the Schmidts weren't being totally upfront was confirmed. "Oh, wow. Did Doug already know, or did he just find out when the police started asking more questions?"

"Oh, he knew. It happened years ago, and the affair was brief. Fortunately, the Sawyers moved shortly afterwards. Even though Doug and I had a rough patch afterwards, we worked through it. Doug knew Lewis had seduced me. I was telling you the truth when I said I was flattered when Lewis made a pass at me. I was home alone with young children and didn't always have time to take care of myself. It felt good to be pursued by a handsome man. But the pass eventually ended up going further. I could kick myself now—and even at the time-- but there's nothing I can do about that now. Doug and I made our peace about it years ago. Until now, when it was brought up in relation to Lewis' murder."

Betty had a dangerous gleam in her eye. "I know Doug didn't kill Lewis, but if I get my hands on whoever told the police about the affair, I can't take responsibility for what I'll do." She looked at the murky blue water. "I'm sure it was Margaret, up to her old tricks."

Kristen followed Betty's gaze toward the steaming water and wondered if Margaret's tricks were now being used to divert attention from the fact that she'd killed her own husband after years of unfaithfulness.

CHAPTER 38

Kristen stared at Betty. She shouldn't be shocked at Betty's revelation. She knew dirty laundry was always aired during a murder investigation, even if it had no bearing on the case.

"So let me get this straight," Kristen said. "The police heard Doug got into it with Lewis right before he died. They did some digging and found out about an affair from decades ago, then decided to call you both in for further questioning?"

"That about sizes it up," Betty wrung her hands. "It's only my guess Margaret told them, but I suppose anyone could have seen Doug shove Lewis when we were sightseeing that first day. To be honest, once we saw you with Doug's walking stick, we thought we should come clean with the police."

They should have come clean long before that. "But they contacted you first?"

Betty nodded. "Not long after you left to deliver the walking stick to the police station, so I'm guessing you were on your way there."

Since the police didn't share any details, Kristen wasn't sure but guessed Betty was correct in her assumption. "Are you sure Margaret knew about your affair with Lewis?"

Betty shrugged. "It's hard to say. She may have known Lewis was messing around but may not have known it was with me. I think she was already used to Lewis' cheating by then, and it was only a short-lived fling between us before I came to my senses."

Kristen was thoughtful. If Margaret didn't know about the affair and hadn't told the police, then how had the police learned of the affair? She could well understand the police knowing about the skirmish between Doug and Lewis—especially since they'd talked to Gunnar early in the investigation. So why did it take the police so long to question Doug and Betty again? Of course, Kristen was probably only getting half the story and had been all along. If only witnesses would be straight with the police in the first place, the process would move more smoothly and quickly. Suspects could be checked out and ruled out, allowing the police to focus on the real killer after the distractions were eliminated.

"Why is Doug so worked up, if he knew about the affair and had put it behind him?" Kristen smiled warmly. "You two seem so happy together."

"We are happy, and I'm so lucky Doug forgave me."

"If he's so forgiving, why did he get into it with Lewis?" Brett asked.

"You've seen Doug in action," Betty said. "He's a big teddy bear one moment but can be a hothead the next. Seeing Lewis after all those years brought it back to him. Even though he knew it was wrong, he felt good— and avenged—after he shoved Lewis. All manly and macho, I guess. But the point is, he didn't need to kill Lewis. He'd already taken care of the things that bothered him in that simple confrontation."

"So why is Doug pouting now?" *Maybe Doug hadn't actually moved on as much as Betty thought he had.*

"Doug, like a lot of men, is full of pride. He didn't like having the police dredge up the past we'd worked so hard to bury." Betty frowned. "I think deep down he's still peeved I had an affair with Lewis in the first place."

"I'm sure Doug will be fine once he's had a chance to sort things out. What better place to think than a geothermal spa? Besides, you've been happily married for years, and this is just a bump in the road."

Kristen had been married for less than a week, so she probably couldn't be considered an expert on marriage, but nonetheless was glad to see Betty smiling at her words.

"Thanks for letting me vent. I feel better already. Now, if you'll excuse me, I'll leave you two lovebirds alone, and I'll find my love." Betty held up her hand, crossing her fingers. "Here's hoping he's ready to kiss and make up."

Kristen smiled and waved as Betty started walking down the path, vowing to steer clear of the couple until their make-up was complete.

"Good grief," Brett said. "You just never know, do you?"

"Nope," Kristen agreed. "Which is why we need to make the most of our time together—especially while we're in this magical country."

"I'm starting to wonder just how magical it is, but I know what you mean. Let's get on with it. A romantic spa afternoon awaits us." Brett steered Kristen down the path—the opposite direction from Betty—toward the main entrance.

"Whatever you say, dear." Kristen was ready for some rest and relaxation on what had turned into a very stressful honeymoon. *What an oxymoron.*

* * *

Kristen walked out of the changing area, a lightweight robe wrapped around her swimming suit, her pink polished toes bared in the flipflops she wore. She shivered from the chill in the air. She knew she'd warm up once she was able to soak in the warm mineral waters, but for now she was freezing. She walked to the foyer outside the changing room, where Brett was already waiting.

"Are you ready?" he asked.

"I'm ready to warm up. I had no idea I'd be so cold at a geothermal area."

"Honestly, the thought of getting undressed in the middle of the winter to sit outside in hot water has never appealed to me."

"You could have mentioned that sooner." Kristen grinned and looked around the crowded main pool. "Apparently we're in the minority."

Kristen and Brett followed the signs that pointed to the main pool. Unsure what to expect, Kristen made a beeline to an area that didn't appear to be as crowded. After a morning of overly stimulating conversations, she was done talking. Besides, wasn't she supposed to spend quality time with Brett? On anyone else's honeymoon, that would be the case, but so far, Kristen and Brett's trip had been less focused on them and more focused on a murder case.

Knowing deep down she would have a hard time totally relaxing with a murderer on the loose, Kristen still wanted to make an effort. Even though the police were still talking to people—like the Schmidts, who Kristen had pretty much ruled out as suspects--she felt they were closing in on the killer. At least she hoped so.

Kristen placed her towel on the lumpy lava pool edge. "Will this spot do?"

Brett nodded. "Looks good to me."

As Kristen took off the robe that covered her red tank suit, she was thankful she wasn't daring enough to wear a bikini as several others were wearing. Even though she knew she'd warm up once she got in the water, the air was cool. She tentatively dipped her right foot into the pool. The temperature was warm but not too hot. "The water feels perfect."

She found a halfway flat section of lava and sat on it, scooting closer to the edge and dangling both her legs into the steamy water. Scanning the pool, she noted most bathers were totally immersed, bobbing around the large, shallow pool that was over two acres in size.

"Testing the waters?" Brett asked as he sat down beside her.

Kristen noticed Brett still wore his t-shirt. "I wasn't sure if the water would be too chilly—it is winter, after all—or too hot, so I'm just chilling, so to speak, as I ease into it.

"We have plenty of time, so there's no rush."

Kirsten looked at the other bathers, her eyes landing on Sam's bright red hair. It looked more subdued than usual since it was wet, but Kristen could recognize him anywhere. She could even see his many freckles glistening with moisture from across the pool.

Curious as to whether the rest of Sam's friends had joined them, Kristen casually let her eyes wander over the rest of the crowd—at least those visible from her more secluded alcove. Since she was already labeled as a busybody, and the memory of the threat from the previous night was still blazed in her brain, she tried to be cautious in her search. Nora—at least in Kristen's mind—was at the top of the suspect list, after lying about knowing Lewis Sawyer, when in fact, she'd worked closely with him. What else had she lied about, or worse yet, what else had she done?

Kristen jumped when Brett touched her shoulder, his low voice interrupting her search of the other bathers. "She's over there." He casually flicked his hand to the right.

Careful not to whip her head to the right too quickly, she murmured in Brett's ear. "How did you know I was looking for them?"

"Come on, Kristen. I'd recognize that 'private detective' look you get when you're concentrating anywhere." Brett grinned.

"We're already acting like an old married couple, I guess," Kristen joked.

Brett shook his head. "I think we have a way to go before we reach the Doug and Betty point, but I can sense you're still stirred up about all this."

Kristen decided to take the plunge—literally—and slowly slid more of her body into the soothing water. "I'm glad you know me so well, and it's a shame I can't just switch off my curiosity, but that's the way I'm wired." She let the warm and tingly water flow over her body as she looked in the direction of the students. They were bantering back and forth as if they didn't have a care in the world. *Maybe they don't*

"I'm surprised to see them here," Kristen said. "I didn't notice them on the bus." Maybe they'd Ubered, or the Icelandic version of hiring their own car.

"If you remember right, you were talking to Margaret up until the last possible minute. We were the last to board the bus and sat in the front seat. It was hard to see who all was on the bus, especially those sitting toward the back, when we had to scramble aboard."

"I suppose you're right. Do you think the police managed to track them down?"

"It's hard to say." Brett stepped into the shallow pool and stood next to her. "They were busy talking to the Schmidts after we left. They probably didn't have time to talk to the students—even if they were able to catch them on the phone."

"That's a good point. The timing was way too tight." Kristen watched as Trever splashed water on Nora. Nora squealed in delight, a radiant smile crossing her normally somber features. She certainly wasn't acting like she'd murdered her former professor and research associate a few days earlier. Kristen bet she felt worse about Lewis' death than anyone else on the trip—other than Margaret, but even that was debatable.

CHAPTER 39

"Now that we've seen them, should we contact the police?" Kristen asked.

Brett was silent for a moment, debating her question. "We should probably let them know the students are here now instead of waiting until we're back in Reykjavik. If the police want to track the students down here, that's their call."

"Then I'll call them right now." Kristen felt honor bound to give the police a heads up. Besides, even though she'd sworn off getting involved, she'd come this far, so why not take the final plunge? She had a suspicion the students had no problems receiving phone calls but were ignoring the officers' attempts to contact them. Why would they do that unless Nora knew more than she was letting on, or worse yet, was the one to kill Lewis?

Kristen got out of the water and rummaged in her bag for her phone. "I should be able to use my phone if I can hook into the Wi-Fi." She looked at her settings. "Darn it. I need a password."

"I bet you could go to the main office and explain the situation. They would probably even let you use their landline."

"I'm sure they don't want the police swarming their peaceful premises."

"Let's hope it doesn't come to that." Brett glanced at the college students. "But if the police want to talk to them, they aren't going anywhere for now. It's a long walk back to Reykjavik if they don't take the bus later this afternoon."

"It will be dark long before then." Shivering, Kristen put on her robe and dropped her phone into its pocket, wishing she'd had a chance to soak in the waters longer before she had to get out again. So much for a peaceful afternoon. But the interruption would be worth it, if the police could touch base with the students. It would be one less piece of unfinished business. "I'll be back soon."

"Do you want me to go with you?"

Brett didn't look all that excited about leaving the soothing water, so Kristen decided to take care of matters herself. Besides, if Brett had his way, she wouldn't have been involved in any of this mess. "No, that's okay. You can stay here and save our spot. I don't want to have to look for another deserted area."

"Don't worry. I'll keep things nice and warm for you."

Kristen used her toe to flick water at him. "I don't think that's a problem in a geothermal area, but thanks anyway."

Kristen slid her feet into her flipflops and walked along the path that wove around the main pool and headed toward what she assumed was the main office. Since they'd already shown their group passes to enter, they hadn't stuck around long near the building, other than to put on their swimsuits in the adjoining changing rooms.

She rubbed the goosebumps dotting her arms as she walked. Not only had she quickly acclimated to the warm water, but the temperatures were in the low thirties, and the midafternoon sun was already starting to sink lower in the sky. She walked for what felt like a mile but was probably only a few hundred yards. Relieved to spot the main building around the bend, she quickened her pace, hoping the building was well heated.

Opening the office door, she walked to the counter. Speaking in English, since her Icelandic vocab wasn't good enough to request a Wi-Fi password, she asked, "I have an important phone call to make. Can you please give me the Wi-Fi password? I'm afraid I can only make overseas calls when I'm hooked up to Wi-Fi."

"We don't usually give our office network password to guests," the lady said, raising her fair colored eyebrows at Kristen. "But if you're sure it's important, I guess it's okay. Please don't share it with others"

Kristen opened her settings and tapped the network password into her phone as the woman recited the code. Kristen was thankful but wondered why the woman had gone against company policy and decided to give her the password. *Do I look that desperate?* "Well, then, I really appreciate it! *Takk fyrir*." Kristen had decided against asking to use the office phone. She really didn't want anyone to listen to her business and sincerely doubted the spa would want to know a possible murder suspect was on the premises. Kristen knew the police would handle things in a discreet manner if they decided to make the trip. *Actually, several suspects are roaming around today and have been with us all week.* Maybe the spa *would* like to know. Kristen brushed the thought aside. There would be time to alert the spa once the police arrived. *For that matter, the police can tell them. Once I call them, my part is complete.*

She left the office area and tried to find a quiet place to call the police. She didn't want to be overheard, but the spa and pool were teeming with people. Even though the alcove they'd been swimming in was fairly secluded, Kristen wanted to call before she went back into the pool area since she assumed reception would be better and less noisy here. Besides, she didn't want the students to see her making a call.

She spotted a bench near a smaller set of secluded bathrooms. At least she could sit down and not be interrupted by a continuous flow of traffic in and out of the changing rooms closer to the office.

Having already entered Officer Helgason's number into her phone, she pulled up his number quickly. As she punched the call button, her fingers felt shaky. Not sure why she was feeling nervous, she cleared her throat, hoping to pull herself together before the policeman answered. The phone rang several times, and just as she thought voicemail was going to pick up, he answered.

"Officer Helgason."

Kristen once again had a case of the nerves, since by then she was expecting to only leave a message. "Um, this is Kristen Matthews—I mean, Kristen Stevenson." *Or was it Kristen Matthews-Stevenson?* At the moment, she couldn't spit her new name out correctly.

"Yes?" The one word was enough to convey his concern, even over the phone. "Is everything okay?"

"I think so." She cleared her throat again, hoping to snap out of her funk. "I'm calling from the Blue Lagoon, and I wanted to let you know that the university students you were trying to contact earlier are also on the same excursion."

"You couldn't have let us know when they boarded the bus?" he asked. "We would have questioned them before they left town."

"I'm sorry. I didn't see them board the bus because I was one of the last ones to board."

"When are you due back at your hotel?"

"According to the itinerary, we are leaving here at five o'clock, so it should be before six o'clock." She heard the normally friendly officer sigh.

"I'm afraid we can't wait that long. Stay away from them, and we'll be there as soon as possible." With that, he abruptly ended the call.

Will do, Kristen mumbled to herself. She sat there, her mouth still gaping open from the policeman's final words. How was she supposed to avoid the students when they were across the pool from them? Granted, it was a large pool, but still … She also wanted to keep an eye on them and make sure none of them bolted before the police came.

Rising from the bench, she was thoughtful as she walked in the direction she assumed would lead her back where Brett was waiting. Even though Kristen was sure Brett wouldn't go out of his way to talk to the students, she still needed to warn him; plus, at a time like this, she wanted to stick close to his reassuring side.

"Hey, Kristen," Trevor said.

Where on earth had he come from? Had he overheard her phone conversation with Officer Helgason? Kristen hoped she hadn't noticeably jumped upon hearing his voice. Trying to keep her voice and actions natural, she said, "Hi, Trevor. How are you enjoying the Blue Lagoon so far?"

Trevor fell into step beside her as she walked. "It's okay, I guess. I'm not sure it's much different than soaking in a hot tub."

From what little time Kristen had spent in the lagoon's pool, she had to disagree. She could almost feel the water's rich minerals soaking into her skin and giving her body a boost. She could well understand how hot baths around the world were thought to be healing waters. "I wasn't too excited about this excursion, but it's one of those must-do things to try when visiting Iceland, so here I am. The water is lovely." Unsure why she was babbling and on edge around Trevor, Kristen took a deep breath to calm herself. She needed to return to the water for some peace and serenity.

"If you're into that sort of thing."

It looked like Trevor had been enjoying himself earlier. What was the reason for his sudden bah-humbug attitude? "If you're getting bored, we're only here for a couple more hours."

"I didn't say I'm bored."

Honestly, Kristen was growing tired of the man's moody attitude. His girlfriend's mood must have rubbed off on him. "Well, then, I hope you enjoy the rest of the afternoon." She started to move away from him when he gripped her arm.

"Not so fast; I'm still talking to you."

Kristen felt her stomach clench. *What's going on here?* She tried to play it cool. "Okay, well, I told Brett I'd only be a few minutes. I don't want him to worry." *Because frankly, I'm starting to worry, myself.*

"There will be plenty of time to catch up with the hubs in a minute." Trevor's hand still gripped Kristen's arm.

She tried to twist away from his grasp. He was starting to creep her out, and her arm was sore. "What is it you want with me?" Not only did he continue to clasp her arm, but he tightened it and starting walking further down the path. Kristen was forced to travel with him. Her heart started racing. *This isn't good.*

"What I want," he said through clenched teeth, "is for you to give us some space."

"I'm perfectly willing to do that," Kristen stammered, then gave herself a mental kick. *I'll be darned if I'll let him know I'm frightened.* "But you'll need to release me in order to give you some space," she said with her newfound muster.

"The thing is, I'm not so sure you're going to back off."

"Well, make up your mind, why don't you?" Kristen's fear was quickly turning to anger at his cat and mouse games. "I'd like to have some more time in the water, and you're preventing me from doing that—not to mention the fact that you're hurting me."

Trevor chuckled. "No problem. If you want some time in the water, that's what you'll get." He continued to drag her down the path, but instead of walking in the direction of the pool where they'd originally come from, he turned on what looked like an isolated side path.

Kristen had no idea where it would take them, but she knew they were going down the wrong road— literally!

***

CHAPTER 40

Kristen's heart continued to pound. Clenching her robe more tightly around her with her free hand, she tried to think things through. Was Trevor the killer? Why? He had no apparent connection with Lewis, other than through Nora.

"Where are you taking me?" Kristen asked. She decided to play dumb. "You've been so friendly the past few days, and we've had fun sightseeing on the same tours, but I really want to get back to my husband."

"If you'd done what most people do on their honeymoon and left well enough alone, none of this would be necessary."

Whatever doubt Kristen had about Trevor being the killer—or at least involved in Lewis' murder somehow—was now gone. "None of what?" she hedged, still attempting to play dumb for as long as she could get by with it.

"Do you think your actions have gone unnoticed?" He turned toward her, a dangerous gleam in his eyes.

"Actions? Why are you paying attention to my actions?" Kristen laughed nervously. "I don't think my new husband and I have had too many public displays of affection."

"Maybe you should have. Then you would have kept your nose out of our business." Trevor shoved her roughly further down the path.

Kristen didn't like how any of this was going. "I apologize if I've intruded on your vacation and asked too many questions. I have one of those naturally curious personalities, but I suppose I should try to tone it down around strangers." Kristen flashed him a smile she really wasn't feeling. She doubted he was feeling it either.

"I agree. You need to tone it down." Trevor said through gritted teeth. "I only wish you'd thought of that sooner."

"Why don't you tell me what the fuss is all about?" Kristen had a feeling she knew, but she wanted to stall for as long as possible, plus see what kind of information Trevor would cough up.

Trevor stopped walking, but his grip on her arm remained firm. "What this is all about? Stop playing games." He shook his head. "I overheard you talking to the police."

Kristen realized her game was up. She tried to remember what exactly she'd told the police. Did her one-sided conversation rate her as a snitch in Trevor's eyes? Was it enough to make Trevor do something stupid? What difference would it make anyway? The police would be there in less than an hour. *Surely I can hold him off until then.* "What makes you think I was talking to the police?" she hedged.

"Come off it and stop playing the dumb blonde. You know way more than you should."

"I don't think I do," she challenged him, which probably wasn't a wise move. "For starters, who killed

Lewis? Are you trying to keep your girlfriend out of trouble?'

"You obviously don't know as much as you think you do," Trevor scoffed.

"Then let me go!" Kristen tried to shrug out of his grip, but Trevor grabbed both her arms. She wasn't sure if he still played baseball, but he was in great shape.

"You're not going anywhere."

"Then you may as well tell me what you know about Lewis' death." *It will be good practice for when you talk to the police.* Kristen tried to remain calm, knowing help would soon be on the way. Plus eventually Brett would wonder what had happened to her, especially if he'd noticed Trevor leave the pool not long after Kristen. *Still, it may take Brett some time to find me. We're definitely in the back forty, and I haven't seen anyone else since I came out of the office with the Wi-Fi password.* The same could be said about the police locating them.

"Know about it? I'm the one who killed him," he boasted.

Kristen couldn't believe he'd blurted out a confession so nonchalantly. She gulped, unsure how to proceed as she stood face to face with the killer.

"For once your big mouth doesn't know what to say." Trevor chuckled, but it wasn't a happy sound.

"What am I supposed to say?" Kristen countered. "It's not every day I find myself arm wrestling with a murderer."

Trevor raised his eyebrows. "Really? That's not what I've heard, which is why I must silence you before you squeal to your police buddies."

He wasn't making any sense. The police were already on their way, and Kristen hadn't known until five minutes ago who'd killed Lewis. *Why is he making matters worse by threatening me?* She supposed killers weren't always thinking straight. She decided to change the subject. "Don't tell me you're the one I have to thank about last night's porta potty episode?"

Trevor nodded, a proud grin on his face. "You've got that right. I wanted to give you one last chance to shut up. But you blew it this morning when you went to the police station, then again a few minutes ago when you called them about me."

"Technically, I called to let them know you were all here. I didn't single you out and had no idea you were the killer. I honestly think you're covering for your girlfriend."

"It's true I'd do anything for Nora—including kill for her."

"What's that supposed to mean?" She wasn't sure she wanted to know, especially if Trevor had the same plan for Kristen.

"You're such a know-it-all; why don't you tell me?"

"I have no clue why you would kill Lewis. You claimed you didn't know him." *Then again, so had Nora, but she'd been lying.*

"No, but Nora did."

Kristen didn't want to let on like she had already known that fact. The less Trevor thought she knew, the better. But since this confrontation was starting to turn into a tell-all, she supposed she was doomed anyway. "Someone with a bright future ahead of them wouldn't kill someone without a darned good reason." Kristen stared him down. As long as she'd come this far, she wanted to know the full story.

"Because he 'done her wrong.' as the expression goes."

"How so?" Kristen should be afraid for her life, but this far into the game, she was honestly curious.

Trevor threw her a disgusted look. "That old man not only put the moves on Nora during a research field trip, but then he tried to take credit for the research she'd been conducting as part of her master's thesis. When he published her research under his own name, he cheated her out of recognition that would have been a big boost to her career after college."

"Oh, wow." Although Nora and Trevor had a right to be upset, most people would have filed a complaint with the college and the scientific journal that published the work, but they wouldn't have resorted to murder. "Is that why you chose to kill him with arsenic?"

Trevor scowled at her. "You claimed you didn't know much about the investigation, but evidently you've snooped around enough to know arsenic was involved, plus have an idea about why I chose it."

Crap! So much for me playing stupid. "Lewis' wife told me he died of arsenic poisoning," Kristen babbled.

"You spent enough time with her, so I'm sure she was bound to come clean eventually."

"She needed someone to talk to, that's all." Kristen eyed him. "Since her husband was murdered on their first day in Iceland."

"Right." Trevor leaned in closer, until he was right in Kristen's face. "How'd you know arsenic would be a significant murder method?"

Kristen shrugged, or tried to, since Trevor continued to grip both her arms. "Margaret mentioned her husband was a geology professor who researched arsenic levels in Illinois groundwater."

"Come on," Trevor scoffed. "That witch doesn't know the first thing about what her husband was working on—not to mention who he was working with."

"I think she knows more than you realize," Kristen argued.

"The only reason she kept him around was to pay the bills. That piece of work has expensive tastes." He glared at her.

Before the murder, Kristen would have agreed with Trevor, but Margaret's well-groomed exterior had gone downhill, and who could blame her when she'd been on an emotional rollercoaster since Lewis's death. "I'll admit she does dress better than the rest of us, though what we're wearing—when we're fully clothed—is more appropriate for Iceland's winter weather." Kristen shivered, from nerves as much as the cool air.

"Getting a little cold, are you? Maybe you should get in the water." Trevor's eyes blazed. "I'll let you pick your poison, so to speak. Death by drowning, or ..." Trevor reached into the pocket of his swimming trunks and pulled out a vile.

Kristen felt the air sucked out of her lungs. She could only assume arsenic was in the vile. "Where did you get that?"

"Where do you think?"

"I'm guessing you stole it from Lewis' research lab." Kristen wondered how he'd gotten away with that, much less gotten it through airport security and customs. "Wouldn't a dangerous chemical be under lock and key?"

"That wasn't a problem when my girlfriend still had a key," Trevor snapped. "Besides, it was extracted from groundwater, and that's easy enough to tap into. Nora's research supported that. Don't you think it's poetic justice that he died from the very poison he was studying? Although he was trying to keep it out of people's tap water; whereas I made sure it was in his."

"He drank water laced with arsenic?" Kristen's eyes widened. "How'd you manage that? For a dose enough to kill him relatively quickly, wouldn't he have tasted it?" Kristen remembered reading that arsenic had a garlic odor to it. How could Lewis not notice? Especially if he worked with arsenic contaminated groundwater for a living? Or, maybe he'd gotten used to its odor.

"Details." It was Trevor's turn to shrug. "Maybe he thought it was pure Icelandic water straight from a glacier. How the heck would I know? All I know is he drank it, and a few minutes later he was dead."

Kristen shuddered at Trevor's matter-of-fact attitude. "Tell me how you got him to drink water tainted with arsenic."

"Easy." Trevor seemed to be enjoying himself now. "I had Nora switch water bottles while he was waiting for his wife in the hotel lobby when we first arrived in town."

"Didn't he recognize Nora?"

Trevor shook his head. "She kept a low profile. Between trying to steer clear of him and wearing full winter garb, he probably didn't glance twice at her. She came up from behind and switched the bottle while I asked him a question."

"Both you and Nora were involved in his death?"

He shook his head. "She just wanted some revenge. She added a trace amount of arsenic—just enough to make him feel sick. She didn't know I'd added more to the bottle--enough to kill the jerk."

Kristen remembered Gunnar telling them he'd seen Sam and Trevor having an angry discussion with Lewis before he died. "Did you know the Sawyers' would be on this trip?"

"Of course. Do I look like the type to carry poison around with me?"

"Not really. In fact, you totally deceived me."

Trevor laughed. "That apparently wouldn't take much. Despite the fact that you didn't catch on right away, you're still too dangerous. I can't have you ruining my future with Nora."

"I think you've already done that." Kristen wondered if Nora could also be implicated in Lewis' murder. Now that Kristen had answers, she tried to edge away from Trevor, but his hold on her didn't loosen. Still, she kept walking backwards, hoping someone would come upon them in the secluded area. *Ironically, this would be a perfect spot for those wanting privacy, like Brett and me.*

She wasn't counting on bumping into something, namely a lump of lava on the pool's edge. She lost her balance, fell backward, and ended up submerged in the warm water. If the circumstances were different, she wouldn't have minded, but unfortunately she'd dragged Trevor along with her. The pool was shallow, but that didn't mean Trevor wouldn't try to cover his tracks, and what better way to do that than drag her underwater? Counting herself fortunate she hadn't injured herself when she fell, she concentrated on trying to keep Trevor from injuring her.

Kristen took advantage of them both landing in the water to scoot away from him while Trevor recovered his balance. She put distance between them and began to crawl out of the pool. Since she was nowhere close to a ladder, she had no choice but to grip the lava chunks to pull herself up. She was halfway out of the pool when Trevor grabbed her left foot and yanked her back into the water so quickly she lost her balance and went underwater. Not being a great swimmer under the best of circumstances, Kristen fought to keep her wits about her. She shot back up, thankful the water was only about a meter deep along the edge. She used her feet to lash out, splashing water in Trevor's face as she scrambled away from him, backing up against the water's edge. When the moment was right, she'd grip the wall and use her upper body strength to try to propel herself upward.

Trevor spit water out of his mouth. Kristen didn't like the look on the face she'd once thought was handsome. She'd also thought he had a pleasant personality. Neither of those traits were evident now; Trevor had shown his true colors in the past few minutes. Seeing the murderous look on his face gave Kristen a burst of energy. She used her arms to grip the lava, pull herself up, and launch herself upward and out of the pool. Sitting on the lava, she jerked her feet upward as Trevor came closer. She wouldn't allow herself to be pulled back into the pool. She tried to stand, wincing as her feet touched the rough lava rock. Somewhere along the way, she'd lost her flipflops—not that they would have been much help on the lumpy rocks. She had no idea where her phone was. Groping the robe that clung to her as it dripped water on the path, she felt the phone, still safe in her pocket. Had it soaked up too much water to be of any use? Even if it was still in working condition, how was it possible to use her phone to ask for help without Trevor seeing her? She assumed she was still hooked into the spa's Wi-Fi and could possibly manage an S.O.S. text, but even that would take too long.

Realizing she wouldn't be able to use her phone before Trevor got out of the pool, she used what little head start she had and began to run back the way they'd come, hoping she would be able to find help. She'd just rounded a bend in the path when her left arm was jerked backward.

"Not so fast." Trevor twisted her arm and thrust her back toward the water.

"Not so fast," a loud, authoritative voice mimicked. "You're about to be arrested for the murder of Lewis Sawyer."

Kristen looked up, her heart pounding, to see Officers Helgason and Grimsson, plus reinforcements on either side of them. Brett stood behind them, relief crossing his features. She ripped her arm free of Trevor and ran into Brett's waiting arms. She clung to him for dear life, realizing how dear her own life was and how close she'd come to losing it.

CHAPTER 41

"Didn't I tell you to stay away from them?" Officer Helgason asked once Trevor was taken away and the other students had been rounded up for questioning.

Kristen's earlier gratefulness at the police arriving just in time to save her from Trevor's clutches vanished and was replaced with weariness. To say she'd been through a lot was putting it mildly, and she wasn't up for a scolding. "I was on my way back to the pool after calling you. Trevor must have been following me. It's not like I invited him to join me."

"Don't take offence," Officer Grímsson said. "We feel bad that you were in danger. We were relieved to arrive in time."

"I'm sure my relief is even greater," Kristen said. "By the way, how did you make it here so quickly? I think it took us around forty-five minutes by bus."

"Between already being in the car on the southwest side of the city when you called, plus driving like crazy to get here, we arrived in record time."

"I'm glad you did, but I'm sure it seemed like hours to Kristen," Brett said, his arm protectively around Kristen's shoulders.

Kristen looked up at Brett. "It seemed like ages before you found me."

"I'm sure it did. After you'd been gone a few minutes, I started looking for you, but this spot is way off the beaten path. I ran into the police when they arrived, and, fortunately, they know this place better than me." Brett pulled her closer. "I panicked when I noticed Trevor had left the pool. He must have been keeping an eye on you. I could kick myself for not seeing him leave, or I would have been right on his tail."

"It's not your fault," Kristen assured him. "How could we know he was the killer? He didn't seem to have any connection with Lewis."

"The fact that he and Sam were seen having words with Lewis should have tipped us off."

"It's okay. I'm safe, the killer has been caught, and that's all that matters."

"She's right," Officer Helgason agreed. "We'll do our part by making sure we have a solid case against him."

"I'll be glad to do whatever I can to help with that," Kristen said. "Is there anything you need from us? We'll be in Iceland for a few more days."

"We'll confirm everything you told us earlier today, so all we'll need from you is a statement about this afternoon's incident," Officer Grímsson said.

"I'll get that to you as soon as possible." Kristen pulled the blanket the spa staff had provided closer around her. "But can we go somewhere a little warmer? Maybe the spa could muster up a cup of coffee."

"Of course," Officer Helgason said. "The spa staff said we can use their office conference room. It won't take long, and then you can get back to your vacation."

Kristen couldn't wait to put the day behind her. She was ready for a new beginning with the man she loved.

"Good, because we're ready to finally start our honeymoon."

* * *

Kristen stared out at the Atlantic Ocean near Iceland's southernmost village of Vík, about a hundred and ten miles southeast of Reykjavík. While the tiny town that only boasted seven hundred and fifty people was charming, it was the water and its unusual black sand and pebble beach that attracted Kristen. The temperature was mild; thirty-seven degrees in January would be a considered a blessing at home. The sun shone brightly, but the wind off the water was brisk. Kristen didn't mind, as the breeze helped to clear her mind and finally free her of the past few days. While she and Brett had enjoyed their time in Iceland leading up to yesterday's final events, she was excited to finally be able to truly relish their time together.

They had taken the excursion bus that morning, before the sun was up, were staying overnight in Vík, and would take the bus back to Reykjavík the next day. Besides spending time on the ocean, there were plenty of other things to see and do, including Vík's surrounding cliffs and glacier. They would explore the tiny town—the biggest one for miles away—and enjoy a lovely evening in cozy lodgings, far away from the rest of the travelers.

Now that the murder was solved, she was able to hang out with the others without questioning them and being suspicious of their answers. After wrapping up their official statements, Kristen wasn't sure she'd be up to celebrating. But she had a blast at the group gathering the previous night—minus Trevor and Nora, who were either arrested or being questioned further. Sam and Alicia had known nothing of what they'd done and had wisely distanced themselves from their friends. Kristen and Brett had been the guests of honor at a hearty Icelandic dinner at the hotel, with rounds of Gull bought by the other travelers. Everyone was glad Lewis' murder was resolved. Kristen was happy Margaret could at least find some closure in knowing who had killed her husband and why. Kristen doubted Margaret would spend long mourning his loss after discovering the truth. Knowing of Lewis' many affairs was one thing, but learning he had also stolen research—at least once—was another. Their whole marriage, and much of Lewis' career, had been full of deception.

Kristen knew her own marriage would have its share of ups and downs, but that was normal. After yesterday's harrowing, near-death experience with Trevor, she wanted nothing more than to settle down with Brett and worry about their own lives without getting involved in any more murder investigations.

"What are you thinking about?" Brett asked. "I know your mind is taking in more than just this amazing scenery."

"I was thinking about how happy I am now that the murderer has been apprehended." She snuggled closer and kissed him. "Then I thought about how lucky I am to have such an amazing man for my husband."

Brett grimaced. "An amazing man wouldn't have let you run off by yourself yesterday."

"No one could predict things would end up the way they did." Kristen smiled.

"But I should have known. That's how things always end up with you."

Kristen pouted. "I hope you don't regret marrying me."

"Of course not. I'm pretty sure you'll keep me on my toes for what I hope is a very long marriage." And he sealed the deal with a very long kiss.

Acknowledgments

Writing mystery novels is a dream come true. I love mixing creative writing with my biology and conservation background. I also enjoy travelling, and having Kristen and Brett take their honeymoon in Iceland was so much fun! All the parks and natural areas in this book are real, but the businesses mentioned are not.

I thank my family for their patience, support and help when I squeezed valuable time into our busy daily lives for writing and editing.

I am grateful to my editor, Donnell Whiting, for her insightful, practical suggestions.

Special thanks to Sherrill Cannon, Norma Good, and Beverly Gray for giving *Land of Ice* a final proofread.

Thanks so much to KJ for bringing my photos to life with her amazing cover design!

I appreciate my co-workers, who never fail to provide me with valuable input.

Thanks to loyal Rachel Raccoon and Sammy Skunk book readers – they have inspired me to continue writing about nature, but this time for adults.

Lastly, thanks to all you readers! I hope you enjoy the seventh book in the Nature Station Mystery Series, *Land of Ice*. It's been a pleasure to write and a true growing experience.

About the Author

Photo by Alexandra Powelson

Born and raised on a farm in Northwestern Illinois, Jannifer Powelson's interest in writing, conservation, and the natural world was sparked at an early age. Books in the Nature Station Mystery Series encompass her passions of writing, photography, nature, and reading mysteries.

Powelson is also the author of four books in the Rachel Raccoon and Sammy Skunk series. These books use entertaining storylines, colorful and realistic illustrations, and photos taken by Powelson, to educate children about nature.

Powelson works as a conservationist and resides in northwestern Illinois with her husband and two daughters. Ms. Powelson is currently working on the seventh book in the Nature Station Mystery Series, *April Showers*.

Other Books

Nature Station Mystery Series
When Nature Calls
An Unnatural Selection
Freak of Nature
Flower Child
Bee in her Bonnet
Leaf Peepers

Rachel Raccoon and Sammy Skunk Series
Rachel and Sammy Visit the Prairie
Rachel and Sammy Visit the Forest – A Guide to Spring Woodland Wildflowers
Rachel and Sammy Learn About Trees
Rachel and Sammy Learn to Conserve

Made in the USA
Columbia, SC
10 May 2022

60217559R00181